BENNY

a "Special Boy"

NOVEL BY JEFFREY FLAGEL

ISBN: 978-1-963565-71-3 (Paperback)
ISBN: 978-1-963565-72-0 (Ebook)

Library of Congress Control Number: 2025901773

Printed in the United States of America

Published by:

QUIPPY™ QUILL

info@thequippyquill.com
(302) 295-2278

For my beautiful wife, Kristy,

Since coming into my life, I have envied no man – or woman
for that matter!

BENNY
a "Special Boy"

CHAPTER OUTLINE

My fists are clenched with such extreme force that I've left little blood or strength for the rest of my body. I can't feel anything over my rage. I've been pacing around the house for what seems like hours. Finally, I hear Gail's car approach the house and pull carefully into the driveway. After several agonizing seconds, she opens the car door. She is taking her sweet time. The door slams shut, and she starts the short walk up to our porch. I hear her footsteps – each one wrenching my heart. She's walking as if she has all the time in the world. I'm about to explode. Before she can insert her key, I throw the front door open, slamming it against the inside door-stop and shattering the small stained-glass piece embedded high on the door. In one furious movement, I step out of the house and shove her with all my strength, striking her with both hands just below her shoulders and knocking her backwards and onto the cement floor. It is a cool night in Seal Beach, California, and though I am barefoot and wearing only boxers and a t-shirt, I feel no chill.

I grab a chunk of her thick, jet-black hair and pull her to her feet, then blindly backhand her and watch as she flies against the porch siding, her glasses slicing into my knuckles and now flipping through the air behind her. My fist continues on its path, slamming into the porch light, breaking the outer glass and lightbulb into pieces. She is screaming at the top of her lungs, though I hear absolutely nothing except my own angry breathing. The light that once illuminated our porch is destroyed. I can't see much in the darkness, but I sense that the back of my fist and knuckles are bloody and broken. Still, I am not in any pain. I feel nothing whatsoever.

Gail collapses to the ground, holding the side of her head. Blood is dripping from her face and down her arm. My senses are gradually returning. Sounds are coming back. Excruciating pain is shooting down my right arm and through my hand, pulsating with every heartbeat. She made me break my hand, and now she is wailing uncontrollably. Marty is at the top of the staircase just inside the front door screaming for me to stop. He doesn't get it. The neighbors are opening their doors to see what the shouting is all about. I can see their porch lights come on. Those bastards are all talking about me. Don't they have their own miserable lives to worry about? My son won't shut up.

I turn my head towards the open front door and yell, "Knock it off Marty, goddammit. Go to your room, now!" He knows I mean business.

Mike, our neighbor who is also a city fireman, shouts to me from across the street, "Hey Benny, is everything okay?"

"Gail just fell again Mike, everything is fine," I explain, then flash him a forced smile so he gets the message.

I turn my eyes down at Gail with a warning glare that she had better keep quiet. The neighbors back away from view, but I know they are still watching from slightly open doors and partially drawn window shades. I grab her upper arm with my good hand and drag her as fast as I can across the threshold inside our house on College

Park Drive. Out of the corner of my eye, I see Marty running back towards his bedroom upstairs. He is such a momma's boy. I hear all three boys running around upstairs, crying, but out of sight. Gail is still howling; once she starts the performance you can never get her to stop. I pull her into the small half-bathroom immediately to the right of the front door to try to clean us both up, and to get her out of earshot from the kids, and from the nosey neighbors.

We barely clear the bathroom door – just enough for me to shut it behind us. I wet a hand towel and start gently dabbing Gail's face. Her howling has turned to whimpering, with occasional flinches and crying out when she feels I have dabbed her too hard.

"Oh Benny, Benny, what did I do?" she keeps repeating with tears in her eyes.

Hearing this somehow calms me. She really loves me. In that moment, she is looking at me as if I am her entire world, as it should be. Look what I've done to my wife, to my true love. Why couldn't she get home on time? This could all have been prevented if she just did what I told her. She knows the rules.

I rinse the towel and hand it to her to hold on the right side of her face while I go to the kitchen to get some ice. As I pass the staircase on my right, I notice that Marty has been joined by Alan and Andy at the top of the stairs.

"Get your asses back into your rooms, now!" I threaten the boys with my teeth clenched.

They scamper quickly back to their respective rooms, doors slamming shut in succession, faint sounds of them crying, wanting to help their mom – but stupid they are not.

Entering the kitchen, my first priority is to reach for the Cutty Sark bottle. I look for a glass, but absent the use of my right hand and in a hurry to dull the pain, I awkwardly remove the lid with my one good hand and turn the bottle over in my mouth. Three good swigs, and I put the bottle down and proceed to rinse off my hand in the sink, wrapping it loosely with an old kitchen towel. I replace the bottle in the liquor cabinet, retrieve a bowl, fill it with ice cubes, and turn back toward the bathroom.

As I pass through the kitchen doorway, my thoughts return to Gail, and a feeling of calm comes over me. I am even smiling. She will be even more loving now. She will be so much more conscientious about pleasing me. She will feel sorry for making me worry about her and will do anything to make up for her selfishness. Sex will be more exciting, at least for a while.

My euphoria is short-lived as I recall the agony she put me through, waiting for what seemed like hours for her to get her ass home. She left the house at 7:00 p.m. to attend the Temple Israel choir practice, as she did every Wednesday. She knows to be home by 10:00 and is usually earlier, but tonight I sat and waited as 10:00 came, then 10:01, 10:02, 10:03, then ten after, and then twenty after… It was 10:35 when she finally pulled up in the driveway. By then, I was so incensed I couldn't see straight. She has no respect. She was intentionally disobeying me, or talking about me, or talking to another man, or worse.

I'm walking with purpose now, getting angrier as I mentally rehearse the upcoming interrogation, "Where the hell were you?" "Why were you so goddamn late?" "Who were you talking to?" "Are you cheating on me?"

I want to slam the door closed but I can't get sufficient leverage in the tiny bathroom. Gail is still crying. I begin peppering her with questions, but she's unable to catch her breath and say anything, let alone to answer even one of them. I'm getting more and more livid as I recall how I felt every minute that passed beyond her curfew. Selfish bitch. I'll kill her if she's cheating on me.

She is recoiling as I become more enraged. I'm inches from her face, racing through my questions and giving her as little time as possible to concoct her answers. Why does she do this to me? Why can't she just tell me the truth?

She finally gains control of herself and tells me that she got to talking with Beth, the temple choir director, and lost track of time. She's apologizing over and over again. What more can I say that I haven't already said? She promises it will never happen again. I don't know whether I should believe her story. I'll have to subtly check it out next Friday night at the Temple. I have friends there too, dammit.

Suddenly, I feel a sharp pain in my left arm. I shake my head in an effort to focus. My memory is cloudy. Gail's image is fading. I'm blinking to try to regain my senses, but my eyes aren't cooperating. A shooting pain surges through my upper body. Pressure is building in my head. I'm trying to click my jaw to pop my ears, but it isn't working. I lift up my right arm from my lap, and stare at the back of my hand for several seconds, remembering the night so many years ago when Gail pushed me to the edge. I hold my right hand with my left, and try to feel the pain I once felt – to see the damage once inflicted by the combination of Gail's head and our cheap porch light. All evidence of that night is long gone.

But now, my left hand is bloody. Its fingernails are torn with bloody skin attached, and both hands are shaking. I place both arms on my chair, and gaze blankly in the direction of the TV. I look away and slowly turn and focus down onto my lap. There is blood on my shirt, and lots more blood pooling on my right thigh, and all over my lap. I think I've wet my pants, but I can't be sure. The TV is blaring but I hear nothing. I'm shaking uncontrollably, sweating profusely, yet I am calm. It is so hot and stagnant in here. My breathing is slow and shallow. I need more air. I need a drink. Where is my Cutty? Where am I? What year is it? What happened in this room? Where the hell is Rosa? There is so much commotion in our tiny apartment, yet I can no longer hear or feel a thing.

I can't walk without her help. I can't dress, or eat, or shower, or function without Rosa. I can't make sense of my thoughts, nor articulate anything that makes sense. Rosa understands me, at least most of the time. Where the hell is she? I need her, now.

I flash back to fifteen minutes before. Rosa is cooking lunch in the kitchen. I can smell her chili sauce simmering on the stove. I love her chili. I want my lunch right away, and I'm trying to call to her but she isn't listening. My voice isn't what it used to be. The TV volume is all the way up. I'm watching The Price is Right; the crowd is laughing and I can't talk or hear over the noise. Rosa is once again on the phone with her daughter, whom I hate with a passion for no reason other than she hates that her mom wants to be with me. She's a flaming bitch as far as I'm concerned. I reluctantly let Rosa talk to her sometimes, or she will get irritated and scold me like a child. She is staying on the phone, whispering, laughing, and enjoying her conversation, and she knows I am sitting in this prison, unable to move on my own, or say what I need to say.

"Get the fuck off the phone… I need you, now!" I demand.

Finally, she hears me, and with the phone still in her hand and held up to her ear, she walks out of the kitchen and over to me to see what I need. She notices I've peed myself. I'm so angry, tears are streaming down my face; my fists are clenched with what little power I have anymore. She has a few more things to say to Laura that I can't quite make out, then finally says goodbye, hangs up and puts the phone down. She starts explaining to me in her thick Hispanic accent, like a disappointed mother talking to a child, that she was only on the phone for a few minutes and she would help me when she was finished. Bullshit. I need you right now!

I am so angry I can't spit any words out. Instead, I let my fists fly. While sitting on my chair, I throw both arms over my head and grab Rosa by the hair. I am holding her with my right hand and with my left, hitting her hard over and over on the mouth, nose and ears – anywhere I can make contact. She falls onto the table next to my chair, knocking over my lamp, my drink, my pills, and all of the other paraphernalia that once laid there. She is crying, screaming for me to stop, making excuse after excuse as if this is my fault. Why didn't you just know I needed you? Why were you laughing and having fun talking to that bitch, Laura?

Rosa falls to the floor and is scratching and pulling at the furniture and carpet, using any leverage available to get away from me. I use my walker to get up, and with a sudden burst of adrenaline, lift it up off the ground, reach out my arms and hit her again and again with it as she continues to try to crawl away. I don't know how much contact I've made, but she is bleeding everywhere, and I know I've ripped one of her ears from her head with the leg of my walker. I can see it dangling there. She manages to create space between us, and somehow makes it back into the kitchen. I slowly get myself settled back in my chair, replace my walker, take a couple of deep breaths, resume looking in the direction of the TV, and assume Rosa will now finish making lunch and take care of me like she is supposed to.

She is crying and moaning so loud it is deafening. Why are women so dramatic? I again demand help changing my pants. I'm sitting in my chair busying myself straightening up my walker and the table beside me, when all of a sudden she comes up to me from behind and lunges at me with a carving knife. I'm not sure if it is because I was able to move slightly to the side in time, or if she tripped as she approached me, but she barely missed my back and head. Instead she falls over my shoulder and slides head first into my lap, stabbing me in my thigh on her way down. She rolls off of me and onto the floor, crawling away as fast as she can, leaving a trail of blood across the living room carpet and hallway floor tile. She disappears into the bedroom. There is lots of blood on me, but I feel no pain. There is so much commotion, but all sound, and all sensation has ceased. I am shaking, and sweating, and full with frustration and rage, but there is love, and a calm comes over me, even a smile. Rosa understands me. She loves and needs me so much. I'm sure she's learned her lesson. She is probably getting a change of clothes for me, and will be out in a minute to apologize, help me change, and get lunch finished and on the table.

I met Rosa almost two years ago at Mission Manor retirement home in Riverside. Marty and Alan moved me there after Joan died, having decided that I could no longer take care of myself, nor the house Joan and I had shared in nearby Beaumont for more than twenty years. They hired Rosa to come to my room daily and help me manage my medication and acclimate to the retirement community life. She is an attractive Mexican woman in her early fifties – a loving caregiver who helped a handful of other old people in the same God-awful place.

Three months after moving in, I was kicked out of Mission Manor for punching an old lady. She deserved it. Even Rosa said she was a nasty old woman. Nell is an ugly, 91-year-old bitch who intentionally got in my way in the hallway between our rooms. Finally, I had enough of her nasty attitude. She just stood there, refusing to give any ground. I was fuming. I could barely think through my anger.

I finally said, "Move that goddamn walker out of my way, old lady."

She just snarled at me and replied, "Why don't you just move *your* mean old fat ass?"

You bet I hit her. She and other old bitches in that place didn't like me, and I didn't like them. They cheated at Bridge. They made noise in the hallway outside my room. They didn't treat me like a lady should treat a man. They should have been warm with lust when I showed up, shower me with attention, and compete with one another for my affection. They should respect my intelligence and look to me to lead the Bridge club, as I am without a doubt the best player there. But no. Instead, they were crotchety old bitches that were just plain miserable. It's no wonder their husbands were dead. They probably killed themselves to escape the misery.

After being kicked out of Mission Manor, Rosa said that I could come and live with her family. She took care of me the way I should be taken care of – better than Mother, better than Gail, and certainly better than Joan. After a few months living with her, she couldn't resist me. She let me touch her anytime and anywhere I wanted. She lay naked with me in my bed, and made me feel like the special boy that I once was – the best looking, funniest, smartest and most talented in school. I was finally getting the love and attention I deserve from a woman. She couldn't get enough of me, and even though I am almost thirty years older than she is, Rosa thought I was the most beautiful man she'd ever met. I am in control. She will do whatever I want her to do. I'll have her all to myself. I am her world and she will cater to me and only to me. Unfortunately, she is married and sneaking around her husband to be with me. How much does Rosa love me? Enough to leave her husband of 30 years, her daughter, and even her job, to move into a small apartment with only me. We've been living together for a year now. I wish Mother were here in California to see this.

"See Mother, I don't need you. I am Rosa's special boy now," I say aloud to myself, imagining Mother is standing in front of me. God I hate her.

Back in my chair, looking at my bloody hands, I am remembering Joan. Poor Joan. She didn't deserve me. She didn't excite me like Rosa does. She didn't take care of me like she said she would. She got what she deserved. Good riddance.

At Loma Linda Hospital, I sat in the stiff visitor's chair in Joan's room where she was recovering from her latest procedure. This time she had to go under anesthesia to clean a deep wound in her leg. There were no get-well cards in sight, no plants on the bedside table, and no balloons drifting toward the ceiling. Our visits had become too routine to bother notifying anyone, so I had nothing to look at but Joan. She looked like death. Her skin was pale and purple and sagging so severely it looked almost unattached from her face. She even smelled like rotten flesh. As much as I hated what had become of her, I felt bad for Joan, since she always tried to care for me as I deserved.

She gave me everything that Gail couldn't. We'd been sleeping together for several months before I left Gail and the kids. I was the only thing in Joan's life that mattered. She showed me the adoration and respect I deserved. Her life was me and only me, unlike Gail who insisted on performing in the Temple choir, and making friends with everyone and anyone. She pitted me against them, and I couldn't compete. Mother and Gail both could have taken a lesson from Joan.

Forty-two years later, thanks to Joan, I was reduced to my miserable life of changing bandages, living in a disorganized pig sty, parking in handicapped spaces, waiting all day for simple meals to be prepared, and having to help grocery shop – all to accommodate Joan. It had been almost twenty years since her Lupus was diagnosed. The medication completely destroyed her muscle tone, and her skin was bruised and sickly. She had virtually no pads on her palms or feet, and needed thick cushioned slippers just to shuffle across the floor. A simple scratch turned into a life altering gash, needing constant care and treatment, all of which fell on me. She had only a few of her original teeth left, and her false teeth were old and no longer fit in her mouth. She could hardly eat, and our bed was a disgusting pile of toxic towels on top, and a virtual pharmacy surrounding it on dinner trays and side tables. Sex stopped years ago when the disease and the medication caused her insides to go raw… and of course Joan was too much of a prude to be at all creative in the bedroom.

The only shred of life I was able to enjoy, I found elsewhere. I found sex, and even love, though those encounters were short-lived. I even left Joan for a couple of months and took up with an old girlfriend I had in the tenth grade, but she didn't treat me as she had back then – like the best looking, most talented, smartest and most popular boy in the school. I threw her out faster than I had lured her in. Nobody treated me like Joan did. She cooked, cleaned, and did whatever I wanted, whenever I wanted it. I was her entire life. There were no family or friends to interfere. I just had to force myself to be content until some excitement came along. But she turned me into a caretaker. She didn't touch me. She couldn't please me anymore. There was no thrill in my life. I couldn't remember when there ever was with her. Joan the mistress was much more enticing than Joan the wife. I loathed her. She just wouldn't die.

Two nurses entered and urged Joan to try to start her physical therapy. It had been three days since the procedure, and she was still in great pain. She told them she'd love to comply but just couldn't will herself out of bed. The nurses continued their attempts at coaxing, but Joan couldn't even maneuver herself upright with their assistance, let alone to try and stand up out of bed. She was too weak, and too frail. Everything hurt. I sat in the room watching all of this, getting angrier and angrier at her, at the nurses, at the hospital, and at the doctors. Her surgeon told me that morning that Joan couldn't stay there; I was going to have to send her to a rehab facility in Riverside, or bring her home and hire home help to take care of her.

Who was going to pay for this? I didn't have insurance for home care, or any kind of rehab or nursing care for that matter. Get up, goddammit. Why can't you just stand the hell up and walk two steps for God's sake? I was livid. The nurses left, and Joan lay there listless, staring at me as I sat in this awful chair at the foot of her bed. She could see how angry I was. Or could she? She looked lifeless. But then again, how could I tell? She closed her eyes and turned her head away from me. I cussed under my breath. My fists were clenching; I was fuming with anger and resentment. My jaws were biting down so hard I thought I would break what few healthy teeth I have left.

Mother would never approve of any woman treating me this way. She was right all along; Joan wasn't good enough for me. I deserve to be with a beautiful, smart, popular girl from a good Jewish family. I am Benny. I am the most attractive, smartest and most talented boy in school. Girls cannot wait to be with me, and then brag that they have had me. And yet here I was, relegated to taking care of my drooping wallflower of a wife who could give me absolutely nothing anymore, as if she ever could. Nobody loved me like Gail, or like Mother. But they abandoned me too. I hate them all.

I was so enraged I could hardly think straight. I couldn't stand the thought of having to taking care of her for another minute. But who was going to take care of me if not Joan? As much as I despised her for making my life so plain and depressing, she did everything for me. I knew nothing of managing our finances or paying bills. I had no idea what to do at tax time. I couldn't handle the stress of dealing with cable or utility companies. I wouldn't grocery shop or cook, no matter how miserable or disabled Joan became. I am Benny. I support you, and you should be thrilled to take care of me. Mother would insist on it.

My fists clenched around either end of a spare pillow I pulled from Joan's hospital room closet. The muscles in my arms were pulsating, fists and knuckles shaking. I walked up to the side of the bed, tears in my eyes, my face red with rage, and inched up towards her head, which was still turned in the other direction. The nurses were busy with their shift change. We were alone.

I'm angry and frustrated that the memory of that afternoon in the hospital with Joan is murky at best. I struggle to remember, but I just can't. I'm stuck in my chair, in the center of our living room, still waiting for Rosa to come back out from the bedroom and take care of me.

I survey my surroundings, not sure what has transpired. I can smell the chili sauce cooking in the kitchen behind me. The TV is so loud I can barely make out the whimpering coming from the bedroom to the right of the kitchen. I hear Rosa whining, presumably begging for help. I recognize her hand reaching out from the bedroom. She is on the floor. My eyes follow the blood trail from the bedroom entry all the way back to my living room chair. Someone is pounding on the front door, but I ignore it. I feel like I am losing consciousness.

Drowsy, then somewhat aware, then feeling faint, then quiet, then loud again. I am rising above myself, looking around the living room, then traveling from room to room throughout the apartment. There are blood streaks on the wall – smeared hand prints, I think. Broken dishes have landed on the kitchen counter and floor. Knick-knacks are strewn about, and a large bloody kitchen knife lay at the foot of my chair. Blood has pooled on my lap. Chili in the pot is boiling over, falling on the electrical elements of the stove, creating smoke and small fire bursts. Rosa is on the floor of the bedroom, her hands and face are covered with blood. She is moaning yet unable to articulate. What happened? What have I done? I am moving around the room, watching myself sitting motionless in my chair. Am I dead? Am I dying? Is Rosa going to die? I have somehow sailed beyond the present, not clear what I am experiencing and whether I will return. I see myself and my disheveled living room in one direction, and in the other direction, my small childhood house on Grove Street in Shaker Heights, just outside of Cleveland. I am peering from the front yard into our dining room where Mother, Dad, and me and my brothers, Jimmy and Donald, are all sitting eating dinner. I must be twelve or thirteen years old. I am the oldest. I am the one whose hair is combed the nicest. I am the best looking of the brothers, sitting next to Mother as she praises and scolds me at the same time.

Looking back toward the bloody chaos that is my living room, I try to make sense of so many confused scenes from my life. There are people I recognize reaching for me. My Grandma Eve invites me with open arms and outward palms. Dad is looking at me with his usual stern expression, motioning for me to follow him, somewhere. Joan has her arms outstretched, calling for me to come to her. She looks like she did on our first camping trip together. The sky is somehow visible through our living room ceiling, and it is a beautiful, cloudless blue. Bright lights reach out to me from all directions, each seeming to represent part of my past. Why is Mother not here for me? I can't go anywhere without her. I can't leave Rosa.

I open my eyes. I am in my living room, sitting in my chair. I feel fully conscious now, but weak and dizzy. It is so warm – so hard to breathe. The smell of burnt chili fills the air. Blood is all over the apartment. The knocking on the door is louder and louder. Maybe I'm dying? Where is Rosa? She loves me. She needs me to love her. I am her whole life.

"Open the door, this is the police," I hear them barking from outside. I want to get up, but I can't...

I am drifting in and out of my body, and back and forth to and from the present and the past. I'm trying to understand what is happening in this moment, yet I am being drawn to a kaleidoscope of memories from my life, each beckoning me to follow back in time and relive a moment from my past. My movement around those scenes is slowing, the light adjusting to allow focus, an increased awareness of each moment. I see Mother. She is so beautiful. I hear music. Her music.

I watch Mother as she plays the piano in our living room. I remember the sweet sounds of the Bach piece that she so eloquently played on that evening so long ago. Her face had little emotion. Her eyes were wide open, yet her hands and shoulders rose, moved and swayed with the music. She was a natural; so beautiful as she sat there in her holiday dress, with her holiday apron still adorned.

I am reliving this wonderful moment from my childhood, from when I was only seven years old. Time had stopped. I am no longer experiencing the chaotic flashing of a lifetime of experiences and emotions. I am no longer thinking about Rosa, or Joan, or Gail, or the confusion that is my life now, in the present. I am here in my house on Grove Street with Mother and Dad, where I once belonged. I look around and let the feelings of warmth, love, and family engulf me. I also feel familiar feelings of fear and self-doubt, but I ignore those. I sense the aroma of Mother's wonderful cooking. It is our Thanksgiving dinner. Even through the yummy smells of turkey, stuffing and yams cooking, I smell Mother's perfume. Her hair is perfect. It was always perfect.

It is a ritual that Dad started when I was a small toddler. With our holiday dinner cooking in the kitchen, Dad summoned me and my brothers to sit in the center of the living room floor. Any guests that we may have, and we often entertain extended family and Dad's most important partners and clients, got the best seats on the expensive leather couch and matching chair in the center of the living room. Once everyone was seated, Dad adjusted the lamps in the room so as to enhance the lighting on and nearby the baby grand piano, and then took his place on his favorite rocker chair in the corner of the room with a clear view of everyone, and all that transpires. When the room was ready and all were seated, and when my brothers and I were sitting quietly and attentively, Dad would point to one of us to go and invite Mother to come and play the classical piece of her choosing.

On this Thanksgiving, I got the nod. Yes, with two of my Dad's partners from work, and my Grandma Eve and Grandpa Max all celebrating the holiday with us this year, I had the honor of going into the kitchen and inviting Mother to come and play for us.

I entered the kitchen, making sure my shirt was tucked in, my tie was tight and perfectly straight, and my hair adjusted so I look my absolute best. Mother was basting the turkey again, making sure it was cooking properly and on schedule so that the entire meal would be ready and served together, on time and delicious, as Dad expected. She turned suddenly and was startled by my stealth approach. She spun around and knocked over an empty gravy boat which was sitting on the counter top next to the oven. She managed to save it from hitting the floor and breaking into a hundred pieces. She was angry with me.

"Benny, what in the world?" She continued, "Can't you be still and behave for one evening?" "I swear I don't know what I'm going to do with you."

"But Mother," I pleaded, "…Dad chose me to come and ask

you to play the piano for everyone, I am sorry I made you knock the dish off the counter."

Mother looked at me with a half-smile, feigning regret for having just lectured me for this untimely accident, turned towards the sink, and proceeded to wash and dry her hands thoroughly. She reached into her purse, removed a small mirror compact, and proceeded to check her makeup, lipstick, and hair. When she was completely satisfied that she was presentable, she reached out to hold my hand, and I quickly grabbed it, imagining that everyone sitting in the living room will see that Mother is holding *my* hand and letting *me* lead her to her thoroughly polished and finely tuned piano.

Once Mother and I arrived and she had taken her place at the piano (and I back on the floor), Dad scanned the room slowly, and announced our Thanksgiving tradition where Mother performs a classical piece for the family, and for our guests. Before motioning for Mother to begin, he added how proud he is of all of the wonderful accomplishments he and his partners have achieved at the firm this year, which of course enabled us once again to enjoy this wonderful evening and share it with family and special friends. After he concluded his very detailed and perfectly crafted introductory remarks, he looked at our guests and then deliberately turned to Mother, giving her a loving smile, his chin high with pride but also with a look that communicates his high expectations. He then waved as if to motion everyone's attention to her. It was Mother's turn to shine.

"Thank you, dear. Today I have chosen to play Bach's Piano Concerto No. 5 in F-Minor," she says with a gentle smile to the crowd and a loving nod to Dad.

She adjusted the piano bench, stretched her hands across the keys, brushed a small piece of lint from the keyboard, and began softly playing. She had little facial expression, but her body language was so very fluid and full of emotion, and her hands reflected her deep passion with each and every note she played. I wished that I could play the piano like Mother. But I don't think I could ever be that good. Johann Sebastian Bach could not have played it with more grace. It was absolutely lovely, and I was once again mesmerized by her presence. Mother was so talented, and beautiful, and looking mostly at me, her special boy.

Before dinner started, Dad stood up to give thanks for our country, for his wonderful family, for the firm, for good friends, and for all we enjoy. During dinner, we were expected to behave, hold the silverware correctly, never place our elbows on the table, and never interrupt the adults. We had to wait for conversation to stop before getting the attention of Mother to give us an additional helping of…something. I always seemed to have a hard time sitting still. I would kick one of my brothers under the table, or feed table scraps to our dog, Sparky. And I almost always got caught.

After dinner was over, I asked to be excused from the dinner table; and once Dad approved, I walked alone into our living room. I looked around to make sure no one else was near, and proceeded to walk up to the piano and run my hands across the keyboard. I wanted so much to play like Mother, to show her how talented I was and make her proud. But I knew that I could never be as good as she, and

I also knew Dad would be very disappointed if I tried and failed. I couldn't fail.

Dad was the most popular among all of our friends at Shaker Heights Country Club, and at close-by Temple Beth El. So many of these men were wealthy business owners, and Dad's firm did their taxes. In fact, Dad did the taxes himself for the most important of their clients, since he had established such trust and close friendships over the years. Dad golfed with them no less than twice a week, weather permitting. At least once a month, he let me come with him on the weekend. He taught me a basic golf swing, but spent more time showing me how to be an obedient and effective caddy. He occasionally let me swing at a few balls when he warmed up before his matches. He must have thought I was pretty good, as he would never have allowed me to embarrass him at the Club.

We hardly saw him, between working such long hours at the office, and golfing and socializing with his friends. Mother was so proud of him, constantly reminding us of the incredible respect he has earned in the community, and how hard Dad works to provide such nice things, in such a nice home, and in such a wonderful neighborhood.

Dad was very cut and dry when it came to his expectations. He said on so many occasions, "Do what your Mother says, the first time she says it."

There was no room for misinterpretation. If I was bad, I was scolded most of the day by Mother and reminded that I will 'get it' when Dad gets home. And true she was to her word, and he to his obligation. Without emotion, Dad received the bad news from Mother, grabbed me hard by the arm and marched me into my room, where he proceeded to spank me over and over until I was crying profusely and unable to sit down. Sometimes, when he was extremely angry, he would start immediately with the belt. Sometimes it was on account of the severity of my misgiving, other times it was because Mother caught him in a bad mood, or I gave him a look that immediately set him wrong. There was very little conversation, other than me pleading with him that I won't do it again, and him telling me, with gritted teeth, that he works hard all day and that I must behave and do what Mother says. Period.

But on this Thanksgiving in 1941, other than knocking over the gravy boat by accident, I was a very good boy. Dad chose me to usher Mother into the living room to play for family and guests. Later that evening, after I had privately longed to be able to play the piano like Mother, as I was helping to clear our dinner table I overheard my parents in the kitchen, talking about me. Apparently Dad had seen me walk up and run my hands up and down the piano keys. They were discussing whether it was a good idea to introduce me to some piano lessons. I was excited and worried at the same time. Excited that I could learn the piano and please Mother, and worried that I couldn't measure up to her incredible standards.

The following January, Mother found a piano teacher who would come to our house twice a week, for one hour lessons each. I was required to practice a minimum of one hour per day, every single day except lesson day. On that day, after dinner I was to show Mother and Dad what I had learned the previous week, and what lessons I was supposed to practice for the upcoming week.

I was learning piano, certainly that it was much harder than I thought. I didn't like to practice. It was taking way too long to learn to play anything that I could show off to Mother. I guess I just didn't like the piano. The worst part was knowing how disappointed my parents were going to be – in particular, Mother.

My grandparents emigrated from Russia in 1908. They owned livestock and sold meat in Kiev, and when they came to America, they moved to Cleveland where many of their Jewish friends and acquaintances from their village had located. Grandpa Max had just enough money to buy land and cattle, and to rent storefront space in downtown Cleveland. He opened a small meat market on Franklin Street. Grandma Eve helped grandpa in the store, and in a very short time they built a successful market, called Max's Meats. Mother always said that Grandpa Max's success was on account of his wonderful, friendly personality. Everyone that knew him loved him. He was an honest, respected business man. Mother would use both of her parents as examples when telling me and my brothers who we must strive to be like when we grew up.

Mother was born in September, 1913. By that time, Grandpa Max and Grandma Eve had built a stable business. They had a nicer home and more money than most of their friends, yet they were very caring and giving people. Many of those that had made the long journey to America couldn't afford to eat on a regular basis. My grandfather saw to it that they ate. He made sure that any extra meats were packaged up and given to families in need.

By the time Mother was ten years old, Grandpa had put her to work delivering groceries in our mostly Jewish neighborhood. Mother would tell him about the needy families, and he would have Grandma

Eve deliver to certain of those families, but only after grandpa discussed the situations with his inner circle at Temple. Because there were so many that needed help, and extra meats and groceries were limited, my grandparents had to be selective. It was an unspoken rule that help was given to Jewish families only, most all of which were either acquaintances of grandpa's, or recommended by his close group of friends at Temple.

Mother was raised to be a very proper young lady. Her name is Grace, and she was reminded constantly that she was expected to earn that name every day in the way she behaved and communicated. Some of Mother's friends used to call her Gracie, but grandma and grandpa disapproved of this nickname because to them, it minimized the expectation. So Mother always proudly went only by the name Grace, and corrected anyone that referred to her otherwise.

Mother worked hard from a young age to help support her family, and was expected to set an example for her younger sister and brother, and even take care of them for long periods while her mother and father worked at the store. Glenda was six years younger than Mother, and Teddy was two years younger than that. Not only did Mother make her parents proud by being a straight-A student at school, but when she arrived home from the mile-long walk home from school, she would take care of Glenda and Teddy until Grandma Eve arrived home with meats for Mother to deliver to families in their east-side neighborhood. Mother would finish sometimes after 7 or 8 p.m. on weeknights, and then have to concentrate on her studies before going to bed around 10:00. On Saturday after Shabbat services, she took care of Glenda and Teddy until late afternoon, while her parents cleaned and organized at the store. On Sunday, the entire family would work at Max's Meats, where Mother was responsible for teaching Glenda and Teddy to help around the store, and of course make sure they were presentable and behaving appropriately in front of customers.

Mother was growing up to be a very beautiful young woman, and she knew it. All of the boys had crushes on her. She had her first boyfriend at sixteen years old, yet she kept a respectable distance even from him. She had been raised to be a courteous and responsible young lady, and that is precisely how she came across. Her parents loved that about her. Not only was she still a near-perfect student all through high school, but she was a gifted piano player, a trusted daughter, and a loved and respected older sister. Mother was the epitome of a sophisticated young lady – one who exuded confidence and intelligence, but also showed compassion and 'grace' for and with all those who knew her.

Mother went off to college at The Ohio State University in Columbus, in September 1930. She loved school, and continued her academic prowess and overall popularity that she had earned throughout her childhood. After completing her freshman year, Mother's family decided she should leave school to help Grandpa Max full time at the shop, since he had been sick of late and unable to continue his grueling work schedule. Though disappointed, Mother was the perfect daughter, and supported her family's decision completely. She figured she could go back to school anytime… that her father's health would improve and things would be back to normal soon.

Mother worked full time at her parent's store for the better part of a year. By then, it was looking doubtful that she would return to school to continue with her college education. Within a year of returning home, Mother met Dad at a Temple picnic. Grace's life was forever changed on that afternoon in June 1932. Grace was by far the most attractive and confident looking girl he'd ever seen. He nervously approached her and struck up a conversation. And although Mother was initially unsure whether she should go out with him, she eventually acquiesced later that summer, and one year to the day after first meeting, on June 25, 1933, they were married at Grace's parents' house in Cleveland.

I was born in October 1934. Mother was barely 21 years old. By the time she was 27, she had all three of her boys. Mother loved me so much, but she seemed to be always scolding me on account of my behavior, and teaching me manners. Dad was gone most of the time, either working long hours or socializing with his many current and prospective clients, most of them from Shaker Heights Country Club or Temple Beth El. Mother was in charge at home, and she had little patience for disobedience – for embarrassing her and Dad. He had too much to lose if I misbehaved at one of their gatherings at our house, or worse if we were all out together in public. Mother was responsible to control us, or more accurately to control me, as my brothers were always so perfect and obedient. Mother never spanked me; she would simply report my bad behavior the moment Dad walked in the door, and he would deliver severe spankings and belt whippings without discussion and with little emotion.

As much as I tried, I could never fool Mother. She knew what I was thinking before I could complete the thought. She would stop me from doing something wrong before I ever started. Probably saved me some pretty painful whippings in retrospect. Mother doted on me. I was a good-looking young boy and teenager, and Mother always bragged about how angelic I looked. She was constantly primping me – fixing my hair, licking her fingers and wiping dirt from my face, and whispering in my ear. Always the whispering.

She would repeat, "Benny, stand up straight." "Benny, get your elbows off the table." "Benny, stop that or you'll get it when your father gets home."

Hard as it was, my mission then was to keep Mother happy. Not just to avoid upsetting Dad, but also because she was so loved and revered by everyone we knew. I loved listening to Mother brag about me to everyone when she was proud of me. She would call me her 'special boy.' She would always say that I was the most handsome, smartest and most talented of all my friends, and that I should behave and act like a gentleman.

As a young teenager, I was attracted to many girls, and I was sure they were interested in me. No matter what I was doing, I used to look around to see the girls staring back at me. I didn't even have to show off. They loved to watch me. After all, I was the most handsome, smartest and talented boy in school. I got in so much trouble with Mother, and in-turn, with Dad, because I was attracted to the wrong girls, and because I was caught doing some bad things with one in particular.

It seemed I went from Mother's special boy to the boy who was always in trouble with my parents. I felt so guilty for making my beautiful Mother have to suffer through my mistakes. Why can't I just behave and do what Mother wants? But as I got older, my questions changed. Why doesn't Mother tell me how special I am anymore? Why don't you approve of my girlfriends? Why am I marrying the wrong woman? Why is my house not clean enough? Why don't I make enough money? Why must you always tell me to lose weight, and that you are embarrassed because I'm so fat?

As I sit in the middle of my living room so many years later, blood everywhere, waiting for Rosa to take care of me like the special boy I am, I think of how much I miss Mother. She's 102 years old and living in Florida. I should call her. On the other hand, she'd just tell me that Rosa is wrong for me. Bitch.

I am traversing through time, needing Rosa, missing Gail, and I am being pulled towards another memory. My family is back at home in Shaker Heights, getting ready for a family dinner at the Club. I can see myself in my Sunday best clothes. Mother criticizes me, again, as if to expect bad behavior. I was almost eleven years old.

Our family was headed to the Club on a Sunday night to celebrate the end of World War II with Dad's business associates and friends from the Jewish community. The Club's restaurant manager, Jacob, saw us as we entered the main dining room foyer and came over to personally greet Dad and Mother. Dad was one of the biggest benefactors at the Club. He was on the board of directors, and had a hand in much if not all of the community and charity work that the Club sponsored. He was also there at least twice a week to golf, and several times had invited Jacob to join him and his business associates in a round of golf.

Jacob made sure that we had the best table in the dining room, and as he led us there, he made sure to parade our family by the most prominent of the Club members. It probably took fifteen minutes to get seated, since Dad had to engage with everyone along the route, showing off his elegant wife and perfect family. Mother's job was to make sure that her three boys were perfect gentlemen.

Once seated, Mother made sure we correctly placed our napkins on our laps and sat attentively as Dad asked Jacob for drinks for the family. Once those arrived, he stood up and 'clinked' the side of his bourbon glass with a spoon, getting the attention of most of his friends and others in the room. Jacob made additional noise against another glass on our table to help Dad make sure everyone was paying close attention. Dad spoke quietly but firmly, and the room was still. Everyone wanted to hear Dad's words. He asked that everyone hold hands at their respective tables, and bow their heads in prayer. He proceeded to thank the soldiers and their families for their incredible sacrifices, and added a short prayer for the millions of Jews that were murdered during the war, and the poor families that were left behind. I think I detected his voice cracking with emotion during this speech, though we almost never saw this sort of emotion from Dad. He ended by saying that his family wished them all happiness, health and prosperity in the future. After a couple seconds of complete silence, the room erupted in applause. Dad was a great speaker. Everyone loved him. At that moment we were all very proud of him, and of ourselves, because Dad believed strongly that we were a reflection of him, and vice versa.

During dinner, Dad and Mother ate very deliberately, making sure that all proper etiquette was followed. They watched and coached with their eyes as we picked up the fork and knife, making sure we were holding utensils correctly, and efficiently handling our dinners without making a spectacle. As the meal was drawing to an end, Dad went off with other men to the cigar room to talk business, while Mom socialized with some of the ladies in the dining room. Usually, the ladies with the youngest (or worst behaved) children didn't move from their tables. Women with older and better behaved children would get up and walk around to socialize with the other ladies. There was a bonus room adjacent to the dining room where older kids were allowed to go and be together before, during and after social events. I asked Mother if I could be excused to go to the bonus room with some of my friends from school. Even though most of the kids that were allowed to use the bonus room were thirteen years old or older, Mother said okay, so long as I behaved and didn't embarrass her in front of hers and Dad's very good friends at the Club. She had issued me a challenge. If I could behave in this room and make her proud, then next time she would trust me to do the same. I happily agreed to her condition. Jimmy and Donald were too young, so they stayed with Mother.

George and I were both going to turn eleven years old soon, within a month of each other. George and his family were also at the Club that evening. When he saw that I was excused to the bonus room, he asked his mother if he could go with me. They too were reluctant to let George go, since he was younger than all of the kids in that room. But seeing that Mother let me go, George was allowed to go with me. We felt pretty good about being trusted to go to the bonus room without supervision. When we got there, we saw so many older kids from school, and most of them kept their distance, as playing with us would make them look bad. There were boys and girls in the room, most around thirteen or fourteen years old. As we were studying all the kids in the bonus room, I saw Diane, a very pretty girl from school who was eleven years old and one grade higher than I was. I was sure she liked me. She was always staring at me. I sure liked her. I told George that I liked her, and he proceeded to go up to Diane and tell her so. I was mortified, until I saw her smile and look in my direction.

I was as nervous as I've ever been, but all I could think of was Mother's words, that I was "…the best looking, smartest and most talented boy in school." How could she not like me?

I cranked up the courage and walked up to her and stood close to her. I asked her if she liked me. She was very embarrassed, but finally spit out a, "kind of…"

So in front of George and others that were in the room, I put my hand on one of her shoulders, leaned over and kissed Diane on the cheek. She didn't move a muscle. In fact, because she just stared at me after I kissed her, I went ahead and kissed her again, this time on the lips. Her plain stare changed to complete shock. Tears started down her face. She turned and started to run away. But when she did, my hand got caught in her hair bow, and it came off in my hand, but not before her head jerked back causing her to fall on the floor. I could hear her crying, calling for her father as she exited the bonus room. Her hair was a mess, and she had lost one of her shoes running from the room. I couldn't believe it. What was her problem? All I did was kiss her. I was sure she would like it, and like me even more. I was so mad at Diane. But at that moment, I was afraid. I knew Mother would be so disappointed, and Dad was going to kill me.

It didn't take long before Dad burst into the room with Mother in tow, followed by my brothers. Behind all of them were Diane and her parents, standing together watching and waiting to make sure I would be punished for my actions. Diane fetched her lost shoe, and stood back with her parents, still crying. Dad grabbed me by the upper arm so hard I thought it would come right off. His fingers were digging into my flesh. I wanted to scream. He told me that I had embarrassed him in front of all of his friends, and that I must immediately apologize to Diane and her parents, and convincingly. He said quietly, so only I would hear, that I would pay for my behavior when we got home. I apologized, crying all the while, but mostly on account of the belting I knew I was going to get when we got home. After I apologized, I'm sure I saw Diane giving me an evil smile as Dad pulled me away. I couldn't believe what I had just seen. My muscles started to tense. All senses disappeared, except for the anger that enveloped me. I hated her… and couldn't wait to get back at her. Someday.

My Violin

After failing at my brief attempt at piano lessons, Mother and Dad were reluctant to invest much in any new interests, at least not right away. Mother was very disappointed that I never really applied myself. She told me many times that Dad spent his hard-earned money to get me lessons from a reputable piano teacher, and I never took them seriously. She shamed me to no end. But during the six months where I attempted to learn piano, I would frequently overhear Dad telling Mother that the violin is a much more practical instrument for me to learn. He said that they could teach me to play it as a part of the school orchestra program, and buying a cheap used violin would not be a problem, since it could easily be resold or donated back to the school if things didn't work out.

Dad thought it was a reasonable investment to try to cultivate my apparent interest in music, and that there was no better instrument, at least in his opinion, than the violin. Coincidentally, Dad was on the Board of Directors of the Cleveland Symphony Orchestra. He would surely love it if I could learn the violin. This could be my chance to get Dad's attention – to really excel at the violin and make both my parents proud. But Mother was not ready to trust me right away. It was going to take some time and something special for me to please her again.

Just after my 8th birthday in October 1942, only five months

"

after quitting the piano, I was again apologizing for my failure at piano, and pleading with Mother to let me play the violin. I wanted to make her proud again. I wanted my Dad to notice me, and for him to want to take me to the Symphony. I wanted him to ask me to play in front of his clients, and to brag about me to his friends. Mother sat me down and told me how disappointed both she and Dad were that I never seemed to want to put in any work to play the piano. She told me that for her to be able to play as she did, she had to practice for hours every day. She took no days off. And she accomplished all of that hard work while working at Grandpa Max's meat market and babysitting her sister and brother. I didn't apply myself, and this upset my parents more than anything else.

Just a few weeks after that initial conversation, on an otherwise ordinary Sunday morning, Mother and Dad surprised me with a tiny used violin. I was ecstatic. I removed it from its cloth zippered case and just held it, first on my lap, then under my chin like I'd seen professionals do in picture books and newspapers. It was so cool and smooth, so beautiful, and so…mine. I tried to run the bow across the strings; it felt so natural, but sounded pretty awful. Dad told me to stop, for now. He said that Mother had contacted the school and enrolled me in the junior orchestra at my elementary school for the second semester. In the meantime, she was going to take me to the library and check out some books about the violin. He wanted me to learn about the history of the instrument, and read some stories on some of the more well-known violinists. He wanted me to appreciate this opportunity before ever playing a note, and certainly before making a commitment to concentrate on another instrument.

From the very beginning, I loved and exceled at playing the violin. After learning the basics in the junior orchestra during the second semester of the third grade, Mother and Dad agreed to get me private lessons. The music teacher at school had called them at the end of the school year and told them that I had natural ability, and a real feel for the music through my violin. He recommended private lessons, and even suggested some musicians whom he knew that gave private music lessons.

Mother was not going to settle for just any private instructor. She asked Dad to contact the conductor of the Cleveland Symphony and get some recommendations. He found out that the second chair of the violin section of the orchestra also gave private violin lessons to intermediate and advanced students, but only by referral. Normally I wouldn't have been considered either, at least not at that point, but because of Dad's connections with the orchestra's Board of Directors, he agreed to take me on. I immediately took to his tutelage, catching on to both the music in a literal sense, as well as the feel and the comprehensive aspect of the music, which cannot be taught. It is either there, or it's not. From the beginning, Dad made it clear that regardless of my progress, these lessons were expensive, and I had better keep working hard and make Mother proud. After Dad's initial intervention, my success or failure became Mother's responsibility. Dad had too much responsibility at work and in the community to be concerned with mine or my brothers' daily issues. Make Dad proud. Do not embarrass him outside the home. Those were our simple but non-negotiable rules growing up. And Mother reminded us of these almost every day.

For many years to follow, Mother made sure I had the best instructors, since keeping my original instructor wasn't possible once he took a job with a larger orchestra in Chicago. Mother enjoyed my playing so much that she would even accompany me on her piano. She was so fluid in her play, she brought out the best in my playing. She and I seemed to really connect with our music. I was her special boy again. Mother was so proud of me, and I of myself.

Almost five years after starting on my small, used violin, Mother gave me the most beautiful brand new violin for my Bar Mitzvah. She looked so beautiful that day in her stunning white gown with the beautiful roses on it, and she couldn't wait to give me the violin the minute we arrived back home. She was so proud of me. I was most certainly her special boy again.

I was in our high school orchestra, even though I was just a lowly freshman. All the girls loved me. As I performed, I could see them all staring at me, giggling with their friends. And I could see Mother beaming from the audience. That pride was going to be short lived, however. She was becoming more and more upset at my shrinking practice time, as my priorities were quickly shifting from studying at school and on my violin, to impressing the girls.

I am pulled swiftly back to the present, staring at the TV after having this fight with Rosa that I can't even recall. As I again scan the entire room, I focus this time on what I'm actually staring at. Is it the TV, which continues to blare so loud it is muffling the sounds Rosa is making in the bedroom? Looking again, high on the wall behind the TV is the painting of a violin that Mother gave me when I married Gail. I'm sure at the time it was her way of showing me what I could have had, who knows. Regardless, it is a very beautiful violin; a bow lay next to it, along with a metronome, round wire-rimmed glasses and sheet music scattered around it on a wood floor. I've kept that painting for all these years. That's what I'm staring at. As hard as I try, I can't remember what happened to my beloved violin.

Dad

Dad was the fourth of five children, and the first to be born in the United States, in 1907. His parents, Grandpa Josef and Grandma Marie, emigrated in 1904 from Zhitomir – a small mostly Jewish community in what is now northwest Ukraine. Dad's younger sister died of a brain aneurism during childbirth when she was only 21 years old, which tragically also resulted in her baby's death. Dad had two older sisters and one older brother.

Like Mother's parents, they settled in northern Ohio where many of their friends from their village back home had also relocated. Grandpa sold fresh vegetables and other groceries back in Zhitomir, and took up the same business in Cleveland, initially working for an established grocery store downtown. Grandma had her hands full raising her five children on Grandpa's limited income. My grandparents moved the family to the east side of downtown Cleveland in early 1914 when Dad was six years old, since Grandpa had an opportunity to be a partner in a small grocery store there. They also lived in the apartment directly above the store.

Unfortunately, Dad didn't have many stories describing his parents; what kind of people they were, what they did as a family, what caused them to have to leave their homeland and start all over again in the new world. The memories that Dad often repeated were how incredibly hard his parents worked to support his family, how loving and nurturing his mother was, and that his youngest sister with whom he was so very close had died tragically in her early twenties. He once told us that his brother was an outcast from the family, but he never discussed the circumstances. Whether Dad carried more memories from his childhood and growing up in Cleveland was a mystery to me. He didn't want to discuss it. He believed in what lie ahead, and not what had happened in the past. Even when punishing me he seemed in a huge hurry to inflict as severe a lesson as he thought appropriate so we would never have to discuss it again. He didn't want to talk about transpired events. After my punishment, he would talk only about what is next, about tomorrow, about how my behavior must be to a certain standard going forward, always reminding me of the consequences if not. I could never make up for what had happened previously. This was both good and bad. The good was obvious; I had what amounted to a clean slate every time he put his belt back on and left my room. The bad news was that I couldn't forget the disappointment I had created, and there was nothing I could do to make up for it.

Dad graduated from East Side High School in Cleveland in June 1925. He didn't play sports, though he did play the drums in the high school orchestra. Most of his spare time was spent working for my grandparents every day after school. He was the first in his immediate family to go to college. And not just any college. After graduating high school, Dad started working at Republic Steel Company as a bookkeeper, and was attending the YMCA Community College part-time. After three years of full-time work and part-time school, he applied and was accepted to the New York University

School of Commerce, one of the most prestigious schools in the eastern United States at the time. As with everything else he took on, Dad was a dedicated student. He believed it was his responsibility to study hard, achieve as high marks as possible, and make his parents proud. And as was Dad's life in a nutshell, he was successful. He graduated in the top 10% of his class, even considering he balanced his full class load while working part time for a local CPA firm in New York City. After earning his Bachelor's degree from NYU in June 1932, Dad returned home to Cleveland, where he took a job as an accountant with Bonwit Teller Department Stores. He also started right away studying for the CPA exam, which he would have to return to NYU to take, but not until he was confident that he could pass it the first time. This level of confidence would likely take a couple of years, since he wanted to have some accounting experience under his belt, and make sure he would not fail that test. It was well known that the CPA exam was very difficult and complex, that only a very small percentage of applicants passed on the first attempt. He was determined to be one of those elite.

On June 25, 1932, just two weeks after returning home from NYU, Dad and his parents attended the Temple's B'nai B'rith picnic where Mother and her entire family were among the guests present. Dad and Mother met for the first time over an outdoor lunch and iced tea. The way Dad tells it, he noticed the most beautiful girl across the park lawn and couldn't take his eyes off of her. Nothing and no one else at the picnic even registered anymore. He had never seen anyone so beautiful. As the afternoon progressed, Dad was growing afraid that the day would pass before he got up the courage to talk to her. He finally followed her up to the food tables, walked up next to her and introduced himself. Dad was immediately smitten. Grace wasn't just pretty, she was elegant. She was well spoken. She was confident. They talked for quite some time before Mother's parents came to gather her up, as it was getting late in the afternoon. He knew he had to pursue her. He was convinced she the woman with whom he would spend his entire life. In Dad's mind it was only a matter of time before he proposed, she accepted, and they were married. It was important to Dad that he earn the trust of Mother's parents, and show them all that he was going to be a successful businessman, and of course, good husband material. Dad's ultimate goal was still to become a CPA and start his own accounting firm in or near Cleveland – possibly even Shaker Heights, which was a growing upper-middle class suburb where many Jewish families were settling. The timeline for accomplishing all of this had taken center stage in his thoughts of late, since he wanted to make sure he was on his way to building a successful career before getting married, finding a home and having a family.

Dad was doing very well at Bonwit Teller and spending all of his spare time studying for the CPA exam, and, of course, courting Mother. Dad proposed to her in October 1932. They were married June 25, 1933, one year to the day after meeting at that B'nai B'rith picnic. The following December, he was finally ready for the CPA exam. He traveled back to New York, convinced that he was well prepared to pass the test, pursue his professional ambitions, and secure a nice home so that he and Mother could start their family. Not only did he pass, but he scored 100%. Throughout his life, one of his proudest accomplishments was passing that exam with a perfect score. I can't recall how many times I've heard that story, and the consistent message that accompanied it – that hard work, dedication and loyalty are all necessary elements to achieve true success.

Dad worked full time for Bonwit Teller through mid-1934 while he was gaining clients of his own, on his way to opening his own accounting firm. He and Mother bought our home on Grove Street in Shaker Heights in July 1934. From the very start of their marriage, Dad was busy building his business and expanding his social footprint. He was determined to increase his client base, and in the process make a nice home for Mother and his future family, which started none too soon when I was born in October 1934.

Dad was rarely home, especially between January and May every year, during tax season. But even during the balance of the year, Dad worked hard. He personally handled the books of Bonwit Teller for many years after having worked for them as an accountant, and for several other large and small businesses in and around Cleveland. Even though taxes were filed in April, he had many clients that needed his counsel year-round. He was a busy man, and a very successful one. And he was much loved and respected at our Temple, at our Country Club and throughout Cleveland's east-side communities.

When my brothers and I were growing up, Dad relied on Mother to enforce the same rigid orderliness at home that he prided himself on maintaining in his accounting practice. He would half-jokingly refer to this division of work as their respective 'departments.'

"Oh, that's Mother's department," he'd say, when referring to laundry, or cooking, or cleaning.

And when it came to the day-to-day management of me and my brothers, he would tell us that this was, "…Mother's most important department."

Sure, he would be the one to physically deliver the punishment. But Mother determined the infraction and severity. Mother was the one who remembered everything I had ever done wrong, which many times increased the severity of the punishment. Most important, Mother and Dad were always on the same page. There was never any disagreement that I remember, and as a result I never had any thoughts of trying to gain sympathy from one or the other. They were a well- oiled machine when it came to parenthood, and anything else for that matter. What Mother said, went. And Dad loved being able to depend on her to keep us in line, in addition to her other 'departmental duties'.

The community all saw Dad as a gentle giant among them. Not in size or stature, but in his actions, and in the soft spoken way he was able to make his point. I also saw him as a man of few words. But for me, I wish there had been more. We never had deep or warm conversations about life, about feelings, about girls, or other soft subjects that I wished we could have talked about. Mother took care of all of that, at least those subjects she was willing to discuss. Dad talked about practical things. How to save and invest money. How to earn respect. Why it was so important to keep your promises. How and why it was important to study hard and do well in school.

The first time I challenged Dad to a foot race out front of our house, I was eight years old. He seemed to be in a pretty good mood after work one summer night, and I thought I could show him how athletic I was, and make him proud. I was the fastest runner in school, even though I was shorter than most of the boys. Dad accepted my challenge, even said he'd spot me three seconds before he started running. He even said he'd beat me wearing his work shoes and dress slacks.

We went out front, stood on the street in front of our house, and after making sure I was ready, Dad said, "Go," with authority.

I was so fast. I thought there was no way he would catch me. But five seconds after starting, he buzzed past me, finishing several seconds before I reached the end of the block. I was disappointed, but also happy that Dad agreed to give me a chance. After the race, Dad reached out his hand to shake mine, like a gentleman should.
I shook his hand, and at the same time I said, "Next time I'll beat you, Dad."

He just turned away towards the house, laughing. The smile I was sporting quickly drained from my face.

Mother and Dad would not approve of Rosa. She doesn't come from a wealthy family. She's definitely not Jewish. Heck, she's not even an American citizen. Mother would be livid. I can just imagine the anguish tearing at her insides; if she were here or I there with her at her nursing home in Naples, Florida, I'd be enjoying the hell out of torturing her. Rosa might not be their idea of the perfect mate for me, but she practically worships me. She does absolutely everything I ask of her, and satisfies my every need. She cooks and cleans and smiles when she has to change my pants, no matter how terrible, and even intentional, the mess might be. She loves me and treats me special, like I deserve to be treated.

When Marty and Alan decided I could no longer take care of the house I shared with Joan, they moved me into Mission Manor. And although I didn't outwardly object, I was miserable at the thought of losing my home and with it, what independence I had left. Most of my things were gone. The boys saw to that. What happened to all of the cash I had carefully stashed throughout the house? Where were all of my pictures from my childhood? I had so many mementos, and now I have nothing but a bed, a tiny couch, a recliner, a dresser and an old TV. I've gone from a nice 1700 square foot house filled with memories to a 500-plus square foot piece-of-shit sterile cheap motel-like room. There's not even room for a dining room table, since the kitchen is only about 30 square feet. There was no need for one, actually, as meals were included. Regardless, that was one more swipe at my independence. I now had a tiny kitchenette, with a teeny tiny refrigerator, with a few teeny tiny soft drinks that had to be turned on their side so they could fit.

Everyone at this place was old and decrepit. Worst of all were the ugly old women. There's no way I wanted to touch any of the old biddies in here, let alone even think about it. All of them were the same, except for the few shift managers or kitchen workers who were in their 30's or 40's, cute but married, and all looking at me like a pathetic old inconvenience. Before moving to Mission Manor, I'd been able to sneak around with some middle-aged ladies I would meet in our neighborhood, both before and since Joan died. But not anymore. Not at this pathetic place. Or at least that's what I thought at first.

I was having trouble adjusting to Mission Manor. I couldn't manage the smorgasbord which was my medication regimen. I was lethargic all the time, couldn't put two sentences together, was missing meals, never showered, never participated in any social activities, and rarely left my room. Two weeks passed, and the management called my sons and suggested hiring a part time caregiver to help me acclimate to my new home. Marty asked me how I would feel about having someone to assist me, and I agreed that it would help. The managers gave him a couple of recommendations, and after making calls and interviewing them on the phone, they selected my caregiver. They assured me Rosa had lots of experience and came highly recommended. When I met her, she seemed very sweet and accommodating, yet firm and sure of herself. She organized my meds, made sure I was awake and attending all meals, helped me in and out of the shower, and as I became more and more incontinent, she cleaned and changed me. She would go to the grocery for me to fill my tiny fridge in my tiny kitchen with tiny drinks or even tinier snacks. She brought me Depends, and helped me adjust to those. What I liked most about Rosa was that she really seemed to like me. She told me how smart she thought I was. She took my side when the stupid old ladies were complaining about me. She listened to me, even though it was hard to recall and express my thoughts. I was becoming very dependent on her. In only a couple of weeks, I was getting mad when Rosa wasn't there. I didn't like the fact that she had other residents she was caring for at Mission Manor. I wanted her there, with me, all the time. I wanted to be her special boy. Her only boy.

I had to accept the fact that she had others to care for, but I was calmed by the knowledge that Rosa liked me best. She responded to my flirting. I could manipulate her easily by crying. When my depression took over and I became melancholy about my life, about Mother's criticisms, Gail's flawed priorities, Joan's pathetic existence, or my kids' indifference to me, Rosa would sit next to me on the bed and cuddle me like a child. When she thought that the old ladies at the home were flirting with me, she became visibly angry. I really pushed her buttons when I told her that Nell and Ellen had both brushed up against me in the hall and had given me long stares in the dining room, smiling at me before turning and walking away. Rosa was pissed. After that exaggeration, Rosa started telling me things about Nell and Ellen that really upset me. She would tell me that they giggle at me, and tease me behind my back. They didn't like me at all. It was a game to these old man-hating bitches. Or was it Rosa's game to get me angry at them, and more dependent on her for protection?

When Rosa would prepare me for showers, she would intentionally rub me briefly, knowing it would get me excited. After a couple of weeks of this teasing, she started reaching in and stroking me while showering. We couldn't let anyone know, or Rosa could lose her job. Maybe that wouldn't be such a bad thing, since I wouldn't have to share her. But for the time being, it was our little secret. She also started telling me about her loveless marriage, including her lack of intimacy with her husband. I wasn't sure exactly where this was leading, but I was more excited than I'd been in years.

We seemed to take turns riling the other. I would wink at the young shift managers, or even some of the disgusting old ladies, making sure of course that Rosa was watching. And in her tit-for-tat and sometimes even perturbed response, she would tell me how much those old ladies hated me, making fun of me every time my back was turned. I knew what she was doing, and even though her comments were somewhat belittling, I didn't mind the game. But my hatred of these ladies, in particular Nell – the mean old bitch whose room was next door to mine – was growing quickly.

I was so upset that day, just having been told by Rosa, again, that Nell was spreading nasty rumors about me, that when we confronted each other in the narrow hallway outside our rooms, it was 'on.'

Nell turned towards me and snarled, "Move your fat ass out of the way, old man."

My arms were tensed and shaking with rage. My teeth were clenched so tight I thought my jaw would snap. I managed to growl back at her, "You fucking bitch!"

She looked at me with such disdain; I couldn't remember anyone ever daring to look at me like that in all my life. It was like slow motion – the way she walked slowly past with her walker, first giving me that nasty look, and following that with a condescending and dismissive laugh. I was sure that she intentionally landed her walker on my left foot as she moved past me. I was so incensed I couldn't think. I turned and with my right backhand, hit her as hard as I could on the shoulder. I didn't care that she was 91. Screw her. She yelled. It sounded like a wounded animal. Certainly an ugly one.

I hit her again, calling her a bitch once more, this time louder and with more purpose. As I raised my fist like a hammer to hit her a third time, the maintenance man grabbed my arm and pushed me back against the wall and pinned me so I couldn't move. Nell wasn't hurt. She didn't even fall down. She's a manipulating bitch who was teasing and disrespecting me, and now she was trying to get me kicked out of Mission Manor. She deserved it. To hell with all of you old rag dolls. Where was Rosa when I needed her? Helping another ugly old bitch? I need you here, now.

It was July 2014 – barely four months after moving into this shithole, and I'd been kicked out. Good. At least I would get away from these miserable old men and pathetic wrinkly old women.

Marty and Alan were mad at me. I'm sure they didn't know what to do with me next, since getting me accepted into another facility would be near impossible considering what had just happened. Lucky for all of us, Rosa came to the rescue. She said that I could live with her family (husband, daughter, in-laws, dogs, etc.) indefinitely. Given the extreme flirting we had been up to, I wasn't sure how this would turn out. But I didn't care. I was happy to be going to live with Rosa. She treated me special, the way a man like me should be treated.

Rosa was 23 when she was first married, in Mexico City. She had told me that she and Frank had an arranged marriage, which was still apparently commonplace in their strict Catholic community. I always wondered why she told me the part about having their marriage arranged; maybe it was an excuse to tell me that she had essentially a loveless marriage. Probably made cheating more acceptable, I didn't really care. They both came to California on a work visa in 1991, when Rosa was 30 years old. She had Laura in the United States two years later, in 1993. Frank applied for citizenship almost immediately after Laura was born, but Rosa wanted to go back to Mexico, and of course take her daughter with her. She missed her family, and wasn't in love with Frank. She longed to be back with her friends and tight-knit community, and not have to try to fit into the chaos that was Southern California. Frank was not going to agree to giving up his daughter, so Rosa stayed, always planning to return, and always planning to take

Laura with her. Unfortunately, Rosa never applied for citizenship. Frank had earned his, and Laura was a citizen by birth. Rosa was going to have to be very careful going forward.

Frank and Rosa both started performing caregiving services at retirement communities in the Riverside and Redlands areas. Both had performed similar services in a large Mexico City retirement home, and they had taken care of Frank's parents until their death. They were more than capable of doing this sort of work, though neither had degrees, and were not certified in any related profession. But both were loved by all of the seniors who they cared for. Even though their marriage may not have been a happy one, they were both very kind, empathetic and effective caregivers. Both had been hired by Mission Manor in 2002, and they enjoyed a fairly decent living, though they worked all hours of the day and night, depending on the needs of their 'patients.'

By the time Rosa felt that she could leave Frank and return to Mexico, Laura was thirteen years old. She was an American. She loved and excelled at school, had many friends, and was not interested in moving to Mexico. That was not her home, and never would be, if she had any say in it. Her mother was upset that Laura felt this way, but she wasn't surprised by it. Rosa knew she would have to maintain her current situation until Laura was on her own, when she could finally leave Frank and start her own life.

As it happened, Laura turned 21 in September 2014. One month later, Rosa asked me to move out with her, just the two of us, into a small apartment. She wanted to leave Frank and be with me.

She told Marty and Alan that she loves me. And I love Rosa.

I don't remember feeling this excited since high school, when Diane and I 'did it' while hiding in the orchestra room at Shaker Heights High School. I got both things I wanted that day – Diane's virginity, and revenge for making a fool of me a little more than four years earlier in our Country Club's bonus room.

Mother had long since forgotten about the time I kissed Diane in the bonus room at the Club when I was almost eleven years old. I hadn't, though. I saw Diane every day at Shaker Heights High School, and still noticed her looking at me all the time. On the outdoor quads, in the hallways, even outside the orchestra room – I knew she was passing close to me just to look at me, to see if I was looking back at her. Well I was, but not because I liked her. It was because she was cute and popular, and surrounded by even more cute and popular girls. I was turning back to look, but not at her. I was looking at anyone but her, because I never forgot the evil look she gave me after letting me kiss her at the Club. She was a tease, and I wasn't going to let anyone screw with me like that again. I could tell that these other girls really liked me, but I was pretty busy, and too young to drive so it would be hard to ask any of them out on a date, or have any privacy even if I could. Besides, Mother wouldn't approve. I didn't recognize any of them from Temple or the Club.

I had school every day until 3:30, and on Mondays, Wednesdays and Fridays I had orchestra practice at the school until 5:30. Tuesdays I took private violin lessons with the 2nd chair violinist in the Cleveland Symphony, and on Thursdays I was invited to sit and practice with the Junior Symphony. The Tuesday and Thursday activities were held at the Performing Arts Theater from 4:00

until at least 6:00. I really enjoyed my Thursday afternoons with the Jr. Symphony, though I had to be on my best behavior. I was the youngest person there. These people were extremely serious about their work, since they were next up if one of theSymphony musicians dropped out or had to miss a performance. I learned a lot at these sessions, but I had to be invisible, except when I got to play along with my violin. Mother dropped me off and picked me up every day, and during those rides she'd asked how I was doing at school and with my music. I loved those drives with Mother. When she dropped me off downtown on Tuesdays and Thursdays, she always reminded me that I was her 'special boy,' and I should remember to do my best and impress the other musicians.

It was unusually warm for late November in Cleveland, and on this particular Friday it was so nice outside I didn't even wear a coat to school. Once 3:30 came around and it was time for school to end and orchestra practice to begin, I made my way to the orchestra room only to find a note on the door. Practice had been cancelled, as our instructor had gone home sick after lunch that day. I was heading to the office to call Mother to come and pick me up early when I saw Diane and her friends gathered together in the outdoor quad walkway. I decided to walk up and join their little group. I wasn't paying much attention to Diane, though as the small talk continued, the other girls left one by one to either start their walk or catch their rides home from school. That left Diane and me. Shades of the Club four years ago. This time though, she was really flirting. Her body language was telling me she wanted me to kiss her, but I knew from experience that I had to be careful. About ten minutes into our somewhat pointless conversation, she asked me if I wanted to go for a walk. So we started, first walking around the quad area, then inside past the lockers and towards the empty orchestra room. While we walked, Diane talked about how she liked watching me play the violin. She said I was the best of the group. She said she liked my haircut, and told me that it made me look cute. About time she noticed.

As we got to the orchestra room door, Diane leaned up against me and kissed me on the lips. It was a short kiss. She pulled back for an instant to see my reaction. For a moment I remembered again how she got me in so much trouble at the Club. I had harbored my anger and resentment toward her for all these years. I had vowed to get back at her someday, and for a moment I thought that this could be my chance. But then she leaned forward and again we were kissing, this time much longer, much harder and much wetter, and we were sliding through the open door of the orchestra room. As we slipped through the door, I instinctively shut and locked it behind us. My heart was beating so hard and fast; I could hardly contain myself. We continued kissing as we made our way to the back of the room, and inside the instrument closet. There wasn't much room in there – it was dark, carpeted, and secluded; all really good elements for what I was hoping would happen next.

We both got down on the floor, and were awkwardly kissing and pressing against each other. I had kissed girls before, but hadn't gone any further than that. Mother would be mortified. But here I was, and I couldn't stop. She let me put my hands up her blouse and on her breast, and all I did for a minute or two was hold the one breast while I kept kissing her. She was so warm and soft. I didn't know how much longer I could hold off. I pulled my hand back from under her blouse and proceeded to quickly undo my belt and pull my pants and underwear off with one free hand. As I started reaching under her skirt to find and pull down her panties, she grabbed my hand and held it firm and still, stopped kissing me and told me in a very soft voice to stop. I had already pulled her underpants half-way down her legs, but for a brief moment I stopped as requested, gave her my best attempt at an expression of love and understanding, and resumed kissing her slower and more softly than before. I didn't want to stop. She started this, anyway. When she responded to my kissing her, I quickly resumed working her underwear down and off of one of her legs. I gently but quickly rolled on top of her and no sooner did I enter her, I had an orgasm, some inside of her, but mostly outside and on her body and her blouse. I went to kiss her again and she turned her head and pushed me away.

She wouldn't kiss me, or even look in my direction. She just lay there and cried. I was fuming inside. What the hell was this all about? My muscles tensed up remembering that night at the Club when I was ten years old and Diane was eleven. I remembered her teasing me, and the look on her face when I gave her what she wanted, then watching as she took great pleasure in turning on me and getting me in so much trouble with my parents.

I stood up, and as I pulled on my underwear I noticed a small amount of blood on my hand, and now on my underwear. I paid no attention. I finished putting my pants and belt back on, reached down and wiped my hand clean on the carpet, and turned to leave. Just before I started heading out, I looked down at her. She was still crying. I glared at her with the same smirk-filled smile that she had given me all those years ago after I'd kissed her at the Club. A little payback, right Diane? Not so great, is it?

Diane continued to cry as I walked out of the orchestra room with my head held high, thinking to myself she got what she wanted and in the end, what she deserved. I wasn't sure what happened to Diane after I left her in the orchestra room at about 4:30. I didn't see her again that afternoon, and I really didn't care to. Mother arrived at school to pick me up on schedule, at 5:30. She asked me how practice was, and I promptly lied and told her it was fine. No, it was great! That night, when I took my bath, I snuck my underwear in with me and washed them thoroughly. I squeezed out as much water as I could and laid them under my bed to dry. I certainly did not want to have to explain the blood to Mother.

The next day, Saturday, it was still very nice outside and Dad was home all day, which was not typical, since if he wasn't at work on Saturdays, then he was at some Temple event, or golfing with clients or friends at the Club. He was taking his time reading the morning newspaper, and I approached him and asked him if he wanted to throw the baseball around in the yard. I hadn't thought about Diane at all that morning. Dad said yes, and we grabbed our mitts and an old baseball and went out front and across the street to a greenbelt area where there were no houses. We played for about fifteen minutes. Dad seemed relaxed and although he was always in quiet contemplation, usually thinking about work or some other important social obligation, he seemed to be enjoying the quiet time with me.

After playing catch, I asked him if he felt like racing me again. I had raced him a few times since the first time he beat me so bad, even after giving me a head start. Each time he had beat me, and each time he laughed at my false confidence that next time would be different. But I was feeling pretty strong, fast, and extra grown-up that day. I was wearing my new gym shoes, too. That should have given me a little advantage over Dad's weekend loafers. Dad agreed, and although he again offered to give me a head start, I refused. I told him I would beat him fair and square.

Dad's face got very serious, very quickly. I had issued a challenge, and in the process even got a little cocky refusing his offer of a head start. The race began. I was surprised that even though we started at the same time, I was keeping up with Dad, and was even a little ahead of him in the middle of the race. My excitement was short lived, when about three-quarters down our block, Dad buzzed past me, finishing first by plenty. He let me think I had a chance for most of the race, then turned it on at the end. He wasn't even tired when we were finished, whereas I was huffing and puffing to catch my breath. As was the custom, he walked up to me to shake my hand. And as was my custom in response, I would reach out and shake his hand.

This time though, before I was able to tell him what I usually do – that I would beat him next time, after which he would always laugh – he stopped me and said, "Benjamin, don't say it." We both knew it wasn't true, anyway.

As we were walking back to our front yard towards our house, a car raced down Grove Street and came screeching to a sudden stop in front of our house, parking right in front of our driveway. It was Diane's father.

When I was in high school, I dreamed of being a fighter pilot. I would be soaring high in the sky in my F-86 Sabre, in command of all that surrounded me. I would shoot all the enemies down; no one would be able to out-maneuver me. The girls back home would all wish they were mine. Mother would brag to all of her friends about her son the fighter pilot. All Mother's friends would gather around her to support her while her special boy was bravely fighting wars abroad. The community would honor me with a parade when I arrived home. I would be the town hero – the envy of all other boys, and all the other mothers. The President would award me the Medal of Honor for killing so many enemy combatants, and saving so many American lives. I could learn to fly. How hard could it be?

I brought up the subject of going into the military and being a fighter pilot one night over dinner after school and orchestra practice. Dad's look went from relaxed and enjoying his food, to very stern, and visibly pissed, presumably ruining his dinner.

He glared at me for several long seconds and said, "Benjamin, you are going to college, period. Now eat."

Mother looked at me as if to say, "Goddamn right." But she never said a word. Again, Mother and Dad were one in everything they believed, no matter who delivered the message. I was mad at myself again, for thinking I'd hear something different this time. My brother,

Jimmy, just looked at me and grinned. He was the fortunate beneficiary of all of my ill-timed comments and actions. Mr. Goody-Goddamn-Two-Shoes. Of course, I could enlist in the Army at seventeen years old, if I wanted to. I only had a year to wait. But I doubted that I'd be able to become a pilot without some serious training, not to mention Mother and Dad would likely cut me off, and somehow force my hand. That dream would have to wait, if not be permanently shelved.

I was a great golfer. Dad had taken me out on so many occasions, and now I was playing in the Club's Junior Handicap League, and even working part time for the resident golf pro. My handicap was only 10, and I was getting better all the time. Every time I was out on the course, I imagined the packed gallery of fans yelling for my attention as I made my way to the green, after a perfect shot from mid-fairway. They knew I would birdie the hole, and I didn't disappoint. All the girls in the stand would melt as I walked by. I could have had any of them. They were all so unbelievably cute. I thought I'd throw Mother a bone and let her weigh in. She would love that. Besides, it was easy to know which of the girls she would approve of. Jewish, rich parents, in the local vicinity. These were key starters. Then, bonus points for being members of Temple Beth El, even more if they belonged to the Club, and automatic acceptance if they met all of the previous criteria and were also either clients or friends of Dad's. As I was out golfing, daydreaming about my golf prowess and the obvious benefits, Dad would quickly bring me back to reality by grabbing my arm and telling me sternly to focus.

"Concentrate, Benny. Work on your chip shots. Stop your daydreaming and be serious for a change. What is wrong with you?"

My music was probably the one thing I was most comfortable with. I knew I was good. The best, in fact, for my age – any age, for that matter. My teachers were in awe of my style, the natural vibrato flowing through my left hand, the swaying of my head and shoulders. The music flowed through me. And while I was actually playing, and not just sitting there waiting to play, I didn't think of girls, or Mother, or anything else. I was in a serene, unimaginable zone. I felt every single note, every string and every stroke, and many times it was all I could do to stay focused on the conductor, as it was so easy for me to get lost in the piece, and in my own playing. Unfortunately, as was life, I had to conform to the other members of the orchestra. It was when I stopped playing that I would quickly scan the room, first for Mother, and then to see the expression on every young girl's face in the audience.

I had decided that one way or another, even if I had to go to college, I was going to be rich and retire at 40. I had so many options, I just had to pick one. With lots of practice time, I could keep up my golf game and be a professional. If I continued on my path working such long hours and with such excellent instructors, I could be a violin virtuoso. With the money I made from either of those paths, I could invest in a business and make tons of money. I wouldn't even have to work, because I'd hire people to manage my businesses. Dad talked all the time about investing, and saving. He could help me to do both, and then I would buy a department store, or a restaurant, or just be a real estate investor, and be able to achieve my dream of 40-and-out. How hard could that be?

Dad was a realist. He had worked his entire life to do well in school, get good jobs, start his own business and build a community of support – all towards achieving his idea of success. No matter how good I might be playing golf, or the violin, priorities were priorities. Education. A respected profession. Community leadership. Anything else was nothing more than a hobby, and with no plan other than daydreams, he had no patience for unrealistic visions of grandeur. Dad came into my bedroom on the same night I brought up being a fighter pilot at dinner. He stepped over to the bed and sat down on it, and I slid over to give him room. I treasured the few times he did this. I felt special, like he was taking time out from being the most important man in our community to spend time with me. Most of those chats were life lessons, typically with a tone of encouragement. This one started that way, but quickly deteriorated, his voice and expression becoming angrier as he softly spoke to me:

"Benjamin, you are smart and talented, but you are losing focus. You are not concentrating on the things that are important, the things that can make you a success. Over the past year, your grades have dropped and you have no explanation. Your teachers say you are daydreaming. You are not practicing violin at near the levels you had before, and the instructor that Mother and I pay good money for is baffled. You do not take golf seriously; you are always looking around you, seeing who might be watching, imagining you are playing in the goddamn

U.S. Open. You have humiliated, embarrassed and shamed Mother and me with decisions that unfortunately you can never take back." He took a breath and continued:

"You do not wake up flying planes or owning businesses. You must study and work hard. You cannot be a violin virtuoso without complete dedication. Complete. Not partial. That goes for any type of success. Success is not an entitlement. You must do what is right and work harder than anyone. You must earn back the pride that Mother and I expect to have in you. And by the way, no golf until things have significantly changed. You do not have a choice."

He proceeded to stand up, remove his belt, pull my covers back… and then stop and stare at me for the longest time. I'd been punished before, but never had I seen my father so angry. After standing there, belt in hand, seething with anger for the longest time, he put the belt back through the belt loops of his pants, leaned over and grabbed a handful of my hair, and lifted my head up off my pillow. He brought his face level with mine.

With such anguish on his face that I had never seen; his lips quivering, arms shaking, and even tears rolling down his face, he said only two words to me: "Fix this."

He let go, dabbed his face with his handkerchief, replaced it in his rear pants pocket, walked out of my room, slammed the door, and left me to my thoughts. I was 16. Dad never struck me that night, and I was never physically punished again. I wasn't sure if I would have preferred a spanking to Dad's looking at me with such despair and disappointment. I didn't sleep at all that night.

Jimmy had become Dad's favorite, quite strategically and with purpose, I think. Jimmy did well in school, and managed to stay almost completely out of trouble. He would sit with Dad and talk about what it's like to be a CPA; he even said that he wanted to work at Dad's office someday. It had been a long time since Mother called me her special boy. That really hurt me. I loved her so much, and it was so important to me that she was proud of me. What about my dreams? Was Dad right? Were all of these just pipe dreams; a big waste of time and energy? Would I be able to retire at 40? Maybe I could own a business? Learn how to invest and make a lot of money in the stock market? Could I ever measure up to Dad? He was so dedicated, so hard working, so confident and focused, and so loved by everyone. I didn't want a typical existence. I didn't want to be a goddamn accountant. I was too special for that. Mother always said that I could accomplish anything.

But all I can think of at this very moment, sitting bloody and alone in the middle of this pathetic apartment in Riverside, California, is that none of these dreams ever came true. Thank you Joan. Thank you Gail. Thank you Mother.

I see myself with the Cleveland Jr. Symphony Orchestra at the beautiful Performing Arts Theater – sitting in the second violin chair position. The current second chair fell sick the night before, and they called me early that morning to see if I would be prepared to sit in for her in the event she couldn't make that night's performance. The Jr. Symphony doesn't play many performances, as it is primarily there serving as the 'minor leagues' of sorts; feeding talent as needed to the primary Cleveland Symphony. On this particular Saturday evening, the Jr. Symphony was scheduled to play a 30-45 minute performance as the opening act for the real thing. I was offered the honor because I was first chair of the Shaker Heights High School orchestra, and I had been practicing with the Jr. Symphony nearly two years now. That of course was a perk afforded to me, since my instructor was the second chair of the real Symphony.

I was nervous, as I'd never performed with this group before, and this evening's performance would be led by a guest conductor I wasn't familiar with. We were to play a total of six pieces, ending with Mozart's Violin Concerto No. 5 in A, 2nd Movement. I had practiced this piece with the Jr. Symphony, and coincidentally we had also played it with the Shaker Heights orchestra earlier last semester. It is a very beautiful piece, and this arrangement features violin and viola throughout. After we finished with our fifth number, I knew this

Mozart Concerto was on deck. I began searching the audience for Mother, and for Margi, my current girlfriend. I found them both, though they weren't sitting together. Mother and Dad had season tickets, and because Dad was busy having dinner with a client, she brought Jimmy. I thought about asking Mother if Margi could sit in our second seat, but knowing how my parents feel about her, I just bought her a separate seat as close to the stage as I could afford.

The conductor raised his baton, gently bouncing it on the wooden podium to get the attention of the entire group, and with one wave, we flowed into one of the most perfect classical pieces ever written for strings. Nothing else existed then. I made a point to watch the guest conductor, and also to be conscious of my fellow violinists. No room for error. I needed to shine. I had shivers traveling through my shoulders and arms throughout the entire performance. I was half smiling and half crying. The patrons cheered, and even gave us a standing ovation at the completion of Concerto No. 5. I knew I had played my heart out. I knew it was beautiful. And most importantly, I knew I had made Mother proud.

After our performance, I walked around the back of the theater towards the lobby while the stage was being rearranged for the main orchestra during the brief intermission. As I walked into view, carrying my violin in my beautiful but worn case, Mother came up to me and gave me a wonderful hug. I couldn't remember the last time she had hugged me like that.

She leaned over and whispered in my ear, "You are the best looking and most talented violinist in the orchestra. I am so proud of you. You are my special boy."

I was so lost in that praise that I didn't see Margi standing there, also wanting to congratulate me for my performance. As Mother broke her grip from me, I watched her proud look turn cold at the sight of Margi. I knew Mother wasn't thrilled with my relationship with her, and so I had done my best to keep her away from the family for the three months we had been seeing one another. I didn't quite understand why Mother didn't approve of her. Margi's family was Jewish, and they were members of our Temple. They didn't have as much money as many of Mother's friends, and weren't members of the Club. But still, I was surprised at her disapproval.

I asked Mother last month why she didn't like Margi, and all she said to me was, "She is not right for you."

Her tone suggested I shouldn't delve any deeper, and so I didn't. But I also didn't stop seeing Margi. She was very cute, and she doted on me. She never criticized me like Mother did; in fact, she was always raving to her friends about me; everything I did was perfect in Margi's eyes. Plus, she was extremely affectionate. There wasn't much Margi wouldn't do for me.

I was a senior in high school. I'd been working my ass off for more than a year to recover from poor grades and just not sufficiently applying myself. I had managed to raise my grade point average to a B, but Mother and Dad were still not satisfied. They wanted me to attend a good college, and were concerned I wouldn't be accepted with only a B average. I was working as hard as I could, but I didn't feel very motivated to go to some boring school filled with a bunch of boring people who thought they were smarter than I was. I just wanted to get through college, make money and enjoy being rich. My dream to retire at 40 was very much alive, and going to a school that would require me to work even harder than this was depressing as hell.

I started the college application process. Even though my GPA wasn't the best, I had my orchestra and Jr. Symphony participation to brag about, which should help my chances getting into school. My parents wanted me to apply to Ohio State and other colleges in the Midwest or eastern U.S., preferably those closer to home. I don't think they trusted me, based on my lack of effort and some other questionable behavior in the last couple of years. I did apply to all those schools that they wanted me to apply to. But I wanted to move away from home – out of reach, or at least further from their reach. So I sent an application to the University of Texas, too. I had read a lot on the different culture that was the great state of Texas and was excited to get out and try something new – to prove myself to my parents. Besides, Mother's constant pressure to be her perfect, special boy was really starting to get to me.

I couldn't date the girls I wanted, or if I did, I had to sneak around. My daily schedules were scrutinized minute-by-minute, and my dedication to school and orchestra were constantly questioned. I wanted so badly to please Mother, but it was starting to feel like an exercise in futility. Nothing I did was good enough, unless of course I was performing as first chair in the Shaker Heights High orchestra, or second chair in the Jr. Symphony, or she was able to brag to all of her friends at the Club of my academic accomplishments, or if – and this is a big if – I happened to be dating some beautiful Jewish debutant that met all of her impossible criteria.

I was accepted at The Ohio State University and the University of Texas. Dad put a lot of pressure on me at first to go to Ohio State, though he was disappointed that I wasn't accepted to any of the other colleges I had applied to. I finally managed to get him to agree to let me go to Texas, since it was a good school, and they had a well-known music program and orchestra, the director of which had shown interest in letting me try out. Besides, I had said to my parents too many times that maybe I'd skip college for a year or two and get a job while practicing with the Jr. Symphony and working on my golf game. Dad wanted me to go to college so badly, he reluctantly agreed to send me to Austin, Texas.

Margi and I dated on and off for the rest of our senior year. As June approached, I'd had about enough of her prioritizing her friends or having to go and do chores at home, when I thought she should be spending more time with me. So many girls wanted me, I didn't need Margi anyway, not to mention Mother would sure be happy if we weren't seeing one another. Our relationship had become tenuous. Every day was some sort of dramatic confrontation, or making up for one. One day I'd get mad at her for not treating me like I deserved, and the next day she'd come begging for me to be with her; I'd oblige and we'd have sex, usually in the back seat of my used 1946 Buick Roadmaster Sedan. It was a pretty good arrangement, as I was planning to leave for school in August. Luckily she never found out that while we were on and off that last semester at Shaker Heights, I was also having sex with Cheri, her best friend in the world – or so she thought. August just couldn't come soon enough.

I fell in love with Austin, Texas when I arrived in late August 1952. I rushed with other new freshmen and was invited to join a fraternity on campus right away, and my high hopes for success and independence were soaring. My classes were great. They were so easy. I wasn't used to sitting in theater-type settings, and not having to participate or be called on directly since the class sizes were so large. I felt like I was keeping up, even considering the limited amount of studying I was doing. I auditioned and was accepted in the University of Texas orchestra, on a probationary basis. That was typical for new members, but I wasn't concerned about it since I knew I was really good. After all, I had been invited to play with the Cleveland Jr. Symphony.

I didn't know how bad my grades had become until I was cut from the orchestra after the first semester, for that reason. The other musicians who cleared probation weren't nearly as good as I was, but apparently talent wasn't one of their key criteria. I was upset for a few days but quickly recovered on account of how much fun I was having with life in the fraternity. Besides, it was their loss, not mine. I figured that playing violin probably wouldn't get me rich or famous anyway. Of course I wouldn't tell Mother. She didn't need to know, and I didn't need the added criticism. Most of my fraternity Brothers were from wealthy families in Texas. They all had fancy cars, and what seemed like unlimited spending money. They introduced me to all kinds of expensive Scotch and Bourbon, and hosted parties several times every week where plenty of sampling occurred. Most of them were pretty good golfers too, and I quickly measured up to their high golf standards. The sorority girls loved this fraternity and were always hanging around. Heck, their parents probably dropped them off out front so they'd meet one of the Brothers from a rich Texas family and hook up for life. These girls were so sophisticated, and so incredibly gorgeous, it was hard to concentrate on much else. I was sort of a novelty since I was a Jewish kid from Ohio, but all the girls assumed I was as wealthy as the other guys just by association. Sometimes it seemed like I was with a different girl every week… and no one seemed to mind, certainly not the girls. It was the first time in my relatively young life that I didn't really care if these girls were completely devoted to me. If one didn't scratch the itch, there were three more waiting who would. Besides, Mother wouldn't approve of any of them, and I was never enamored enough with any of them to have to face off with her.

Before I knew it, finals week was approaching in early December, and I was not prepared. I had barely scraped by, attending my classes and turning in the minimum work required by each one. It was too late to do any meaningful 'cramming' which might make up for my lack of studying and concentration. I barely passed most of my finals, escaping with mostly C's for my final course grade on account of my regular attendance and other simple assignments I'd completed during the semester. Between my grades and getting cut from the orchestra, I knew Mother and Dad wouldn't keep sending me money, or paying for school, or more important to me, letting me stay in the fraternity. When speaking with Mother on the phone during the first semester, I was vague when answering questions about my progress. I told her that I was doing fine in my classes, the orchestra was okay, and the fraternity I was in was really great. I would, of course, elaborate on that, telling her about all of the smart and rich guys I was hanging out with at the fraternity house. I could tell that Mother was reserving judgment until seeing my first semester grades. I didn't think much about that at first, preferring instead to drink expensive Scotch with my fraternity brothers while fondling one of many cute brunettes on the fraternity house library couch. It wasn't until finals were over that I really started worrying. When I got my grades in mid-January, I told Mother on one of our too-frequent calls that my grades were not as good as I had hoped, and that I was going to work much harder and improve them in the next semester. She asked what those grades were, and though I tried to skirt the issue, she kept pushing, so I told her my average was around B minus. She didn't say much, and I immediately felt guilty for lying to her. I knew I was going to have to face reality – and Mother and Dad – when I returned to Shaker Heights for Spring Break in April 1953.

At dinner on my first night back at home, I admitted that my grades weren't as good as they could or should be. Of course, I didn't discuss the fraternity activities, though they knew me and suspected as much. They had also taken calls from several of my fraternity Brothers, and got the feeling that the reason for their calls was not to arrange study groups. My parents didn't ask about the orchestra, as that was a secondary concern. Good grades were the priority. Get a good education, be a professional, make Mother and Dad proud. I knew they would be upset, but I didn't think they would make me leave the University of Texas. I expected some restrictions or even some sort of probation, at most. I was wrong. Dad anticipated I wasn't going to take the opportunity seriously, and had already contacted one of his clients, who was also on the Board of Regents at University of Pennsylvania, for a favor. That first night home from Spring break, at the conclusion of dinner, Dad pulled out the application and told me that I could return to Texas to finish my freshman year, but if I didn't have at least a B plus average by the end of this second semester, I was going to transfer to the University of Pennsylvania. I was panicked. I was already two-thirds into the current semester, and I was fairly certain that my academic performance had not improved since early January. In fact, if anything, it had further deteriorated. I had so much work to do, yet I had no idea how I was going to pull my grades up enough to achieve that kind of an average. In the meantime, he arranged for me to move to a regular dorm on campus, and disallowed (and stopped paying for) my fraternity membership. Mother also called the orchestra director and learned the truth about my short-lived probation period; I had been cut on account of my grades.

Dad sat with me as I filled out the University of Pennsylvania application. He proofed as I wrote, making sure it reflected a student who was anxious to be accepted. The writing was more than on the wall. It was everywhere. I was almost positive that my Texas life would soon end, but I wasn't completely resigned to it. I decided to go along with Mother and Dad so my Spring break wasn't too confrontational. I figured that if I applied myself and at least improved my grades, whether or not I could achieve that magic B plus average, they might let me stay there anyway. I was determined to work my ass off and figure out a way to convince them to let me stay there. They were too calm. I think they knew my days in Texas were up, and were only hoping that I'd at least get transferrable credits to bring with me to Philadelphia. No sooner did I return to Austin than I fell back into my same routine, albeit from a different dormitory. I had moved out of the fraternity house, but the guys still invited me to all their parties, and the girls were just as anxious to be with me as ever. I had sealed my own fate.

So, over a year later, I found myself living in a cramped dorm room in Philadelphia. My grades were better than they had been at Texas, thanks to a higher level of oversight and scrutiny by Mother and Dad. The school wasn't bad, but I really missed my Longhorn buddies. They really knew how to have fun. Mother and Dad were now requiring quarterly updates of my class progress, and I wasn't allowed to join another fraternity until I proved myself. The next year, my junior year at the earliest, was my first and likely only opportunity to join, and that was completely dependent on my GPA after finals this year. Luckily I did well on those tests, and my GPA improved to a hair over a B plus, and Mother and Dad kept their word and let me join a fraternity in the coming fall semester.

When I returned to Shaker Heights during the summer

following my first year at the University of Pennsylvania, I worked at the Club as an assistant to the golf pro, helped maintain the greens, and even helped out in the pro shop. I also was able to spend some time with the Jr. Symphony, even though I hadn't taken a private lesson in more than a year, and had rarely practiced unless I was home on breaks. I still had it, and the conductor seemed happy to have me at practices in the event they needed me to fill in. I was playing lots of golf in my spare time, and was even invited to play a round or two with Dad and his friends. One Saturday evening in July 1954, about five weeks before returning to Philadelphia to start my junior year, there was an event at the Club to celebrate the birthday of a good friend of my parents. I wasn't thrilled about attending, but I figured I had a few hours to kill before heading off to be with Margi later that night.

I am a really good dancer, though I have never taken a lesson. I hadn't done much dancing, except at high school dances, or more recently, at the Texas frat house parties. It had been over a year since I'd done any dancing to speak of. But when I did dance, everyone stopped to watch. I had the moves. Music, whether dancing or playing my violin, rushed through me and took me elsewhere, always to a much better place. There, I was in total control, with the confidence of a Hollywood star. Everyone stared. Everyone smiled. And all the girls wanted to be my partner.

After the tedious dinner was finally over, and all of the painful toasts for Mother's friend were finished, a live band started playing. I was looking at the clock, trying to figure out when we might be able to leave so I could sneak out and have a little back-seat nookie with Margi. The music was good. If I didn't have Margi on my mind, I would have asked any random or lonely-looking woman at the Club to dance. I started scanning the room for such a lady, though my heart wasn't in it. I froze as the most beautiful girl I'd ever seen filled my field of view. She was dancing with a much older man, likely her father or maybe even her grandfather. I watched her glide across the floor with incredible grace; she was a much better dancer than her partner. She had long dark thick hair, unbelievably fair and lovely skin, and the most beautiful smile in the world.

She was a perfect sunrise; the breath of fresh air that made everything in the world seem right. As the band was winding down that number, without saying anything to anyone at our table, I stood up and walked nervously through the middle of the dance floor towards this beautiful girl. When I approached her and her older dance partner, I turned on my charm, and politely asked if I could cut in and have the next dance.

He put his arm and hand out, palm up, as if to say, "Be my guest."

She flashed the same incredible smile I had seen from a short distance only minutes before and agreed to dance with me. I told her my name was Benjamin, but everyone calls me Benny. Then I asked what her name was. Even her voice was like that of an angel. And she was a fantastic dancer too. The two of us danced like we'd been dancing together forever. It was uncanny. Fate, maybe. It turned out that she had been dancing with her uncle. And it was his wife – Gail's aunt – that was such good friends with Mother, and whose birthday we were all there at the Club to celebrate.

Of all of the memories I've had throughout my life, good and bad, no matter the depression that consumes me, and the dementia that has crept up on me these past many months, the memory of that moment, which happened more than 60 years ago, is one of the most vivid of any in my entire life. It is a feeling I've tried to recapture many times since, without success. I was three months short of my 20th birthday, and Gail was barely 17. It was love at first sight, for both of us, I was sure.

Rosa was coming towards the living room, talking on her phone again. I became quickly upset, since I figured she was talking to Laura again, or one of her annoying cousins. But instead, she removed the phone from her ear and reached out to hand it to me.

"It's Marty," she says. "He wants to talk to you."

Marty usually goes through his standard patronizing questions… How are you? How's Rosa? How've you been feeling? Are you getting up and doing some walking around? To which I always answer, fine, fine, fine and no. I have no desire to make chit chat, even if I could. This time however, Marty sounded different. He immediately told me that he had some awful news he needed to tell me. For a second, I figured he was going to tell me that Mother died. Well it's about time. She's 102 years old for crying out loud. She's tortured me most of my life; made me feel like a failure, when all I wanted was for her to say she loved me, and that I was still her special boy. That said, I'd probably be sad if she died. My objective for most of my life was to make her proud, though I found that to be impossible. I focused again on the phone, and Marty's unusually somber tone. He proceeded to tell me that Andy had committed suicide.

"What did you say?" I said, confused and dazed by what Marty had just said. My mind was racing with questions, but also numb.

Someone committed suicide? Who? Why? My mind had questions that my mouth either couldn't or wouldn't ask. I am tired and lethargic most of the time. My Seroquel is the only thing that makes things come into better focus. It helps me put some of my thoughts into words. It calms me down. I don't think I had taken any that day. I didn't understand what Marty was telling me.

All I could muster was, "Who?"

Marty slowed down the message. His exact words were, "Dad, I'm sorry. Andrew, your youngest son – my youngest brother – killed himself this past Sunday. We don't know the exact circumstances or any reasons why."

I couldn't process it or react at first. He repeated that Andy had killed himself, probably because of the shocked silence. Oh my God. I heard him. I understand. My son is dead. Dead! Why? I haven't spoken to Andy in years. He's hated me for so long, and I've hated him right back. But at the moment all I could think of was my precious little boy, Andrew… how cute he was, how Marty and Alan would both bribe him for their childhood allegiances, how his mother would hold him and love him, and how they would both love me. Why did he kill himself? I didn't ask Marty that question again. I'm not really sure if I processed it completely. I just howled; cried hard and out loud, finally dropping the phone on the floor.

Rosa picked it up as I was inconsolable. She talked to Marty, found out a little more, but not much. Still no answer to the question. Why? All Marty told Rosa was that he was found dead in a hotel room near his home in western Florida, and it was clear that he had shot himself in the head. Marty and Alan were going to travel down there with their wives to comfort Andy's wife and daughter, and to be there for the memorial and funeral. No explanation why it happened; what could have caused my precious and quiet little boy – now a successful doctor – to take his own life?

I hadn't talked to Andy in years, but I had secretly followed his life from a distance, as much as I could. I never told anyone, but when I was able to navigate through a computer, I would do internet searches of him, where I found the website for his medical practice. There were links to patient comments about 'Dr. Andy', as he was affectionately known by the community and his patients. He was a family doctor, but also counseled young people, volunteered at free medical clinics, and was very active in charities in the city and beyond. What could have caused him to do this to himself, with all that he had accomplished, and with all of the love and success he seemingly had in his life? I didn't know his family; we had not been a part of each other's lives since long before he married. But from all I saw and learned from the internet, as well as on occasion when Marty or Alan would talk about him, he had everything going for him. I couldn't stop crying. I couldn't process my boy being dead. What could have led him to do this? Were drugs involved? Why couldn't he have called me? I cried all afternoon. I had wet myself again, and I didn't care. I was sitting on my chair in the middle of the living room, wet and in shock. I pushed Rosa's hand away as she tried to comfort me.

Andy was a good boy. A quiet boy. He had become a doctor, and he did it all by himself, as Alan has reminded me. I was so surprised he had become a doctor. I never saw that in him, or expected that from him. He asked me to pay for part of his college and even to help with his med school tuition. First, I thought it would be a waste of money since Andy would no doubt fail or quit when things got tough. Second, I was pissed as hell, because Andy only showed respect for me when he needed money. I told him to get it from his mom; he loved her more than me anyway, and she and her husband had more money than I did. We hardly spoke after he turned 16. He always accused me of abusing him, blaming me for all of his troubles. I didn't abuse him; I tried to make him tough. Clearly a losing battle. He had invited me to go to counseling with him when he was eighteen years old, after he had overdosed on tranquilizers. I reluctantly agreed to go, mostly because it was my insurance paying for this in-patient psycho bullshit, and I was determined to prove it was hogwash. During that session, which included other parents and their kids in a group, he told me he was mad at me for scaring him, and hitting him, and making him feel 'like a piece of shit,' and other words and phrases I choose to forget. I stood up about ten minutes into this whine-a-thon and told them all that this whole charade was a bunch of crap. I stormed out. I told him to find his own goddamn insurance. As I glanced back before slamming the door shut, all eyes were staring at me, and Andy had his head in his hands, leaning forward, likely crying, again. Screw him. He's a mama's boy just like Marty. Now he's dead. I can't yell at him, or ask him why he's done this. And neither Marty nor Alan will tell me, if they even know. He was weak. He gets that from his mother's side of the family, most of whom have gone through a bunch of bullshit counseling for years, not that they are any less crazy for having done it.

I had nothing more to ask Marty or Alan about Andy's suicide. I have enough problems of my own. Since Andy hasn't spoken to me for so many years, I have just ignored the fact that I have a third son. Marty and Alan are the ones that have been helping by handling my financial and living situations since Joan died more than three years ago. Where was Andy? I know he lived across the country, but he hadn't called, or sent a birthday card, nothing for years. I don't even recall how long it's been. Why should I feel bad about him? A son should respect his father. He should be there for me, as I was always there for him. All he had to do was call me, and treat me with the respect I deserved.

I had also performed internet searches on Marty and Alan, since neither of them talked much about their lives or careers during the few (and always short) visits we shared over the years. I didn't know what I was hoping to find. Was it evidence of successful career achievements or community involvement? Or was I looking for failure of some kind, some justification for an "I told you so," or "You should have listened to me."

Alan became a very successful lawyer, law firm partner and later, a published author. I didn't like talking about his career with him much, and I wasn't about to give him the satisfaction of having bested me. I'm the dad and he's the son and he should be the one who looks up to me, and envies my accomplishments. It always felt so backwards to me. It was humiliating. But to see via the internet and various news articles all of the big cases he'd won and the accolades he had earned; there was a measure of pride and satisfaction in knowing this, though I wouldn't admit it. I was sure that I played a part in making him who he was.

Marty was an enigma. Growing up, he was so afraid of his own shadow. He was a fat and lazy teenager and barely finished high school. No matter how much I tried, I couldn't make him tough. He just wanted to get away from me, to leave home. I thought, well he'll get his, I'm sure. He'll fail and come running back for my advice and counsel, and for my help. It felt like a slap in the face, not to mention my embarrassment in having to tell Mother and Dad that my oldest son was a failure. It took me years to forgive him. But Marty out-achieved me too. He ended up an executive at a global aerospace company. I was so amazed to read on the internet about his professional accomplishments. I suppose I should be proud of them all… but all it did was get me angrier. It's bad enough that they all beat me, and didn't respect my accomplishments. But none of them ever thanked me, not once. Now I'm either avoided or appeased until the current crisis has passed. No wonder I don't like to think about them. Unless of course I need them.

My sons owe me. Andy was a doctor, Alan a lawyer, and Marty a corporate executive. All are successful. All happily married with close relationships with their children. I don't know whether I'm jealous, pissed that they weren't doing more for me, or just fed up with them for not giving me the respect that sons should give to their father. I can't process being proud of them when they don't look up to me as they should. My parents never approved of my decisions, and I had to go through life fighting for their approval, to be Mother's special boy like I had been when I was young. I wasn't going to feed my kids with that bullshit. They were going to be tough. My nickname for all of them was 'Butch.' No accident, by the way. Besides, I gave up any chance I had of fame and fortune so that they could exist. When kids came along, bills piled up. I could never afford to even consider investing, or buying property, or any other method that might make me rich. What did I get in return? Ignored. Hated. They don't think I realize it, but I do. Marty has always kept his distance, Alan comes over to deal with a new crisis, and Andy just blew his brains out. Some thanks.

It's Christmas Day. I know this place; I remember this feeling. I've never been so anxious, so happy and in love. Gail loves me. She treats me like I deserve to be treated, even more special than Mother ever did. No more trying in vain to please Mother. No more watching her out of the corner of my eye to get some sort of positive reaction to my accomplishments. I have loved Mother so much, but her prideful smiles have been replaced with growing criticisms of me. It is no mystery that my parents didn't approve of my marriage to Gail. They seemed to go out of their way to avoid her parents, in particular, her father. I'm sure Mother was jealous. Well she can't keep me under her thumb forever.

My desire to get rich and retire young were temporarily replaced with falling so deeply in love, not to mention some satisfaction for defying Mother's wishes. We were in Los Angeles, where Gail was born and raised. It was my wedding day. Gail was the most beautiful creature I've ever seen. I was mesmerized as she started her walk down the aisle arm-in-arm with her father. One of Mother's gifts to us was hiring a professional violinist to play the Wedding March. It was so beautiful, and reminded me of that place I go when I'm playing my own violin. I imagined that if it were me playing instead of the professional violinist, all eyes would be on me, the handsome groom and the talented musician. Mother would forget her objections for a while. She would be so proud of me. It would be the lobby of the Cleveland Performing Arts Theater all over again. A brilliant performance, and the acknowledgment we both know I had earned. Mother's special boy, as it should be.

Gail and her father walked towards me, and I could see under her thin veil that she was smiling innocently and with so much love in her eyes. He was sporting a stone face, yet with tears in his eyes, though I'm sure they weren't the type of tears you would expect from the father of the happy bride. He no doubt worried that she was only 18. Did she know this man she is marrying? Did she realize that his family is judging us, and that they think they are better than we are? He struggled to give his only daughter away; and not just to any man, but to me. He was unable to hide his anxiety. It's like I understood him completely, and I knew what to expect from him even before he did it.

I'm sure he was also upset that after the wedding and our brief honeymoon in Palm Springs, we would be headed back to Philadelphia so I could finish my degree. I only had one semester to go, after which I'm sure he expected we would move to Shaker Heights to live in the shadow of my parents. I suppose his expression is understandable, knowing that the daughter he holds so dear is not only getting married, but she is leaving home indefinitely, and going with someone he doesn't trust. I tried really hard so that my face didn't show what I thought of him. After all, he is Gail's father, and I had to at least feign some level of respect, if for no other reason than that.

Gail was so perfect, so beautiful and with such a positive, happy-go-lucky smile and accompanying spirit, I knew she was meant for me. I had to be somewhat calculated that summer almost a year and a half ago when I found out she only had eight days left on her visit to Shaker Heights, and her Aunt had a fairly busy schedule planned for her during her final week. I worked hard to integrate myself into as many of those plans as possible, also managing to arrange some private time with Gail on three of those nights. On her last night, I took her to an ice cream shop for a sundae, and then we just walked. We walked through residential neighborhoods and into a local park, by then over a mile from my parked car. We held hands, and would stop every block or so to share a long kiss, and an even longer hug. We laughed and talked about everything. In only one week we had learned everything about one another. We talked about how we'd stay in constant contact after Gail went home the next day, and even after I returned to Philadelphia in about six weeks. We would talk on the phone as often as possible, and hopefully we could figure a way to travel one way or the other so we could spend time together. At one point, I even suggested running away with her, to which she giggled, promising she wasn't going anywhere. She said she would wait for me while I finished school. I believed her. I was sure I'd never find anyone like her again.

My whole perspective had changed. We talked on the phone every day, and I made two trips to L.A. to see her, at Christmas and then again during spring break 1955. Mother and Dad paid for all my travel, though I'm sure financing this romance drove them crazy. It was during my spring visit that I proposed to her. I drove her to the Griffith Observatory, and proposed to her on a clear night, with a million stars shining down on us. I even talked to her father before I proposed. I turned on my charm, and got him to reluctantly agree to give her away. Gail was happy that I asked him, and of course I had her believing that his approval was very important to me. I would never have told her what I really thought of him – that he was a loud, self-righteous, left-wing factory jerk who didn't really care for me from the start. That was one opinion that Mother and I had in common. I would have to really work on that relationship, since I didn't want him to somehow sabotage my life with Gail.

It had been seventeen months from the time I first saw her across the dance floor at the Club, until our wedding day. After the graceful yet long walk up the aisle toward the makeshift chupah, the Rabbi stepped forward and asked, "Who will give this young woman to marry this young gentleman?"

Her mother stood up with a wonderful smile – genuinely happy for her daughter – and moved to stand next to her husband. In unison they answered, "We do." But their tones and expressions couldn't have been more opposite each other.

Mother had complained all morning about the cheap decorations and the reformed 'Rent-a-Rabbi,' as she quietly referred to him, and then later on about the food, and the service, and again, Gail's family. She was not saying these things directly to me, but she made no effort to conceal her feelings; I was sure she wanted me within earshot when she gave her continuous commentary to Dad.

From the very beginning Mother was trying her best to talk me out of this. She had made several attempts to set me up with other girls from the Temple or the Club. Some were pretty cute, and all were from wealthy families. One of them had liked me all through high school. In fact, at one of our Shaker Heights homecoming dances a couple of years before, we had escaped the dates we came with, had a couple of dances, and then snuck away and fooled around in a locker room off the gym. She wouldn't leave me alone after that, at least not until her boyfriend found out about her cheating with me, and with others. She went on the offensive to try to keep him. I'm not sure how that turned out, and I didn't care, since she left me alone after that.

Gail's mother was a seamstress, and her father a leader of his local union at his factory job. They were middle class at best, and my parents were mortified that their oldest son wasn't marrying one of the many women I could have chosen back in Shaker Heights – wealthy, and from well-known Jewish families. Mother was sure that they influenced our wedding being held on Christmas day, because renting the room at the Ambassador Hotel was no-doubt discounted that day. She went on with her complaining, adding that the chupah was dilapidated wood in need of a paint job, the folding chairs looked rusted and uncomfortable, the flower arrangements were cheap and not fresh, and the Rabbi – well Mother thought that the Rabbi had the personality of a boulder. She was saving her grand finale for the reception, I was sure.

It was obvious that Gail's parents didn't even know the Rabbi who was performing our wedding. He had to read everyone's names, not wanting to mix them up or pronounce anything incorrectly. Gail's parents were from Jewish families, but didn't attend Temple and hadn't raised Gail or her brothers with any religion. That didn't bother me, as I was rather tired of the expectation that eventually I would also have to be an involved member of the Temple, and like Dad, to compete with the other men to see who can give more money to the various Temple Beth El chic political causes.

But on my wedding day, amidst all of the complaining and mostly unspoken angst, all I could focus on was Gail, who was about to become my wife in just a few seconds. The Rabbi had finished reading the canned and unremarkable sermon he apparently performs for all weddings – more fodder for Mother later on. He then asked if there was anyone there who has any objections to this union. My eyes squinted as I cringed, waiting for Mother to blurt out something terrible and embarrassing. Or worse, maybe Gail's dad unleashes a tirade. But alas, they kept their objections to themselves, and because most people don't even pay much attention to that standard invitation, the Rabbi moved right along, without hesitation, to the recital of vows and the exchange of our wedding rings. Finally, we bowed our heads as he read the benediction in Hebrew and then in English. Then, for the final tradition of the Jewish wedding, the Rabbi introduced the breaking of the glass, and described the tradition:

"As this glass shatters, so may your marriage never break. The breaking of this glass symbolizes the fragility of our relationships and reminds us that we must treat them with special care, and with love."

He then placed the glass in front of me, and I stomped on it with authority. "Mazel-Tov" was the resounding wish from all our family and friends at the Hotel that afternoon.

Gail and I were husband and wife, and I couldn't wait to start our new life together. As we walked together back down the aisle, I on the left and Gail on the right, I passed within a couple of inches of Gail's father, and she passed just as close to Mother, on the opposite aisle. He looked past me, and Mother looked past Gail, as if it was rehearsed. It was a warm 75 degree day in Southern California, but cold inside nonetheless.

Our wedding was over, and the ballroom at the Ambassador Hotel was quickly converted to the reception hall. Gail's parents had arranged for a late sit- down lunch, since the hotel was closing its event center so the staff could enjoy Christmas night with their families. Mother was no doubt complaining of the food, but at that point I didn't care. I was so happy, seated next to my wife of 20 minutes and waiting for my best man, and our fathers, to give their toasts.

After the best man's short talk, it was Gail's father's turn. I was nervous what he would say. I must say, he was well behaved. Despite his clear anguish for a variety of reasons, he did a nice job. He talked about his daughter growing up to be such a beautiful young woman, and how he wished her all the happiness that she deserved. He was crying, yet this time I believed he was sincere. Gail was touched, and gave him a very warm hug when he finished. Then it was Dad's turn. My father is always eloquent when he speaks, and was careful not to out-do my father-in-law, since he didn't want to overshadow the host. As Dad spoke, my mind wandered. I thought about various times I had disappointed my parents. I thought about Diane, and other times I had upset and embarrassed Dad. I kept trying to bring myself back to today, to my new bride, and our new life which was just beginning. My eyes were watching Dad as he spoke, though I must admit I wasn't always in the moment. Then he said something that triggered one of the most painful memories of my childhood. He was telling a heartwarming story about how I nursed Sparky back to health after she had been hit by a car. I'm sure he was telling the story to show my compassionate side; maybe he thought Gail's father needed to hear it. But it caught me cold. It reminded me of that terrible day when I was nine years old. My stomach turned. Sparky had long since healed from her bout with the car more than a year prior. I was quickly transported back more than eleven years to the day Sparky was taken away from me forever. I was surprised Dad mentioned her, since Mother had warned me that I was never to speak of that day again.

Sparky was a gift from my parents for my sixth birthday. Even though she was in reality the family's dog, from the very beginning it was my responsibility to take care of her. She was our dog when Sparky was fun, and loved, and admired by guests, but she was my dog when it came to making sure she was cared for, and our home was never adversely impacted by her presence. No matter the trouble I would get into at school or at home, I was always conscientious when it came to Sparky. I had gone to great lengths to make sure that her poop was always cleaned up every day, her water dish was filled, and she was walked and fed every day. When I was at school or at practice, Mother would have one of my brothers' help with her feeding and water, so long as I kept the house and yard clean of her messes. Sparky was also very protective of me. When I was punished, Dad would have Mother take Sparky to another room in the house, or put her outside in better weather. When Mother or Dad were mad at me, Sparky would run towards me and turn to bark at anyone she felt was threatening me. Nobody had to raise their voices. She could sense any angst in the room, and who it was directed at. No matter what else was going on in my life, Sparky loved me, no matter what. She was the best friend I had in the world.

When I got home from school, Mother had gone to the market, leaving me a note telling me to be sure to clean up after Sparky, as we would be having company that evening. I played with her for a few minutes, and then got started on cleaning the yard and checking the house, so I was sure to get those things done before Mother got home. I loved Friday afternoons because I didn't have to do any schoolwork that night. I could play with Sparky, or go out and play with friends, knowing the weekend was ahead.

When Mother drove up the driveway, I met her at the car, ready to help her carry in whatever she had brought home from the store. I immediately and proudly told her that I had done all my chores, especially cleaning up after Sparky. Mother smiled and gave me her prideful look, the one I live for. We carried in the groceries, and I gladly carried the heavy bags. After placing all of the cold food in our refrigerator, she looked down at me and told me that she was counting on me to help Dad by keeping an eye on my brothers, and making sure I kept Sparky out of the living room. I was glad to help.

Dad had volunteered our house for a Temple board meeting, since the old Beth El buildings had been flooded the day before by over two inches of rain, and the electricity was still out in the surrounding area. Our neighborhood hadn't suffered much, so it was agreed that those who could navigate through the flooded streets and downed electric lines would come to our house that Friday night in May. As Mother quickly prepared coffee and refreshments for our visitors, Dad accidentally tripped over Sparky as he was making his way to the kitchen to help Mother. No harm done, except he walked into my room and warned me to keep Sparky away from the guests.

Everyone arrived by 8:00. Mother was going back and forth between the kitchen and the living room, serving coffee and dessert.

My brothers and I were in the family room, staying quiet so as not to disturb Dad's meeting. The three of us were playing with Sparky, sitting in a triangle shape, rolling a ball back and forth to each other while Sparky gave chase. I turned my head and saw Mother rushing from the kitchen to the living room, apparently trying to keep up with the demands of Dad's company. I quickly jumped up and ran towards her to see if I could help her. As I took off towards Mother, Sparky followed, assuming we were still playing. I didn't notice Sparky chasing me until she jumped up on me from behind, and I fell into Mother, who dumped a tray of coffee, cream, cups and saucers. The coffee splattered everywhere, and many of the dishes broke on impact. Mother fell into the lap of one of the men, so she wasn't hurt, thankfully. But her beautiful dress was stained with coffee, and some our guests had coffee and cream splattered all over them. I felt terrible.

Dad's friends helped them clean up the mess, and they resumed their meeting. After everyone left our house that night, I lay in bed wide awake, fully expecting a visit from Dad. I lay there for hours, and nothing. I don't know when I finally fell asleep, but I woke up Saturday morning at about 9:00, much later than I normally do. When I got up, Dad was gone. I looked around the house for Sparky. She was gone too. Dad's car pulled up to the house at about 9:15 – still no sign of Sparky. He motioned me back into my room, and I followed. He had tears in his eyes, as he told me in a stern yet calm voice that Sparky was gone. I couldn't believe what he just said. I begged him to change his mind and bring Sparky back. I promised that

I would be Mother and Dad's special boy from then on. He just turned and left my room, saying nothing else. I never learned what happened to Sparky. And I never forgot what I never understood.

Gail and I moved from Philadelphia back to Shaker Heights after I graduated from the University of Pennsylvania in June 1956. Even though I didn't want to go to college, I was quite proud of it when it was all said and done. I ended up with a B average; not as good as my parents would have liked, but pretty good anyway, and most important, good enough to graduate. We moved in with Mother and Dad at their insistence; we needed time to save money in order to afford our own place. Dad even gave us Mother's old Chevy, as they were planning to buy a new car soon anyway. It was hard to have any bit of privacy or space around the house, but because Jimmy was away at Northwestern University in Chicago most of the time, it was tolerable. Unfortunately, no amount of distance under one roof shared with Mother was sufficient. She smothered me and was always hovering over Gail. She criticized her cooking, her cleaning, and her overall way of caring for me. Gail was a good sport about it, but I didn't know how long that would last. I also didn't know how long I could take it. Mother was simply jealous that Gail loved me so much and treated me with such adoration. I was her special boy, and not Mother's. It pissed her off to no end, I'm sure.

While Mother suffocated Gail and me, Dad talked often about Jimmy, his good grades, and his plans to become a CPA like Dad. When he wasn't talking about Jimmy, he was reminding me constantly that I needed to find a job. He went on with the familiar lecture that I needed to save money for my future, and as soon as I could, to get involved in the Temple. Dad was sure that if I found a good job with a local company and joined the Temple, those rich and connected contacts would no doubt create more professional opportunities for me. Here I was, just having graduated from a great school – the one he chose for me – and all he could talk about was the great Jimmy, and nag me about getting a job and plotting out his recipe for my success.

Fuck Jimmy! What if I want to work at the firm too? How come you don't talk about that? I'm smarter than he is, anyway. I could be a CPA, no problem. All I have to do is add, subtract and understand simple tax rules. But why would I want to do that? Sounds pretty boring to me. You and Mother always told me that I was the smartest, best looking and most talented of any kids you knew. I'd always assumed that included my brothers. I'm sick and tired of hearing about Jimmy. I'm sure he'll do fine, and he's a good boy and does everything right. Blah blah. Fine then, go live in goddamn Jimmy-ville. Just leave the car and some food in the fridge so we can eat. Of course I didn't say any of this out loud, but it felt good to have that imaginary one-way conversation and get it out of my system without screwing up my meal ticket.

Only weeks after finishing school and moving back to Shaker Heights, we found out that Gail was pregnant with our first child. We were all very excited, although Mother had to jab me a little about having a child before we can even support ourselves. In practically the same breath, Mother also said that she felt strongly that we should live with them until after the baby was born, to allow me to save money for a bigger apartment. I didn't react right away. I wanted privacy, but I knew that staying with my parents made good sense.

The other thing that occurred to me was keeping the dream to retire rich by age 40 intact. In reality, my dream of becoming a fighter pilot may no longer make much sense, and even aspiring to be a professional golfer might have to wait, since I am now married and with a new baby to support. But my business degree should help me to get a good job, save money, invest and still retire rich. I could still achieve my goal and show my parents, Gail's parents, and of course Jimmy, how special I really am. But now that I have to support a family, I'm going to have to deal with a flatter trajectory towards riches. The dream was still alive, most definitely. Right now, however, I have to be a good husband, father and provider. I went to work doing Accounts Payable for Bonwit Teller in downtown Cleveland. Dad helped me get the job, as he had a long established professional and personal relationship with the owners, dating back to his first job out of NYU. After I was there for a few weeks, their senior managers started asking me to review some of their business growth plans, and even their purchase agreements with some of their larger suppliers. I really enjoyed all of that. It got me interested in contracts, and possibly becoming a lawyer. But every day, I had to come home to Mother. For a very brief moment every afternoon after work, Gail would greet me at the front door with open arms, and a hug and kiss. But standing behind her with arms crossed and a partial scowl on her face, was Mother. She had to clean up after us, even though Gail would go the extra mile to be a good guest, helping Mother keep everything neat and tidy. But it was never good enough.

Mother was careful not to cause a scene. Instead, she would pull me aside and talk in a near-whisper. Even her words were annoyingly subtle. Just say what you mean for god's sake. You're pissed off because Gail doesn't clean the way you do. I got that. Could it be that you are upset that you have to stare at your nemesis all day long, and by the end of the day you feel like a bull ready to charge the taunting daughter-in-law?

All Mother has done for me in the last few years is try to make me fourteen years old again. Or maybe even six or seven. Probably whatever combination resulted in the perfect, special boy who could do no wrong. I don't play much violin anymore. That upsets her. She reminds me of the beautiful and expensive violin she bought for me as a Bar Mitzvah present. She won't take me to the Club and show me off, because I'll have Gail on my arm. That would be embarrassing, since Mother had set me up with several of her rich friends' young daughters, and most of those relationships didn't end well. And lately, she's been telling me I've gained weight, and that people will look at me and judge me differently if I get fat. What is this hell I have landed in?

We managed to get along. Both Gail and I worked hard at pleasing Mother around the house, and I gave Dad a hand in the yard on the weekends. Dad and I even did a little golfing on the weekends when the weather cooperated. Gail was having a difficult pregnancy.

She was sick a lot, and had back problems as she approached full term. Finally, very late on a Friday night in late February 1957, Gail went into labor. I drove us to Mt. Sinai Hospital in a snow storm, arriving just after midnight. After more than 30 hours of labor, at 6:20 in the morning on Sunday, Marty was born. My healthy baby boy was born, and Gail was fine, beautiful as ever, and taking a well-deserved rest.

A little more than six months after Marty was born, we convinced ourselves that we had to leave Mother and Dad's house. But not just the house. And not just Shaker Heights. We wanted to leave Ohio, and the Midwest, altogether. I started thinking about it in June. Dad was again talking about Jimmy's joining the firm after graduation, this time using the word 'partner' in the conversation. Mother's criticism was at an all-time high, now including Gail's day-to-day mothering of Marty. I started researching law schools in the Los Angeles area. Gail had already discussed that possibility with her mom, and of course they were excited at the prospect of having their daughter and new grandson with them full time, if only temporarily. We made the final decision in August when I was accepted for the upcoming semester at Loyola Law School in Los Angeles. We packed up our few belongings, and Mother and Dad drove us to the Cleveland Airport. They held Marty as long as they could before handing him back to Gail. Dad didn't say much.

As I hugged Mother, she whispered one final jab in my ear, "Benny, you are making a big mistake, one you won't be able to take back."

She was stone-faced, and after making that comment, turned and walked back to the car. What could I say, with Gail and Dad there, and us seconds from walking away and boarding our airplane? I let it go, rationalizing that I would prove her wrong. We will build our family, I will finish law school, and I will show them all. We boarded TWA's Boeing 707 for our non-stop flight to L.A. No more worrying about pleasing Mother, or making Dad proud – at least no more hourly reminders. We were on our way. Marty screamed the entire flight.

We left our car behind. Dad gave it to Jimmy. He told me that he and Mother would be coming to visit as soon as they could; they missed Marty already, and wanted to get to know Gail's folks better. I wasn't looking forward to that, but I figured it would be some time before Dad could get away from the office and his community activities for such a trip. I had saved a little money, and Dad handed me a check for $500 at the airport. That was so huge; I wasn't sure how I was going to afford a car in L.A., which was absolutely necessary to find and start a job, and get myself to school. I was sure that I could now afford a decent used car in L.A. I was very appreciative, and hugged and thanked him as we headed for the plane.

I felt like a free bird, having escaped Mother's grasp. We could raise Marty as we saw fit. I would start law school, and in time graduate and get a good job. We'd have a huge house, a manicured lawn, and a family that looked up to me, their special dad and husband. But when I closed my eyes during the long flight to L.A., I couldn't help but think about Mother, and her obvious disappointment and disapproval at how and with whom I am living my life. The more I thought about it, the angrier I got. But I couldn't shake the sadness I was feeling, either. I missed being her special boy.

Gail's mom picked us up and drove us to their house on Kinnard Avenue. Though I was still excited to start over, I wasn't sure how much better this might be, since Gail's father didn't hide the fact that he didn't like me. But it was our fresh start. We settled in, and once I secured my classes at Loyola, I immediately began looking for a job. My plan was to work full time and go to school at night. I wanted to start saving for an apartment, and move as quickly as possible. I knew that we wouldn't be happy; at least I wouldn't be happy, until we had a place of our own to raise our family. Within two weeks, I had purchased a used car and found a full- time job at North American Aviation in El Segundo as an entry level cost analyst.

I started my classes a few days after I started my job. My classes were Monday, Wednesday and Thursday nights from 6:30 to 10:00. I also had a Saturday morning class, from 8:30 until noon. Two weeks into this schedule, I came home Saturday afternoon, anxious to greet my wife and baby boy. The first thing I saw when I entered the house was Marty. He was crawling around the living room floor playing with his toys, with no one else in the room. He looked at me and smiled, although I was more interested in knowing where Gail or her folks were. Why was Marty alone? As I walked into the room towards Marty, to my left I saw Gail and her parents sitting around the dining room table with a young, handsome guy, maybe a couple of years older than me. One of Gail's old friends had come over to the house to say hello, and they were all catching up on old times, keeping an eye on Marty from the adjoining room.

No harm done, except this fellow was seated very close to Gail, and she was giggling like a schoolgirl when he spoke. Her father seemed to be enjoying the look on my face, though I tried to hide my angst. I had worked all week, and when I wasn't working, I was at school, or studying, or trying to carve out time for Gail and Marty. I put my school things in our room, and came back out and played with Marty in the middle of the living room floor until it was time for 'Charlie' to leave. As he was leaving, his hug and very light kiss on Gail's forehead, which seemed to last way longer than appropriate, made me angry as hell. I bit my tongue until Charlie was long gone. After he left, and Gail's mom was with Marty, I pulled Gail into our bedroom and shut the door. I tried to keep it calm and quiet, but I was so angry, my teeth were clenched and arms tense and shaking all the way down to my fists. I told Gail I worked so hard, and then had to come home to see some old boyfriend making a move towards her. Of course she denied it, which made me angrier. It scared Gail.

I didn't touch her, but she backed towards the door and said, loud enough to be heard outside our room, "Benny, you're scaring me."

Gail's dad, who was likely waiting to pounce from the other side of the door, stood inches from it and said with anger and authority, "Hey, is there a problem in there?"

I offered an immediate, defensive and biting response of my

own, "None of your business. Everything is fine."

He didn't say anything else, at least not right then, but I had no doubt he wanted to club me over the head with a baseball bat. The cat was out of the bag. There was no more pretending when it came to our feelings towards each other, which put Gail square in the middle.

We moved out the following January, to a small apartment about two miles from the house, and two miles closer to school and work. Having our own place definitely helped me relax into my busy routine, and spend as much quality time as I could with Gail and Marty. Not even two weeks after we moved in, we found out that Gail was pregnant with our second child. She was due in September 1958.

We probably would have been fine with waiting a little longer, but both of us were thrilled at growing our family. My revised goals were still intact. Finish law school, get a great job, make lots of money and make everyone I've ever known envious of my wonderful life.

Mother and Dad called us shortly after we moved into our apartment. As has been their habit for my entire adult life, they were both on separate phone extensions so they could both participate in the conversation. I told them about school, and work, and Marty. Mother didn't ask about Gail, but I offered the latest anyway, including the fact that we were going to have another child. Their excitement seemed to me to be luke-warm, as they were probably concerned that we were moving too fast, and I was still in school and not earning enough money. Not seconds later did Dad share that Jimmy was going to graduate from Northwestern this coming June, and was going to work as an accountant at the firm while studying for his CPA exam. He also shared that Jimmy is talking about going to law school after getting his CPA license, in theory to be a tax law expert in the firm. Good grief.

I had a son of my own. All I could think about at first was not becoming Mother. She looked at me with disappointment all the time, worried about what her friends thought of me, and killed my dreams with her own inflexible and unrealistic expectations. That would not happen with my son. My cute little baby looked at me as his entire world. I could do no wrong. I would throw him in the air and he would smile, and sometimes laugh with the cutest of expressions. He had an infectious smile, and the fattest pinch-able cheeks. Marty is going to know how much he is loved, no matter what choices he makes.

In these moments when I am his world, he is the greatest gift. But he cries a lot. He is awake and crying most nights. Gail tends to him, but I still lose sleep – lots of it. It makes it very hard to concentrate during my long days, and even harder to study or relax at home. Gail is always coddling him, when I think he needs a firm hand. Stop that incessant crying, already. Just tell him no. Put him in his crib, shut the door and let him cry. Come and pay attention to your husband; he will learn to stop crying. But instead, Gail cradles him, softly shushes him, and even sings to him. Mother never sang to me, and I turned out just fine.

Marty has put a strain on my relationship with Gail. After long days working and going to class, I want her attention, yet she's always with Marty. On my days off, I get on the floor with him, play with him, and once again I am his hero. He doesn't scream around me. Maybe it's the coddling that's causing him to cry so much. I tell Gail to stop babying him, and she just walks away and does it anyway. I'm the one working and going to school so we can retire rich one day. I have to tip-toe with Gail; I don't want to get mad at her, which always turns out bad for me. So I decided to try some Scotch at night. It used to help me sleep when I was at college. I picked up some Cutty Sark – my brand of choice from my fraternity days – from the neighborhood liquor store. It seems to help me sleep through the noise and stress.

Growing up, Marty became more and more of a crybaby. He was afraid to wrestle with me. He cried when I told him to say 'Uncle' when twisting his arm behind his back. He even cried before I touched him. He didn't want to play basketball with me.
He would look up at me, start crying and say, "Daddy, I don't want to play."

Gail said I never let him shoot; I was too physical with him, and I got mad when he tried to beat me. Of course I didn't let him shoot. That's the objective of the game. Life is competitive. Basketball is competitive. Is he going to cry every time he has to confront anyone? I'll teach him to complain about our games, and especially to tell mommy behind my back. I'd grab his arm forcefully, swat him hard until he said he wouldn't tell mommy again, and then tell him to be a big boy and play tough.

When the games were over and we were back in the house, I always apologized to Marty after I was forced to punish him. He is my son, and I just want to help him be stronger. He needs to understand why daddy was upset and what I was trying to teach him. Yet as I apologized and reiterated his mistakes back to him, all I got was angrier, especially watching his out-of-control crying and gasping for breaths between sobs. He wasn't listening at all. Momma's boy. I work so hard, and come home and carve out time to spend with my son, and this is the thanks I get? He was going to learn, goddammit. What in the hell is Gail doing to him, anyway?

Marty never looked up to me like I looked up to my dad. He never wanted to race me in the front yard. He just cried and ran away. I longed for the days back when Marty was a baby. I threw him in the air, he laughed. I crawled on the floor, he crawled after me. Then he was four, and cried more, and crawled to mommy for comfort some of the time. Then five, and then six, and he would run from me instead of after me. And of course, bringing up the rear was Gail, who would jump in between me and my son, and make all kinds of excuses for him. It took all my energy not to just grab her and push her out of the way. Let me teach my son. He needs to learn. He needs to respect me. He deserves these spankings.

The older Marty got, the more complicated my life got. When I finished law school, Marty was four years old. Mother and Dad would call us every week, and always ask about the boys, and about my job. It felt like a weekly interrogation, to which there were no right answers. Are you moving ahead at work? Have you been saving to buy a house? Have you joined a Temple? How are the boys doing in school? Have you been watching your weight, Benny?

I stayed with North American Aviation, and became a senior cost analyst in the B1 Bomber group. They also had me review complex supplier contracts. I was making slow progress at work. Not rich, at least not yet. Alan was two years old, and my relationship with Gail was much different than when we first met at the Club, got married, and lived together in Philadelphia – when all my hopes and dreams were still alive and well. When it was just Gail and me, I was her entire world. She wanted to be with me. She wanted to dance with me. We were always touching. I could do no wrong. I was definitely her special boy. But everything changed with Marty, and moving to L.A., and working, and law school. I was doing everything I was supposed to be doing, but I wasn't getting any happier.

In July, 1970 when Marty was thirteen years old, we celebrated his Bar Mitzvah. I dreaded the family coming together, Mother and Dad judging me, and the money I would have to spend on the party. Yet for a brief moment I found some relief. I was sitting next to him on the pulpit, and watched him read his Torah portion, and sing his Aliyah's, and read his Bar Mitzvah speech that he wrote all by himself. I hadn't been this proud of him since he took his first steps. In truth, I was surprised that he was so poised in front of so many people, and so articulate and expressive. I placed my hand on his knee, and smiled at him. He knew I was proud.

I whispered to him while standing in front of the entire congregation, "I'm proud of you, Butch."

I thought I saw a tear in his eye. And a smile like he has never shown me. Maybe he just wanted me to be proud of him? Maybe I didn't say that enough. Well maybe I could have if he wasn't always running from me. In that moment, I thought of my dad, and how much I always wanted to make him proud of me. I was never afraid of him. Marty should not be afraid of me. I am a wonderful father.

Three months later, Gail and I separated. Marty then became even more distant. He didn't want to go on camping trips with me, so I would take Alan and Andy. Then Marty got caught up with the wrong bunch of friends and his schoolwork suffered. I blame Gail for that. She had babied him so much, and now that he didn't have his father there every day to keep up the discipline, he continued to fall into this teenaged oblivion. The high school had been calling me, telling me he had been skipping classes, and failing many of them. I finally had enough. About a month before Marty's 17th birthday, I took off work early and drove to the McDonalds where he had been working. I walked behind the counter, grabbed him by the hair and pulled him outside and shoved him in the passenger side of my car.

"You are coming to live with me," I said. "I've talked to your mom, and she agrees. You are going to quit this fucking job and catch up on schoolwork."

I took him home and taught him a lesson, again with my University of Pennsylvania fraternity paddle.

The next year was miserable for me. Marty had gained even more weight; he was fat and lazy, and doing the very minimum to get by. I had to be reminded of his failures every day when I got home from work. I overheard him talking to Andy about being a famous musician instead of graduating high school and going to college. Hearing Marty tell Andy this pissed me off so much I could barely see straight. He had taken ten years of piano lessons, but always made excuses why he couldn't play for me. I could have been a professional violinist. Who better to judge your talent? You think you can be a famous musician? How about graduate high school, go to college and get a goddamn job? Be realistic for a change. I knew I shouldn't say any of these things to him, but I just couldn't help it. So I let loose. I told Marty how I felt about his lack of effort, his ridiculous pipe-dreams, and his disgusting appearance. I couldn't deal with his blatant lack of respect.

Marty left home one day after graduating high school, almost exactly one year after coming to live with me, in January 1975. Alan told me that Marty was living in his car for months after moving out. He would do anything to get away from me. Fine. Deal with the cruel world, ungrateful shit.

Years later and in retrospect, Marty did pretty well. And not as a professional musician. He worked for the same company for 30 years, and was promoted into executive management where he spent the last ten of those years. I was proud of him, but I couldn't stand talking to him about it, because I knew he would want to rub his success in my face. A son should look up to his father – revere him, ask about his accomplishments, and even brag about him to friends. Not Marty. He just ran and hid behind Gail, telling everyone how abusive I was. Such bullshit. But when all was said and done, it is obvious that the foundation I set finally took hold and led to his success. Of course Marty would never have acknowledged that. All I ever got were benign father's day cards in the mail every year, and token visits. He never brought his family to see me. Obviously he was ashamed of his dad.

After Joan died in August 2012, Marty offered to take over my finances for me, since trying to navigate through my bills, bank accounts, IRA, tax form and such was overwhelming. Joan had done all of that for me for practically our entire marriage. But hell, he should do all this for me. I'm his father. It's what children do when their parents need help, right? Marty and Alan talked me into selling the house Joan and I had lived in since I retired 20 years before. And Marty was the one who found Mission Manor. It is his fault that I had to endure day after day with those ugly, miserably bitter old biddies.

I never thanked Marty for hiring Rosa. She is like an angel. It was Mother back when I was her special boy. She takes care of me, and tells me how smart and handsome I am. She tells me I am a wonderful man, and a great father. I love her so much.

My mind is racing in the present, "What have I done to my sweet Rosa?" "Marty, where are you?" "Why don't you ever call or come visit?" "Can you help Rosa? She isn't answering me. I need to talk to you about us. We're in love…"

<h1 style="text-align:center">Alan</h1>

Our second son was born in September 1958 in Los Angeles. Gail was only in labor with Alan for a couple of hours, and his birth was much easier for her. He was healthy and beautiful, and unlike his older brother, he slept all through the night. Alan was a thinker from the very beginning. He seemed to study his brother and behave completely opposite, as if taking a lesson on what not to do. Marty was only seventeen months old when Alan was born, and of course Marty demanded lots of mommy's attention. So even though I was still in law school and working full time, the time I was able to spend with Alan was more private, and of a higher quality. Gail was distracted and couldn't intervene as much when we played. Alan was going to be daddy's boy. He was going to be tough, and he was going to look up to and respect his father. I could see it in him from when he was just an infant starting to crawl.

The two boys played well together for the first couple of years, but because Alan seemed to do what he was supposed to do without much if any drama, the brotherly bond eventually turned to an early rivalry. Alan never ran from anything. Although Gail was a tender and loving mother, Alan was not a mamma's boy. He loved his mommy, did what she expected him to do, yet was ready and even anxious to climb all over me when I got home from work on those evenings I didn't have school. Alan and I wrestled all the time. He wanted daddy to challenge him. He wanted to show me how tough he was. Marty would play with us, but when I wanted them to say 'Uncle,' he would just cry and give up. Alan, on the other hand, would refuse to give in. I had been wrestling with the boys since they were both old enough to crawl. It seemed to get more serious with Alan when he was about seven years old. He would cry sometimes, but it was out of anger and pain, and not out of fear. At first, I went along, as it felt to me like a sign of his toughness. I was teaching him to be strong. But then, I got angry. He wasn't just wrestling tough; he was being defiant. Those tears of his were angry ones. What the hell? He is tough, I can see that. But I beat him. He needs to treat me with respect, to learn the lessons I was teaching. He is not the teacher. Just say 'Uncle' and admit defeat, for Christ's sake.

As Alan got older, our wrestling matches became more intense. One in particular came at a bad time. I had had a tough day at work and just wanted to come home and relax. That night, Gail attacked me the minute I walked through the door. The water heater had stopped working. Marty had gotten a bad grade in his 5th grade Social Studies class. And to top it off, I had to change a flat tire on my Chevy Impala in the parking lot at work before heading home. After punishing Marty with my U-Penn fraternity paddle, and figuring out what to do with the water heater, I was finally sitting down to unwind when Alan crawled in the middle of the floor, wanting to wrestle. At first I wanted no part in it, but he had this overconfident look on his face that I was determined to wipe right off. He needed to look at me with respect, dammit. I smiled back at him and got on my hands and knees on the floor. Alan was nine years old.

About five minutes into the match, I pinned him face down, pried his left arm from underneath him and twisted it behind his back, smiling as I made the usual demand that he say 'Uncle' to me. I had my knee in his back so he couldn't move. Gail walked in the room and gave me a firm yet passive, "Benny, please stop."

I looked up and told her everything was fine, and to just turn around, and leave us alone. And I said it with a calm, about-to-win-the-match smile. Gail shook her head side to side and reluctantly left the room. I was not going to let go until he said it, and he knew it. I was getting angrier and angrier with him, as he was more and more defiant – red faced and tears streaming down his face in obvious pain. The longer he refused to give in, the more weight I put on my knee, and the more I twisted his arm, until I heard his arm snap. See what he made me do?

Alan did well at school, and always tested high in school aptitude tests. Though we didn't wrestle with any intensity anymore, he would play basketball with me. The first few minutes of the game were always fun, but when I refused to let him score he would get mad. He would try to dribble through me, and I'd knock him to the pavement. I did the same with Marty, only true to form, Marty would never come back for seconds. Alan was pretty tough; of that I was sure. But he didn't know when to concede. It pissed me off that we couldn't just walk away from those games arm in arm, like a close father and son, or at least a handshake as I'd always done with Dad. Instead, he would be mad at me for being too rough, and I would have to get rougher with him on account of his disrespectful defiance. The last time we played basketball was a Sunday afternoon just after Alan's eleventh birthday. He wanted to play a real game, one-on-one, and told me before we started that he was going to beat me this time. He managed to get in a shot or two, but I stuffed all of his other shots, and won easily. Near the end of the short game, he was getting mad and again trying to drive and dribble through me. I was blocking him so hard, he would fall to the pavement on the school basketball court. He refused to stay down, bouncing back and again charging me. He was so mad; his face was as red as ever, and tears starting down his cheeks. All that did was infuriate me more. My jaw was clenched shut, arms tensed and shaking with anger. I finally had enough of this battle and walked furiously up to him to teach him once and for all to show me some respect. He dropped the ball and clenched his own fists in a defensive stance.

I stopped short of him and he said something I never forgot, "If you ever touch me again, I'll kill you!"

I was in shock. I didn't get physical with him again, but I was going to make him pay for his insolence, someday.

After Gail and I divorced in 1971, Alan lived with his mother. The boys would come on camping trips with me, and I would see them most weekends. I hated Gail. I hated my life. I was still working at the same company and had moved into management, but now I was paying Gail most of my salary to keep up with our wonderful house and raise the kids. I married Joan in mid-1971 and tried to make a nice home with what little money I had left. Once we had moved into a decent house, I tried to get the boys to leave Gail and move in with me. But no matter how I tried to entice them, they wouldn't do it. I wanted to cut Gail off – no more handouts. I'm the better parent anyway. I do things with the boys. I take them camping, play basketball, and teach them responsibility. Alan wouldn't even talk to me about the possibility of moving in with me. He'd always go camping with me and do his duty and come see me on the weekends, but we weren't as close as we had been when he was a little boy, and it pissed me off so much I could hardly sleep at night.

When Gail remarried in 1976, Alan could talk about nothing else but his step-father. Francis did this and Francis does that. Francis has a big boat. Francis took me windsurfing. Francis took mom to Europe. Francis is rich. Why the hell am I sending her child support if she has all this money? When Alan was accepted to UCLA, he had the nerve to ask me to pay his tuition. I was so mad at the whole situation, I told him to go have his buddy, Francis, pay for it. After all, Francis seemed so enamored with him and his toys, why wouldn't he want to send his new special boy to college? In typical stubborn form, Alan wouldn't let it go. He told me that Gail wouldn't ask Francis to pay for it. He said I should pay because I'm his father. It took all my inner strength not to knock him to the ground. I don't know how he paid for it, and I don't care. I wasn't going to pay. He has a rich step-father he is closer to than he is to me, and I paid Gail child support for all those years. Let her figure it out. Alan was persistent, though. On a camping trip during the summer after his freshman year, he talked me into making his car and insurance payments, instead of having me listen to his periodic whining about paying his tuition. I took the bait. But I only paid that bill for a year. When Alan stopped coming to visit on a regular basis, and got defensive when I asked him why, I stopped the payments. Let him deal with that.

I had an almost identical uncomfortable conversation with Alan after he graduated from UCLA in 1980 and was accepted to Boalt Law School at Berkeley. He was excited when he told me he had been accepted to such an elite school, but I stopped him short of asking for me to pay for it. I told him I couldn't and wouldn't pay for it. I thought for sure he was bragging about having been accepted to such a great school, intentionally comparing his accomplishment to my having only attended Loyola of Los Angeles. I wasn't going to let him have the satisfaction of showing me up, so I just ignored him for the most part. Besides, Boalt would cost a bloody fortune. For the first time in my life I had no alimony or child support payments, and could buy what I want and spoil myself for a change. I was done sacrificing so much for my ungrateful sons.

After graduating from law school, Alan joined a well-known firm in L.A., and was eventually made a partner. A few years later he joined a much larger firm as a partner, responsible for their entire intellectual property law practice. I didn't talk much to Alan about his career. After all, he beat me in every way imaginable; not to mention he never really wanted to know about my career and my accomplishments. I could have been a professional golfer, or a violin virtuoso. Instead I chose to be a father. How come my sons don't acknowledge my talent? How come they don't appreciate my sacrifices?

Unlike Marty, Alan did bring his family to see me a few times a year. We never talked about much, and those visits were so short, I didn't have much of a chance to bond with my grandchildren. I once tried to show Alan's oldest son a method to use if he were in a fight. You quickly grab a hand and bend it inward hard and fast. Alan saw this and yelled for me to stop. What did I do wrong? He is only six years old; I wasn't going to hurt him. I just want them to be impressed, and to be proud of their grandpa. Maybe I can teach them something, if Alan will only let me.

When Joan died, Alan helped to get my house sold, and with Marty, moved me into Mission Manor. He was there after I punched that old bitch Nell. I even had to apologize to him for doing that. How goddamn humiliating. He helped me move in with Rosa when Mission Manor kicked me out. He comes out to see me when I'm having problems, even though I also know he is mad at me for causing so much trouble. I know he has tried to get me diagnosed with dementia so he can put me in a nursing home. He thinks I need to be restrained, and drugged. I can't believe that my sons treat me this way. After all I've done for them for all these years, this is the thanks I get.

Thank God for Rosa. She loves me. She tells me I am smart and wonderful, and I will never have to go into a nursing home no matter what Alan says.

I was so pissed off at Gail when I found out she was pregnant again. Did she get pregnant on purpose? It was hard enough to make ends meet, and now we would have another mouth to feed. We had never discussed having another baby. That February night when Gail told me she was eight weeks pregnant, I stayed up after she went to bed and drank almost half my Cutty, straight out of the bottle. I stayed downstairs and stared at the TV, thinking about my dream to get rich and retire. I was only 26; there was still time. But she was making it more difficult. I thought about Marty and Alan, and how I was going to be able to split my time three ways, and impart to each of them important lessons about how to be tough, and successful. Would there be enough of me to go around? Would they be upset about having to share time with their daddy? I didn't want Gail to know how drunk I was that night, and I didn't want to say something she would make me regret. I guess she didn't do this on purpose. If she did she'd never admit it anyway. I can only imagine what Mother is going to say.

Andy was born in L.A. October 1961. Marty was four-and-a-half years old, and Alan was three. On the weeknights when I was home and on the weekends, the two boys and I wrestled and played inside and out front of the house. I was bonding with them. It was harder to bond with Andy. He was always playing baby games with

Gail, and by the time I got sick of Marty running from me and Alan trying to beat me, Andy didn't want to play with me. I tried to wrestle with him a few times, but like Marty, he would cry and run away. I blame Marty and Gail for that. Marty, because his example taught Andy how to be a wimp, and Gail, because she discouraged, and even disallowed my playing rough with him. I should have spent more time with him when he was a toddler. He wasn't tough at all.

Andy and I never established much of a relationship when he was young. He was only nine years old when Gail and I divorced, and after that I didn't spend as much time with any of the boys. I would get so mad at Andy when it was my weekend to have them, and he'd go crying to Gail – not wanting to leave her to come visit his father. He would usually come camping with me and Joan, but even then I had to tiptoe around him. God forbid I should upset him and he'd go crying to mommy when we returned home.

I endured this for several years until Andy was fifteen. Apparently life with Gail wasn't so peachy when she moved in with and then married Francis. The two of them went on long vacations, since Francis was semi-retired and living *my* dream. Andy needed guidance, and discipline. He and I had been getting along; we were even having fun on some of our recent camping trips. I finally talked him into coming to live with me and Joan. Maybe I'd finally have the relationship with him I should have had all along. We got him all new bedroom furniture, let him decorate his room as he wanted, and made his life pretty goddamn easy. During the year that he was with us, we had bought him a moped, and a brand new saxophone. I rarely punished him, as he couldn't handle discipline at all. I didn't want him to think he could just up and decide to move back to Gail's, so I worked hard to control myself.

One afternoon after school, he took off riding on his moped with his friends. When I got home from work, he was in the house, upstairs. I didn't see the moped outside in its usual spot, so I looked in the garage and in the backyard, and still no moped. I could feel my blood pressure rising.

I walked through the house yelling at the top of my lungs, "Where is the moped, Andy?" "Andy, where are you? Where is the goddamn moped?"

I was sure he was hiding from me upstairs, so I went after him. I threw his bedroom door open and he was sitting on the bed, head in his hands, crying.

All he could say was, "I'm sorry, dad...I'm so sorry."

He knew I was pissed. My teeth were clenched tight, and my arms were shaking all the way down to my fists. I could barely focus. There were no longer sounds. Things moved in slow motion. That was a brand new moped. I pulled him up from the bed and slammed him up against the dresser on the opposite wall. I punched him in the chest, and then in the arm. I was yelling all the while, but probably not making much sense in my rage. He slid to the corner of the room and coiled up against the wall, still standing, positioned in a cowardly stance to protect his face. I managed to slap him upside his head twice, the second one forcing him down on the bed.

"Where is the goddamn moped?" I yelled.

He couldn't answer, he was sobbing like such a baby. Finally, he told me between sobs that it had been stolen from outside the local music store. I told him to get his ungrateful ass back to that store and find it. He left the house quickly, carrying nothing with him. It was almost dark, about 6 p.m. Two hours later, Gail called. Andy was back over at her house. He had called her from the corner 7-11 store, and she had driven from Long Beach to Irvine to pick him up.

Andy told Gail that I had beaten him. I screamed and cussed at Gail. Once again she had interfered with my being a parent. Andy deserved to be punished. He was irresponsible and careless. He was weak. She hung up on me, but not before telling me he was moving back in with her, and she would talk to Joan about picking up his things. I was so angry, I just told Joan to leave me alone. I stayed downstairs all night, drinking what was left of my Cutty. I called in sick at work the next day. And I rarely heard from Andy for the next two years, until he called me from a hospital psych ward after having overdosed.

Almost a year after his overdose, Andy enlisted in the Navy. I was silently betting against him, since the military demanded discipline. But surprisingly, he did pretty well. He became a Corpsman, was initially stationed in Honolulu, and was later stationed in Des Moines Iowa, where he worked at an Army reserve center. His job was to give basic physical exams to Army personnel before they were activated into service. He never called me, so any information I received was from Alan or Marty, though they rarely spoke to me either.

Years later, Andy called me, and wouldn't you know, he wanted money. He had gone back to school and earned his Bachelor's degree from the University of Iowa, and he had been accepted to start medical school at the American University of the Caribbean School of Medicine. So now, having been virtually ignored for more than fifteen years, Andy wants me to help pay for school. Bullshit. I made it a very short conversation, and it was obvious he didn't really expect me to help.

Also, I wasn't going to pony up any money for some two-bit foreign college. Obviously he couldn't get accepted to any reputable school in the U.S. I couldn't imagine who he would have asked before coming to me. I found out later it was my dad who ended up funding him – wasn't that just the fucking icing on the cake.

Andy graduated from medical school and started practicing family medicine in 2002, when he was 40 years old. I was proud, but angry too. He had ignored me for most of his life. He hadn't appreciated any of my sacrifices. And now he's a doctor, happily married, and a community leader in his west Florida town, and he has bested me, too.

When Joan died in 2012, all of my boys came to the funeral, Andy included. I looked at them from afar, and thought to myself how successful they had all become. I was very proud of them. But I wasn't going to give them the satisfaction of telling them. I never saw, nor spoke to Andy again. Three years after Joan died, Marty called to tell me his brother was dead.

I'm looking at my almost 34-year-old self and beginning to realize that getting rich is getting more and more unlikely. On one of our weekly calls, Dad gave me another opportunity to buy into a business that could make us lots of money. He had called me with these opportunities before, and I never went for it. It felt like these offers were just more criticism of my life – patronizing me and my career, and my home and family. I wasn't going to give my parents the satisfaction of knowing that I needed their help or wanted more money. The last time I'd told Dad about my dreams, I had gotten a lecture and seen an anger in him I'd rarely seen before. I had learned my lesson. Two years later, I found out that this investment – a share in an Arby's franchise in Youngstown, Ohio – had grown to nearly a dozen franchises owned by this investment group. And to top it off, my 40th birthday coincided with the grand opening of the 30th of those restaurants in Akron. And I was no closer to living my dream.

In May 1964 Gail and I bought a house in Seal Beach, and moved to Orange County, a middle class suburb south of L.A. It was a brand new house, two stories, with four bedrooms and a huge yard. I told Gail right away that I wanted a swimming pool. She was concerned about the cost, but it was my money and I wanted to have it, so I contracted with a pool company to build it. The house and pool made me feel like I had accomplished something significant. I wasn't rich, but I had moved my family into a big house, on a nice street, in a very nice, new neighborhood. We joined a new Temple too. Temple Israel was in Long Beach, about a fifteen-minute drive from our house in Seal Beach. It was an established congregation, yet we fit in right away. I was immediately recruited to help on the finance committee, and Gail joined the choir. I had requested and gotten a transfer to North American's Anaheim facility, about a twenty-minute drive from Seal Beach. I was a first-level manager in their Cost Analysis group, our job being to evaluate supplier contracts and negotiate the price of contracts and changes. My job was stable, but growth was slow, and the job itself was hardly exciting. Though I was affording my new house, my beautiful pool, and even a new car, I didn't feel fulfilled.

Mother and Dad would call weekly, but those calls only made me feel worse about my life. "Are you still only a first-level manager?" "Are you saving any money?" "Are the boys doing well in school?" "Are you getting ahead at work?" "Do you need any help from us?" It was like listening to a broken record.

Why don't they ever tell me they're proud of me? The last time they visited, all they did was buy the boys clothes, comment on Gail's poor housekeeping, and criticize me for having built a pool in our backyard. They made me feel like we were goddamn indigent.

But the truth was, my career was stagnant. The money was decent, but I had a long way to go before I'd be making the big corporate money. Who knew when or even if I'd ever get ahead in that job? Some of these men who had climbed to powerful positions spent their entire lives working. I was never going to do that. My weekends were mine. My weeknights were mine. I could run this business with a blindfold, still maintaining my personal time, no problem.

My marriage was also stagnant. Gail was fighting me on everything, and getting on my nerves with her constant nagging. She would complain about me being too rough with the kids, drinking too much, and getting angry all the time. She wanted more money to buy the kids better clothes. She would ask me why I needed a brand-new car every two years. Enough already. Where is all this coming from, my mother? I know she criticizes Gail. She says the house isn't clean enough and the kids aren't clean or properly dressed. They have holes in their pants and dirt behind their ears. When they go to the bathroom, they don't always wash their hands. The criticisms are endless. Gail feels bad, but she just perpetuates Mother's crap by asking me for money to dress the boys nicer. Bullshit. We do not have to please Mother, and you will use the allowance I give you for all of our expenses, including getting the kids clothes.

Gail had also established a network of friends. They were housewives in our neighborhood, and some were also members of Temple Israel. She would meet with these friends most days when the kids were in school. When I got home at night, I could tell that the household chores had taken a back seat, and I was sure this was because she was spending most of the day talking bullshit with these women. Gail had also become very popular in our Temple choir. She was not only a very beautiful woman, but she had a beautiful soprano voice and had become a leader and soloist in the choir. Sometimes I felt very proud of her. But Gail was getting all this attention, and no one appreciated me for letting her participate in the choir and for volunteering my own time in the Temple finance committee. It's always all about Gail. She's so beautiful. Her voice is like that of an angel. She is such a happy and wonderful woman. Everybody loves her. It's bad enough that my talents and contributions weren't acknowledged, but I was getting angrier and angrier that she seemed to prefer being at choir practice, or with these annoying friends, instead of with me or her children. I wondered if other men were coming on to her. Maybe that's why she was dressing so pretty for choir practices?

Even though my job wasn't my dream come true, I was really good at it. I was in a different element when I was at work. I was the smartest one there, and everyone looked up to me. And the women all flirted with me. One of the secretaries, Nancy, made excuses all day long to come talk to me, and she wasn't even my secretary. She would come over to my secretary to bring supplies that we didn't need, and while she was there, she would stand and look into my office area to see if I was looking at her. Of course I was.

I sat in the same place in the cafeteria every day, eating the lunch that Gail had packed for me. Most of the time, a few guys would come over to sit with me, although I was always hopeful that a beautiful woman would come by and grab a spot before one of those guys did. Nancy was coming over to have lunch with me more and more, making sure she was early enough to preempt any other lunch companion from joining me. Pretty soon, she was there every day. In fact, if anyone showed up before her, they left a seat next to me open for Nancy. She treated me like I deserved to be treated. She complimented my cologne, and even my ties. She said I had a sexy smile. I got excited just reciprocating some of her compliments. I knew I could have her if I wanted. All I could think of initially was my first meeting with Gail at the Club when I was only 19, and how smitten I'd been with her. But then I'd quickly jump back to the present, thinking about all the evenings when I get home from work, finding Gail either disheveled after a long day with chores and kids, or getting leftovers ready for my dinner so she could get all prettied up to go and impress all her choir buddies. The more I thought about those things, the more upset I became, and the more flirting I did with Nancy.

We decided to go out to lunch one day, instead of going to the cafeteria. Nancy met me in the parking lot, and we got in my bright red 1967 Mustang and drove off.

Just as we approached the restaurant, she looked over at me and said, "Benny, do we have to go to lunch? I'm not really hungry."

I knew what she meant. I wanted her too, but I had to do some last minute rationalizing before making my move. I pictured Gail protecting my sons from me, and greeting me most evenings looking less than attractive near the end of her day. I imagined other men hitting on my wife. But most of all, I thought about Mother's criticisms. Maybe she'd been right all along. Maybe Gail wasn't good enough for me.

I pulled into a large Thrifty Drug Store parking lot, and parked far away from most of the cars there. After I turned the engine off, I looked over at Nancy. I didn't remember the last time I had been that nervous or excited with a woman. I leaned over and started kissing her; and she kissed me back, deep and hard. I had my hands up her skirt, and she was touching me. I had to stop; I didn't want to make a mess on my work clothes. Before I had a chance to say anything else, she told me that her house was only a few blocks from there, and that we should go there. I figured she was married, so I asked where her husband was. She told me that she was in the process of getting a divorce, and he hadn't been at the house for weeks. I drove the five blocks to Nancy's house, as horny as I'd been since the night I'd cheated on Margi in high school. This woman wanted me, bad. I was about to reclaim that euphoria of being the best looking, smartest and most desirable boy around.

We pulled up to her house, and before I knew it we were naked and on her bed. Sex had never been this good for me. No woman had ever been so free of inhibitions before Nancy. The first time was quick, but we did it again before realizing that we had to get back to work, and not let on that anything was going on between us. We cleaned up and dressed, and were back at work only about ninety minutes after we had left. Nancy didn't come by my office the rest of that day. And I managed to get through the afternoon without letting what I had just done affect me. We saw each other regularly over the next three months. We spent most lunches at her house, and even some evenings. I would call and tell Gail I had a late meeting, and of course she wouldn't question it at all.

By early October, I was getting tired of Nancy's dependence on me. She insisted we be together every work day, and she had begun pestering me to sneak away on the weekends to be with her. She was getting more and more possessive of me. She would even get upset when other attractive women at work would flirt with me. She was needy as hell, and I was just about done with the daily balancing of this exhausting relationship. Then she started concluding our lunchtime rendezvous by telling me that it was time I told Gail about us and talked to her about getting a divorce. She said that she would be a much better wife than Gail was, and a good mother to my kids, and that we would be happy together. Even though Nancy was attractive and exciting, I had no intention of leaving my family for her. After two weeks of her pressing me about Gail, I saved the inevitable conversation for Friday's lunch hour. Instead of driving to her house, we sat in my car in the parking lot at work, and I told her that we needed to end our affair. I told her I loved my wife, and I didn't want to leave my kids and be a weekend father to them. Nancy did not take it well.

She slammed the dashboard of my car with her fist, saying over and over again, "Affair? Is that what you think this is? An Affair?"

I had to grab her hand so she wouldn't put a dent in my Mustang's interior. She sobbed, got out of my car, slammed the door, made a beeline through the parking lot to her car and left work for the rest of the day. She didn't talk to me for several days after that, until one day, about two weeks later, when we happened to meet on the walk to the parking lot at the end the day. She glared at me and asked how I would feel if she called Gail and told her about our 'affair.' I was shocked, and so pissed off I could have ripped her head right off her shoulders. Instead, I followed her to her car, being as outwardly calm as possible, all-the-while pleading with her not to do that. As we approached the car, I looked around us to see if anyone was close by. My jaw was clenched, and my arms were shaking all the way down to my fists, but I didn't let on. Once I was sure nobody was in sight, and she reached the driver's side of her car, I grabbed her by the throat, shoved her backwards against the car door and got two inches from her face.

I said in as threatening a voice as I could, "You stay the fuck away from me and my family."

I slammed her hard into the side of the car, banging her head on the roof before letting go of her throat. She cried and coughed simultaneously. I grabbed her upper left arm with my right hand and squeezed it tight. She was crying and wincing in pain as I whispered the same thing again in her ear to make sure she understood. Nancy didn't say anything about it to anyone, including me, at least not for a while.

I had been drinking my Cutty most every night, feeling the stress of work, of not having the balls to make investments that have come my way, of cheating on Gail. I knew that I was not Gail's special boy anymore. She didn't dress nice and look sexy for me anymore. She didn't plan special dinners for me and only me. It was all about the kids, and the choir, and her meddling friends. Sex with her was boring. There was no passion anymore, and nothing that would even come close to Nancy's aggressive and exploratory 'repertoire.' I was never going to get rich living this life, with this family, and with this wife. As depressed as I would get when thinking this way, I was afraid to leave my home and my kids, and even Gail. I loved her, but I wasn't excited by her anymore. I decided then that cheating on Gail was an effective way of keeping my marriage and my family together. I just had to be more selective, and more discreet. No more crazy women, for sure.

Only a couple weeks after ending my romance with Nancy, Gail got home late from choir practice and I hit her on our front porch in a fit of rage. I had lost all control. I felt no emotion, and no pain – nothing whatsoever. She was showing me up; she was the perfect choir girl with her own perfect friends. I wasn't the center of her life anymore. She defied me by being late. What happened to that beautiful girl that adored me so much? I needed her back.

Nancy and I would pass one another in the corridors at work every day, and sometimes run into each other as we left work in the afternoon. But we said nothing. We avoided eye contact. I was relieved that she never said anything to anyone about our little tryst, and especially the way it ended. If she did say something, it hadn't gotten back to me, at least so far. She had taken a few days off after the confrontation outside her car that afternoon. I was hoping she didn't have marks on her arms or face from our confrontation, at least none anyone would see. Luckily, nobody had noticed anything, me included.

I was lying somewhat low for several months after ending things with Nancy. I certainly did not want to strike up another relationship with anyone at work, especially considering her volatility and the likelihood that she would make life very difficult for me if she knew I was seeing someone else outside of my marriage. I resumed my daily cafeteria visits, and slowly the lunch companions that had joined me pre-Nancy came back to the table. At first they tried to joke about my three- month absence, but when I wouldn't bite, we moved on to the mundane subjects of work, kids and sports.

My boss increased my job responsibilities, which included teaching cost and pricing data requirements for Government contracting. I really enjoyed that, and I was spending more and more time with him, helping in his evaluation all of the employees on the team during the performance review periods. I was still a first- line manager, but I felt like he really trusted me, and I could be considered his successor should he move up or on in the future. Because his schedule was so busy, I had to coordinate with his secretary often to squeeze in time with him in- between his many meetings. I had also been using her for my own administrative tasks over a two-week period since my secretary had gone on vacation with her family.

Joan was not incredibly attractive, but she was a lovely, sweet and accommodating lady. She was so busy with her normal duties, yet made time to do all the work I had left her to do – quicker and with more care and accuracy than I'd experienced. She brought me coffee, and leftovers from her dinner the night before. They were so much better than the boring sandwiches Gail packed for me, I'd throw away my bagged lunch in favor of Joan's delicious leftovers. On father's day, she brought me a coffee mug that said, 'World's Best Dad.' It made me feel so special. From the few conversations we had, she knew how much I loved my boys, and how frustrated I was that my wife got in the way of me being able to bond with them. We were fast becoming friends, and I was also starting to notice some of Joan's hidden but very attractive features.

One of the subjects with which we had much in common was camping. She and her ex-husband had done lots of it, and I had been getting more and more into it over the past couple of years. Gail and I had started with a medium sized family tent, a cooler and a Coleman stove, all of which barely fit in the trunk of my Mustang. We were enjoying those trips, so we purchased a Ford truck and small camper that fit in the truck bed, still utilizing the tent for the kids to sleep in. The five of us had gone on three or four camping trips of late, all in the Southern California desert utilizing our new equipment. I was getting better at the whole camping thing. We never did anything like that when I was a kid; there was no way Mother would be caught dead without all of her comforts. I'd bought some inexpensive fishing gear and had been trying to teach myself and the boys how to do easy fishing in one of the mountain lakes nearby our camp spots. Alan really enjoyed fishing; and as if on cue, Marty had no interest in learning how to fish, at least not from me.

One afternoon at work, Joan walked over to my office with a letter that she had typed for my signature. She was not in a hurry to return to her desk; I assumed her boss was in a meeting, away from his office. We were talking about camping again, this time she was sharing that she was going on her first trip since her divorce about six months prior. She was traveling with the same group of friends that she had camped with many times before. All of a sudden I was nervous, and excited at Joan's sharing this with me. Was it an invitation for me to come along? Was she attracted to me?

I looked at her as if to have come up with a brilliant idea, and asked, "What if I brought my camper and met you there?" I was so nervous; I didn't know whether I had crossed a line. Her answer put my mind at ease, though I detected no enthusiasm in her response. She softly and carefully said, "Sure Benny. That would be fun."

She said nothing of my boys, probably assuming they would be there as well, which made me doubt her intentions. It was too early to worry about that, but I knew if anything were to develop, I was going to have to go on this trip without Gail. I wasn't sure how I was going to work this out, but I was trying very hard to think of a way to either go alone, or with only the kids.

The conversation between Joan and me occurred on a Tuesday, and the trip she invited me to accompany her on was the upcoming weekend. I had to come up with something fast. When I got home from work that same day, I greeted Gail with a big hug, and maintained my happy mood all evening. I purposely didn't react much to some of the reported issues with the kids for that day. I didn't want to wreck the mood. When we got into bed, I told Gail that I wanted to take Andy on a camping trip the upcoming weekend – just he and I. After all, we almost never spent any quality time together. I asked if she would mind staying back with Marty and Alan. She was extremely supportive, saying almost immediately that she thought it would be great if Andy and I spent some alone time together. She was also enjoying the remnants of our pleasant evening together. Those had been fewer and farther between of late, for a variety of reasons. On this night, nobody misbehaved, nobody got hurt wrestling, and nobody got upset or angry. We just ate dinner, joked around a little while mommy cleaned the kitchen, and had a relaxing evening watching television. Gail and I even had some pretty decent sex that night. When we turned over to go to sleep, I lay awake for a bit, feeling pretty proud of myself. I had played everything perfectly.

Joan and her friends planned to leave work a little early on Friday and drive to their favorite campsite in the San Bernardino

Mountains. They would arrive before dark, set up camp and immediately build their campfire and cook a pot luck- style dinner. I took Friday afternoon off, went home and packed up the camper for

my one-on-one with Andy. Gail and the other boys saw us off, and we were on our way by 4:00. We arrived about two hours later, before any of the others, including Joan. I used the extra time to set up our table, stove, and other camping gear so I could help Joan when she arrived. Andy and I went for a walk to check out the grounds. As we were walking, I was reflecting on how my plan had come together. Marty and Alan were old enough to recognize if something were to happen between me and Joan, and they were sure to report whatever they thought they saw back to Gail. Good move to exclude them. Andy, on the other hand, was only seven years old. I wouldn't have to hide anything; he would be oblivious to anything beyond his and my having fun together. During that walk around the campground, I watched and listened to Andy, probably for the first time in his life. He was cute, and smart, and full of ideas and curiosity. He was sharing all these little useless things with me, even though Gail was nowhere near. It made me feel very close with him, probably for the first time in his short life. Even if things didn't work out with Joan the way I'd hoped, maybe this weekend would be time well spent anyway. Maybe I should do this same sort of one-on-one bonding trip with Marty and Alan, too?

When Joan and her camping friends arrived, I was busy helping everyone get their trailers and other equipment set up. I could see Joan looking at me – thinking how wonderful and helpful I am. I didn't want her to know that I was watching her, but I was. She looked so beautiful in her casual camping attire; it was so different than how she looked sitting behind her little desk at work, all manicured for the boss. She had smooth pale skin, a simple but telling smile, and she spoke with a sweet, calming voice. She had a nice figure too, which was hard to notice at work under all those dress clothes. We sat together around the campfire that night, long after all of the others had gone to bed. I had already put Andy to bed in my camper when the other younger kids were also turning in for the night, and then I came back out to the campfire to spend more of the evening with Joan.

We had each had a couple of glasses of wine. But I avoided the Cutty Sark that night. I wanted to be in the moment, and not say or do anything I'd regret. We had moved closer to one another since the nights in the mountains were pretty cool. Joan retrieved a blanket from her small trailer, and after offering to share, we draped it over the two of us as the fire slowly extinguished itself. When it was getting late, I offered to walk her back to her trailer, which was only two spaces down from where my camper was set up. As we approached the trailer door, she turned to me with her arms extended, offering me a hug. We had talked about so many things. Our love for camping, my kids, our jobs, her marriage, and the unfortunate state of my marriage. I told her that I wasn't ready to leave Gail and the kids, but added that it was essentially a loveless marriage. She didn't seem disappointed. The honesty seemed to relax her even more. Our hug was long, and it was rich, full of emotion, and provided the release that we both apparently needed.

With most all of the relationships I had had with women since I was a teenager, we had sex almost immediately. It was exciting, and something I had grown to expect. If they really liked me, then they should want to have sex with me. Why waste my time if this isn't going anywhere? Am I the center of your world or not? But this time, with Joan, there was a quiet confidence that I hadn't felt before. We simultaneously broke our long hug, gave each other a short but sensuous kiss on the lips, and went our separate ways, she into her trailer, and me back to our camper to sleep opposite Andy. Saturday night was much the same, only we shared a deeper kiss at the door of her trailer. My life had all of a sudden become a bit more complicated, again.

I tried so hard to protect my marriage, and what amounted to my entire life all wrapped up in our house on College Park Drive. But here we all were – me, Gail, Marty, Alan and Andy – sitting in our family room only two weeks before Thanksgiving, and I was telling them that I want a divorce. Gail was sobbing uncontrollably; she already knew what I was going to say. I'd been out of the house for more than a month already. We told the kids I was on an important business trip, but they suspected something was wrong. Gail had been a mess since I admitted to having an affair and left the house last month. I had already rented an apartment in Anaheim – a small dingy place close to work that my life would now be relegated to once I went through with this. God I didn't want this. I wanted to stay married, to live in my house with my kids; but that was no longer possible after Nancy's threats. I could just kill her.

Joan and I had been seeing each other since that first camping trip the previous summer. But we kept it as low key as possible. We hadn't gone on any more camping trips, but I had been to her house a few times during lunches, though we never left work at the same time. We would see each other in the staircase of our building at work and if no one was around, we'd share a quick kiss. I also met her twice over the past couple of months at her house after work, telling Gail that I had late meetings that I couldn't miss. It was so hard to leave her bedside on those evening visits. It felt so right with Joan; it wasn't as exciting as it was with Nancy, and Joan was plain in comparison to the women I was usually attracted to. But she was different. She could draw me in just by being so soft, and so very adoring. This was how I deserved to be treated by a woman.

I was at Joan's that fateful Thursday night, in the calm, loving environment that was Joan's bedroom. I wanted so much to wake up in her arms, but I'd told Gail I'd be home by 9:00 and didn't want to raise any questions. I kissed Joan at her front door and hurried to my car. I got in, checked the rear view mirror to fix my shirt and tie, and was about to start the engine when suddenly there was a knock on my driver's side window. My heart sank. It was Nancy, and standing next to her was a large man about our age, no doubt recruited to protect her from my reaction. I rolled down my window and feigned a smile, asking what she was doing there.

She looked at me with a smug smile on her face and said, "Good luck explaining all this to your wife, asshole."

I'd never felt so sick in my entire life. I had to struggle not to throw up right there and then. How long had she been following me? I still don't know who the husky guy with her was, although when she turned to walk away, they were holding hands. I couldn't confront her there. I didn't want to get into a fight with this guy, whoever he was. I didn't have time to go back into the house and tell Joan, though I really wanted to. So I drove home, panicked like never before. Would Nancy really tell Gail about us, and about Joan? If she did, what would I do? What would I say?

I knew one thing for sure; even if Gail forgave me, I would never again be her special boy. I would have permanently fallen off the pedestal she'd once placed me on – where I deserved to be. I would become the groveling husband, begging for forgiveness, and pleading for another chance. She would have the upper hand in every discussion, every argument. I'd have to be the perfect husband, put up with boring sex, and tip-toe around the house all the time. I'd have to stop seeing Joan. God I needed Joan so much. I couldn't let that happen. How dare Gail make me beg. I won't apologize. It's her fault. She doesn't treat me special anymore. She doesn't look pretty for me like she used to. I was getting angrier as I got closer to home. I decided not to say anything to Gail that night. Tomorrow would be Friday, the end of the workweek, and I would see how things went at work before doing anything drastic. I'd keep an eye on Nancy, maybe even talk to her to gauge how serious she was about ruining my life.

I got home about 9:30 that night, after driving around thinking about my situation. Gail was in bed, almost asleep. I crawled in, moved up next to her, and put my arms around her to see if I could recapture the feelings I once had. In that moment, I felt bad for her. I felt love, though a much different love than when we first met. I closed my eyes and actually started tearing up, wondering if this would be the last time we lay together arm in arm. We had sex that night. It was okay, but it wasn't Joan. And once again my mind went back to Nancy. I didn't sleep at all that night.

When I got to work the following morning, I walked very quickly by Joan's desk, dropping a note in front of her without stopping. It said to meet me in the copy room in the southwest corner of the second floor, which was one level below us. I kept walking, taking the long way to make sure Nancy wasn't aware of what was happening. Joan arrived two minutes after I did. I told her what had happened the night before. I had already told her almost everything about my involvement with Nancy, except for that unpleasant encounter in the parking lot. I was still in panic mode, but she had her usual calming effect. She told me not to make any rash decisions and assured me that, whatever I decided, she was there for me. She looked at me, caressed my cheek with her hand, and promised me she would never abandon me, no matter what I decided to do.

She had a tear in her eye; and before we walked out of the small copy room, she mouthed the words, "I love you," without making a sound.

The rest of that day was quiet. I was very careful not to cross paths with Nancy. When it was time to leave for the day, I stayed back and watched her grab her purse and head out of the building before I left my office. I took a deep breath as I exited the building and started across the parking lot. It felt as if I had dodged a bullet, at least for the time being. As I approached my car, Nancy appeared from behind a light pole about ten feet away. Obviously she had been waiting for me.

She wouldn't come closer, but shouted in a voice way too loud for our close proximity, "Hey, Benny." I froze, looked in her direction, and said nothing. I didn't want to make things worse than they already were. She continued, "Is your home number still 827-

3381?"

She turned and walked away quickly. She was alone. The big husky guy she had confronted me with last night was nowhere around. I watched her get in her car and back out quickly, spinning her tires as she darted forward and left the parking lot, clearly not interested in any reaction I might have. She made the right turn out on La Palma Avenue and was gone. I sat in my car and began to panic. What am I going to do now? I can't let Nancy talk to Gail, but I also can't be at the house all day, every day to intercept phone calls. Then, a moment of calm came over me as I recalled my conversation with Joan that morning. She would love me no matter what. And she would never leave me.

The phone rang twice that Friday night. Both times I answered it, and both times the caller hung up. The next morning, the phone rang. Marty grabbed it before I had a chance to pick it up.

I walked hurriedly into the family room, just as he said, "Hello," to the caller. He turned and told me that it was a lady who wanted to talk to Mom. I took the phone from him and said in a terse tone, "Who is this?"

And again, the caller hung up. I knew who it was. And I knew what she wanted. I told Gail I needed to take a drive, and in her usual, predictably trusting way, she smiled and told me to drive safely. I told her I'd be back in an hour or so. The walls were closing in. I needed to make a decision, to formulate a plan. I drove to the local Lucky supermarket and sat in my car in the parking lot. I pulled out a pencil and paper from the glovebox and started adding up what my expenses would be if I left Gail and got my own apartment. Would I have to pay child support? Goddammit, I'm sure one of those bitches Gail hangs around with would help her get a lawyer who would take me for everything. I had given Gail so much. What had she contributed? Nothing. I was the one who'd gone to school and who worked so hard, not her. And now I would lose it all because she couldn't make me as happy or treat me as well as I deserved. As unfair as this all was, I had to face reality. I couldn't bear the thought of leaving my boys for Gail to raise by herself. She'd already made them so damned soft. She can't control them. They need discipline. They need me. But I would always be their father. I would have to make the best of being a part-time daddy. The boys would miss me so much; it might even make us closer. I tried not to think about it, as it made me angry and clouded my judgment. Who knows, maybe Nancy had tried to call again while I'd been out driving and thinking, and Gail already knew everything. I had to act quickly. I started up the car and headed back home.

I drove down our street, pulled in the driveway and parked. When I entered the house, Gail was cleaning the kitchen after feeding the kids a late breakfast. It didn't appear as if Nancy had called; Gail had her usual expression going about her routine. I walked up to her in the kitchen and told her I needed to talk to her in private. She saw my face. It was no doubt drained of color, as I was sick to my stomach over what was about to happen to my life. She dried her hands with a towel and followed me upstairs to the bedroom, telling the kids to be good and play while mom and dad talked. As we climbed the staircase, I thought again about how terrible it would be if I had to beg Gail not to leave me. I thought about what she would think of me, and how mortified I would be, having to deal with her every day after admitting my affair. I couldn't allow that. I had to leave. It was the only way to save face, to maintain the upper hand. I was no longer her special boy, and with every step I took towards the bedroom, I got angrier and angrier at her for this. It was her fault. We both sat on the bed, and I told her I was leaving her. I told her I'd had an affair, and that this woman was probably going to call her and tell her about it. I didn't elaborate, and I didn't mention Joan. She was my fallback and would likely save me in the long run. I couldn't sacrifice that. After absorbing the initial shock, Gail begged me to reconsider. She just sobbed, clearly not wanting to think about what I had just told her. I said I was going to pack some things and get a hotel room near work, and that we would talk in a week or so. I quickly threw together what I needed in an old suitcase, leaving Gail sobbing in the bedroom. I went into the family room where the boys were watching TV. I told them daddy was going on a business trip, and I'd see them in a week or so. They thought little of it, even as I gave them unusually long hugs before leaving.

The following Monday at work, I followed Nancy into the stairwell, surprising her from behind. I didn't know whether she had succeeded at reaching Gail over the weekend, but I was determined to take that threat away from her. I grabbed her arm, not with as much force as before, but enough where she couldn't get away. Before she had a chance to react, I looked at her and calmly told her that I'd told Gail about our affair, and that I had left home and checked into a hotel. She didn't say a word, and although I'd expected some sort of expression of satisfaction, she remained stone-faced.

As I let go of her, I gave her a half-smile and said, "Go fuck yourself." Nancy was out of my life.

In the four weeks that had passed since leaving home, I hadn't been back or seen my boys. I had wanted to stay with Joan, but decided it would be better if I were actually in a hotel, in case Gail tried to find me. I did see Joan often, having most dinners with her, and even staying at her place on occasion. But I'd spent most of my nights at the hotel. I had spoken to Gail a few times on the phone, each time a sob-fest, begging me to come back home. Now, my mind was made up. I was no longer Gail's entire world. I had lost face. I needed to be with Joan.

I sat in what used to be my family room, staring at my swimming pool out the sliding glass door window, having just told my boys I wanted a divorce. Gail hadn't stopped crying since I'd first told her I was leaving a month before. The boys all cried at the news. Alan stood alone in the corner of the room. Marty was hugging me, and Andy was being comforted by Gail. Finally, I stood, separated from Marty, gave a nod to Alan, and turned to leave. As I walked through the door, I realized suddenly that I may have just made the biggest mistake of my life.

June 1993

Joan and I celebrated our 22nd anniversary this month. I took her to Sizzler, since it's close to home and they had coupons in the newspaper. I was going through the motions, but I just didn't have the desire to do much else. I had been transferred to Rockwell's Downey California facility three years prior, to work on the Space Shuttle program. The commute wasn't too bad, about a 30 minute straight shot either way on Interstate 5 to and from our condominium in Tustin. I was made a director, but it seemed obvious that I'd never be promoted to executive ranks, because I wouldn't work more than I had to. I was fine with that. I didn't like it much, anyway. I did legal reviews of supplier contracts which was sometimes interesting, but repetitive as hell.

By 5:00 every afternoon, work had sucked the life out of me. Buyers asking me questions they should research themselves, my boss asking me to do special assignments since no one else could or would, and having to be friendly to some of these idiots every minute of every day. It was pure torture. Then, all I had to look forward to was going home and waiting for Joan to wash every single goddamn piece of lettuce individually and season every single piece of chicken with such excruciating detail, I never knew if or when dinner would be ready. By the time the salad arrived, the meat was cold, the ice had melted in my drink, and she was still shuffling around in the kitchen getting

tableware or something. I didn't even wait for her anymore. I had
exhausted every biting comment I could think of in the hopes of
changing the outcome of her painfully slow process, but to no avail. I
couldn't' help but to sigh out loud, or even pound the table in disgust
on occasion.

Joan was diagnosed in early 1988 with Lupus. Specifically, she
had Systemic Lupus Erythematosus (SLE). It attacked just about all
of her internal organs and most noticeably, her muscles, skin and
orifices. If the disease wasn't bad enough, the medication she had to
take to control the effects of such a widespread anti-immune
deficiency disease seemed to intensify the symptoms, sucking the
moisture right out of her, and along with it, much of her energy. With
all of the various issues that resulted from the disease and the
treatment, the one that affected me the most was her inability to have
intercourse. Add to that, Joan was the epitome of a prude. If we
couldn't have intercourse, there was no asking her to do anything else.
Between her prudishness and her feeling so tired and uncomfortable
most of the time, any special requests I might have were a waste of
effort, though I continued to subtly remind her that she wasn't
pleasing me.

Mother and Dad were still calling us weekly, and our
conversations had become more distant. They no longer asked about
my job. They didn't ask Joan about her life; they knew the answers
and just weren't that interested. And I know Mother. She was seething
that Joan wasn't making me happy anymore. She hadn't approved of

Gail, that is, until I married Joan. Mother didn't have to say anything; I could hear it in her voice. Dad knew I was planning to retire at the end of next year, at 60 years old, and he had no reservations in telling me he thought that was a mistake. He would ask me about my savings, if I had any investments, and what my pension would be – all of which I refused to tell him. If I did, I knew he would be disappointed, even if he was able to keep silent about it. I told him I was going to move to the Southern California desert and golf every day. It would be like being on a permanent vacation. I rationalized that once we moved into this 55 and older golf community in Beaumont, that when I wasn't golfing, I'd be out meeting some attractive widow for some recreational sex. I refused to think about the possibility that I'd be stuck home with Joan all day every day, watching her deteriorate – no longer able or willing to please me the way I deserve. There was no way I was going to sacrifice my needs after all I had done for her.

Joan was slowing down more and more. She took care of the shopping, some basic house cleaning, and did all of the cooking, of course. I couldn't even make a sandwich, and if I could, I wasn't going to admit it. She also took care of all of our bills, and dealing with calling repair people, and even having our taxes done. I didn't have the patience for any of it. Joan saw her mother and sister once a week, which pissed me off every time it happened. They had stopped coming to our house a couple of years prior. I hated knowing that she enjoyed being anywhere other than with me. I am sure they were poisoning her mind against me. Just because they had lousy marriages, now they wanted to recruit Joan into the lonely bitches club. I had no use for them, and they knew it. But Joan wanted to please everyone. She had always been there for me, no matter what. Too bad she couldn't please me anymore.

I hadn't had sex in so long, and not just because Joan wouldn't, but because I hadn't looked outside our marriage in a few years. We had gotten involved in a camping club, and between that, my job, and seeing the kids occasionally, I didn't have much time to sneak around. In a way, it was kind of a relief not to be hiding anything. We had gone from having sex whenever I wanted it, to having painful sex, to her not wanting it at all. I couldn't believe there was nothing she could do – no medicine she could apply or take that would enable her to please me. I also couldn't believe she wouldn't please me in another way. I got tired of asking. It was hopeless and just got me angrier with her. I was better off looking at alternatives.

I was so lonely, I started thinking about my high school girlfriends. I thought about Margi. She wanted sex all the time; I never had to ask twice. I also thought about Diane. What happened to her after our experience in the Shaker Heights High School orchestra room? I always wondered. I would think about her more than Margi. With Margi, there was no mystery. I knew every inch of her. There was nothing more to know. Besides, she'd be an old lady by now, and was starting to get fat when I met Gail. But Diane… she was always so cute. She always stared at me like she wanted me; just those teasing glances and inviting smiles were so exciting. Even though I got in a lot of trouble after the one and only time we'd had sex, I'd pictured what I saw of her body a hundred times over the years. She had such silky smooth and fair skin, and her stomach was so flat and strong. I remember seeing her thighs, and thinking how muscular and beautiful they looked. Her hips were narrow but so sexy looking. With every breath she took, her body moved, seeming to beckon me closer to it. I was sure she wanted me to be her first. I wished we had been able to have sex a second and third time. I wanted to explore her more. I would show her what a wonderful lover I was.

I made a few calls to some old friends in Shaker Heights. I would feign interest in the last 35 years of their life, while really probing to find out what ever happened to Diane. After long arduous conversations with three different people I hadn't thought of since high school, I discovered enough about Diane to know where to look next. I learned she had a daughter. She had been married, but was divorced. I found out the last name she went by now, and approximately where she was living. I was getting excited just thinking about Diane after all these years. Would she want to talk to me? Is she still as sexy? Of course she was older, but I imagined the beautiful, sensuous person that Diane had become. I couldn't wait to find out.

I found Diane's phone number the first day I started searching Cleveland's east side directories, using the information my old friends' had provided. I had to think some more about what I was going to say to her before I just cold called her. I played out different scenarios in my mind, and prepared myself to call her the next day. I wondered if calling during my lunch hour, which would be about 2:30 or 3:00 in the afternoon in Cleveland, would be a bad time. Maybe she had a job? There was no other time I could call; Joan was always home and I didn't want to call from there. I called her at noon, with my office door closed. I waited as the phone rang four times, and it was finally answered by an answering machine. I didn't immediately recognize Diane's recorded voice, but I decided to leave a simple message. After all, I didn't know if she might have a boyfriend, or a roommate, and I needed to be pleasant but measured with the information I left.

"Hello, Diane. This is Benny, from High School. I've been thinking about you lately, and was hoping we could catch up on old times."

I left her my work number, and told her to give me a call back if she'd like to talk. I didn't know what to expect. Would she call? Would she even remember me?

Diane called me back a few days later. We talked at least twice each day for four months before finally reuniting in person. Not only had Diane thought of me many times over the years, but she said her marriage wasn't happy because she compared her husband to me. She wouldn't elaborate about her ex-husband, so I didn't pry. She told me she missed our flirting in the quads at school. And she had thought about that day in the orchestra room many times. When I asked her about what happened to her family after that school year, she would change the subject. It didn't matter though. We were hitting it off, and we both wanted to see one another, and soon.

I took a few days of vacation time from work and told Joan I was going on a business trip to a supplier near Cleveland. I didn't tell my parents I was going to be in the east Cleveland area. I spent the entire three days in Diane's bed. We'd get cleaned up to eat – even went out two of the nights. But otherwise, it was non- stop exploration. I had never felt this way before. This was how I deserved to be treated, and loved, even adored. We decided right then that we had to be together. Diane didn't have a lot of money, so I told her that I'd leave Joan, rent an apartment and help her move herself and all of her things to Southern California. I asked her to give me a couple of weeks to work out the details. I dreaded having to do this to Joan, but it was her own fault. She hadn't treated me the way I deserved for years. She didn't please me anymore. I was not her special boy. It looked like Mother was right about Joan, too.

I left her in October, a few days after my 59th birthday. I rented an apartment in Downey, just a few blocks from work. And I moved Diane in. She had lots of furniture – some we were able to use, the rest of it I talked her into selling at a garage sale. Some of it was hard for her to part with since she'd had it for 30- some years. But we were what mattered, and not her 'stuff.' By mid-November, Diane was all moved in, and I was as happy as I'd ever been. We were having incredible sex all the time. Dinner was ready every day when I got home from work. I didn't have to suffer through her poor planning and not having dinner ready, or her not being ready to sit and join me when I was ready to eat. Everything was perfect. Obviously I had to pay for Joan's and my condo, and all of her expenses as well as Diane's and mine, but I didn't care. I would even be willing to work a few years longer if I could come home to this type of bliss every day of my life.

But two months after Diane moved in, I was wondering if I had made the right decision. Diane had joined a women's golf club. They not only golfed most days when I was working to support her, but they frequently stayed in the club and played cards and drank expensive wine afterwards, sometimes as much as two or three times per week. I had arrived home from work on several of those nights and there was no dinner ready; only a note telling me where the leftovers or the sandwich fixings were. She wanted to have wine with every dinner meal, and not cheap wine, either. She would sneak away to talk to her daughter. Was I an embarrassment to her? Why couldn't I be in the room when she talked to her? I knew her name was Tracy, that she was a nurse, and she lived in Cleveland. But that is all I knew. It seemed that Diane was starting to keep secrets from me. When we made love, she smelled like wine, lots of it. Did she need it to have sex with me? She was starting to look old, and nothing like the sexy young girl I remembered from high school.

Joan called me at work every day. She missed me. I even called her from home on the nights Diane expected me to make my own dinner. Joan still loved me, and still wanted to help me. I was sure I had made a mistake. Joan was not exciting, but she was the only woman who had ever treated me special all the time. She was always there for me, even when I wasn't as good to her. I decided to go back to Joan. She wouldn't make me feel like I'd done something wrong – not like Gail did. Joan even suggested taking money from my retirement savings to move Diane back to Cleveland. And so I did.

Diane had been golfing, playing cards and drinking with her

friends, arriving home on this Friday evening about 9:00. She came in the house, looking tipsy from the drinking. She came over to give me a hug, and I turned away and headed into the bedroom. She followed me, asking what *my* problem was. I got very angry, very quickly.

"My problem?" I said. I walked towards her with purpose until I was less than a foot from her face. "My problem is that you're drunk, and this isn't working. I'm sending you back to Cleveland."

She started crying, and violently pulling on my shirt sleeves. Her words were unintelligible from the heavy crying and the effects of the wine. She tore the left sleeve of one of my dress shirts, which set me off. My teeth were clenched so hard I thought they would break. I picked her up by her shoulders and threw her towards the head of the bed, slamming her against the headboard, face first. Her lower lip was bleeding pretty badly, and blood was getting on everything. Goddammit. Now blood is all over the bed, and the sheets. I remembered soon enough that the bed and sheets were hers, so I quickly stopped worrying about that.

I retrieved and handed her a hand towel wet with cold water, and told her to pack up her shit. I told her I had already called a mover, and that they would be here the next day to load her things. I also told her I had booked a one-way plane ticket for her from Los Angeles to Cleveland.

She just sobbed and rambled on, "I gave up my apartment back home to be with you. I quit my job. I gave up most of my things for you. I'll have to live with Tracy, it's not fair to her."

The sobbing continued, and she kept repeating, "Benny, there are things you don't know; there are things I haven't told you..."

As I turned away, tired of her whining, she added, "Benny, it's about my daughter. It's about Tracy. I need to tell you about Tracy."

Who knows what hard luck story she was about to tell me. What about her goddamn daughter? She had refused to tell me anything about her before. She had hidden from me when talking to her, and wouldn't discuss the subject even when I asked. I didn't care what her problems were anymore. I was done with Diane. I was already packed. Everything I needed was already in my car.

I cut her off mid-sentence. Walking out the front door, I turned back towards her and told her she was not the person she claimed to be. I said good-bye for the last time. She had done this to herself.

When I arrived back home at our Tustin condo that night, Joan greeted me with a big hug, and a hot dinner she had prepared for my homecoming.

I woke up on a Sunday morning dreading the conversation I was about to have with Rosa. She wanted to go to church. She wanted to meet Laura for lunch. She missed her daughter. Sure enough, she was kissing my ass – being overly sweet and accommodating as she helped me out of bed, to the bathroom, and into the shower. She even rubbed me to try to get me excited, but I knew why. I didn't even wait for the question.

I interrupted in the middle of one of her patronizing comments, "I need you here… you can't leave me."

I didn't mention that bitch of a daughter of hers; I just left it at that. Had to save something for when the conversation got uglier.

Most Sundays, I win. I cry, and she feels so guilty; she can't leave me. Instead, she makes me feel better, cooks me a wonderful warm breakfast and disappears to the bathroom afterwards to shower and get ready for the day with me. I know she sneaks in a phone call with Laura, but after convincing her to stay with me, I try not to get too upset about those, since she makes those calls in private and they are only a few minutes long.

"But I miss my daughter… Benny, surely you can…" is all I let her say.

Although I still have trouble putting words and sentences together, I told her that her daughter is a bitch, and that she hates me, and of course I added some tears for effect. Rosa wouldn't leave knowing I need her so much that it made me cry. She never does. This time was different, though. Rosa didn't believe me, or at least that's how it appeared to me. She didn't have that sympathetic look on her angelic face anymore.

She looked at me like Mother used to look at me when I disappointed her. "No Benny. You can handle yourself for a few hours without me. I'm going to church, and I'm going to spend time with Laura."

She helped me to my recliner in the center of the living room and turned on the TV for me. She said she would make me breakfast in a few minutes. Why was today so different? Had I humiliated myself for nothing? Was she really going to defy me?

I was livid. My whole body tensed up with anger. Tears poured from my eyes and snot out my nose, but these tears were angry ones, and not the ones I gin up to get my way. My teeth were going to break from the pressure. Rosa knew I was mad, and she hurriedly placed me in my chair and made her way back into the bathroom to continue dressing and getting pretty for this 'alleged' meeting with her daughter. I wanted to grab her and shake her. I needed to hit her – to slap her face on account of her disrespecting me. It took all my energy to control my anger. I am supporting her, goddammit. She has food, and shelter, and gas for the car – all because of me. She belongs to me, and should be happy to do what I want, and when I want it. But my congestive heart failure prevents me from yelling. I cough almost every time I try to take a decent breath, or say more than a couple of words. My mouth doesn't always say what my mind wants it to anymore. I want to yell at her and tell her, clearly, how terrible she is being to me, but I can't. So once she was back in the bathroom and out of sight, I stood up from my chair, unfastened my pants, pulled them down and peed all over the carpet. Fuck her. Clean this up, Bitch.

By the time Rosa appeared from the bathroom all dressed and made up for church, I had removed my pants and underwear, thrown them aside and was sitting naked from the waist down in my recliner. She saw the mess. She said nothing. Normally she would treat me like a small child – talking baby talk but cleaning up my mess and telling me she loves me, and I don't have to do these things. Not this time. I heard some loud banging and slamming behind me and was momentarily concerned that she might be coming after me to punish me for messing up the living room. Although she was angrily tossing things around in the kitchen, she wasn't coming for me. Out of the corner of my eye, I saw her nervously pour a bowl of cereal, and put it on the dining room table with a small glass of milk, a spoon, and a glass of water with my morning pills. She also placed there some rags and carpet cleaner. She grabbed her purse and sweater and as she got to the front door, she looked over in my direction and told me that when I was tired of staring at my own piss, I could clean it up myself. Then she told me to get my own breakfast; she was leaving, and would be back home when she was finished with church and visiting with Laura. This was a first; Rosa had never before walked away from me when I needed her. All I could think of was how I was going to get even with her.

I needed to talk to Mother. She would understand how I feel. She would say the right things. If she were here with me, she would cradle my head close to her body, comforting me. She would tell me that Rosa isn't good enough for me, that she doesn't treat me the way I deserve to be treated. I wanted to call her, but Rosa always dials for me. She has all of the phone numbers saved on her cell phone. We have a home phone, but how would I find her number? Maybe I could call Alan or Marty. But where are their numbers? I never make my own phone calls. Joan always did this for me, too. The new-fangled telephone receivers were frustrating for me, so I made her do it. And cell phones? Forget about those. Once I tried to navigate a cell phone, and when I couldn't, I threw it across the room and just missed hitting Joan in the face. And that was in the late 90's. Nowadays I can't even get the damn things to turn on, let alone find a dial tone and the numbers to dial with.

I picked up the house phone, which was on the table beside my recliner. Luckily there were three numbers that Rosa had printed on a small piece of paper – her cell phone, Marty's number, and Alan's number. Rosa had put the entire number (including the '1' that has to be dialed before the area code), so if I needed to use the phone by myself, any confusion would hopefully be eliminated. I dialed Alan's number. It went straight to fucking voice mail, so I hung up. Then I tried Marty. Thankfully he answered. He went through his feigned attempts at showing concern as to my well-being, but I let him off the hook and just asked if he could read Mother's phone number to me. He did, I forced a 'thank you' and hung up.

As I was dialing Mother, all of our recent history filled my mind, including her criticisms of Gail, and Joan, and of my own life. I was too fat. I could have made so much more money had I stayed in Shaker Heights and married a rich, Jewish girl from the Temple. And the most hurtful criticism of all: How could such a special boy with such talent, good looks and a promising future turn out like you did? I'm not sure if those were the exact words, but those were definitely the sentiments. I hung up the phone after one ring, and before Mother answered. I didn't need to hear those things again. My mind went back to those wonderful times so long ago when I would overhear her bragging to her friends about me. Such a talented, smart and popular boy. Her special boy. So I picked up the phone and dialed again. Three rings, four rings… and Mother finally answered after the fifth ring.

It's still hard for me to remember that Mother is 102 years old. She doesn't hear or see well, and forgets things. I'm 21 years younger. Seeing and hearing aren't issues for me, but memory and speech are. Mother gets around better than I do. Marty and Alan tell me she can still walk without a walker, though she chooses to have one with her just in case, since her sight isn't good. I can barely get out of my chair, or out of bed, without Rosa's help. Mother has trouble with her plumbing, but she is very proper (still), and won't allow herself to be too far from a toilet. I really don't care where I am or who I'm with when I lose control. Rosa will clean me up. Marty told me that Mother has a wonderful attitude; he thinks that's why she's lived so long. That's just goddamn terrific.

I needed to hear Mother's voice. I need her to tell me I am still her special boy. I want to ask about Dad. Mother always talked about him like he was perfect. Was he really? I could never measure up. He let Mother be the bad guy… I never really got to know him. Only now was I mourning his death seven years ago. I never got to tell him I loved him. I never got to ask him if he was proud of me. As I grew up and started my own family, my relationship with Dad became more distant. He and Mother were critical of Gail, though Mother was always the spokesperson. They didn't think she came from a good or prominent enough family. They didn't think I made enough money. I was getting fat, and looking this way would negatively affect my success in business, not to mention it simply embarrassed them. When Gail and I divorced and I remarried, Mother said Joan wasn't smart or pretty enough for me. To add insult to injury, she was Catholic. Still, Dad never said a word. Was he as disappointed as Mother was? Did she truly speak for them both? I always looked up to Dad – at his incredible accomplishments, his seemingly perfect marriage, his status in his community. But I couldn't make him proud of me, at least he never said. And being around him was a constant reminder of my own failures. I wanted to talk to Mother about all this and more, but I doubted if I could spit any of it out. Even if I could, she probably wouldn't hear me. Once she answered the phone, it took several introductions, each louder than the last, until she knew she was talking to me.

As much as I wanted to say to her, all I could muster was, "Hello, Mother. I'm so sad and depressed. I just needed to hear your voice." Mother understood me perfectly.

She took no time at all to absorb what I had just said, and replied, "Benny, what do you want me to say, that I am sorry you're so miserable? I have my own problems. I'm an old lady. I sit in my little room all day every day. I've lived a wonderful life, had a wonderful husband for 73 years, and I was a very good mother. It is not my fault that you've made such bad decisions. Look at Jimmy and Donald – they had the same parents and their lives turned out wonderful."

I was so mad; I threw the phone against the wall to the left of my recliner. I also peed myself, this time right where I sat, and with no underwear or pants to absorb any of it. Of all of the criticisms, nothing hurt as much as the comparison to my brothers. Jimmy became a CPA, and then a lawyer, and then for the coup de gras – he became Dad's partner at the firm. And Donald? He was always the quiet one. I was able to manipulate him when he was a kid; I knew he idolized me. But he bested me too. He started his own commercial real estate company in Cleveland, and did very well. He married a wonderful girl from a prominent Jewish family, and is still married to her almost 50 years later. Both of my brothers have good relationships with their kids, and their grandkids. Mine want nothing to do with me. And Mother? I just wanted to be her special boy, again. To reclaim that feeling of being the most talented, smartest and best looking at school. I feel like such an idiot. She's a goddamn bitch. I should never have called her.

Rosa had been gone two hours. I was hungry, yet I had no

intention of eating the crap she left for me on the table. Let the milk spoil, I didn't care. I wouldn't give her the satisfaction of having helped myself to cereal and milk, taken my own medication, and cleaned up the mess I'd made in the living room. I wasn't even going to leave my chair. She can get her ass home, apologize to me and take care of me like I deserve.

Why did Rosa fall in love with me? Was she after what little money I have left? Was it to gain legal residence status? I'm not very nice to her. I know most times she gives in to my demands. But is it that she's afraid of having to deal with my temper, or my acting out? If she's so afraid, why doesn't she abandon me like every other woman in my life has done? What does a young, healthy woman in her early fifties see in an old, fat, miserable old man?

Rosa and I got out of bed, and she helped me get in the shower, handing me the shampoo, and then the soap, and helping me clean my body. She was making sure that I had one hand on the shower safety-grab bar so I stayed balanced. She was being her usual sweet self. Is it because she is afraid of me? Or does she really love me? I didn't ask, since I know what she'll tell me, even if it isn't true. She went back to the kitchen, constantly talking to me from there to make sure I was handling the simple task of balancing myself on something while drying, and then putting on underwear and a t-shirt. I walked slowly over to the bathroom sink, about to brush my teeth. Before picking up my toothbrush, I grabbed both sides of the sink to support myself, leaned forward and stared into the mirror. Who is this old, ugly disheveled bastard staring back at me? I can't even picture sixteen year-old Benjamin anymore. Did he ever exist? Is there really such a thing as Karma? Has Mother lied to me for all these years?

How could Mother's special boy end up so ordinary? Have I even achieved 'ordinary?' Why do I love so deeply, and then hate so fiercely? Why do all of the women I've loved first look at me with such desire and adoration, soon to fade into matter-of-fact, and, in time, into fear? Why did I cheat on Gail? She was the love of my life, and I threw it all away. And for what? Stupid, meaningless sex with Nancy? Forty-two boring years with Joan? And what the hell is with Diane? She just keeps popping up in my life after she humiliated me when we were just kids. Did I force myself on her in high school? No way. She wanted me, and always has. But she must really hate me after our last episode. Right at this moment, staring into my bathroom mirror, I understood why. And now Rosa has found me, and says she loves me. She tells me how special I am, and does whatever I want her to do, for me, and to me. Can that really be sincere? I look like death – the fat, angry version.

I remember that night, hitting Gail on our porch. That was the beginning of the end. I thought for sure she had to be cheating on me; but it turned out she wasn't. I was the one getting bored with us. I was the one who cheated. I was the one who needed that special recognition. I remember getting so angry with my boys, but I never remember why. They grew to be such good men, and good parents. So how bad could their behavior have been? Why was I always so angry with them? Why did I always have to be better than them? Even today, I absolutely hate knowing that all three of them bested me. I can't erase the looks on Marty's and Alan's faces when we were wrestling on our living room floor. They were either terrified, or mad beyond fear. Why didn't they respect me like I did my dad? Why did I marry Joan? There was never any excitement in our relationship. Is it because she saved me at my lowest point, and I thought I owed her? Mother once said to me that I was repaying a debt, and I wasn't in love with my wife. That was the last time I called Mother a fucking bitch, out loud that is.

My whole life I've wanted to please Mother. I remember those times when I was a small child staring at her with admiration, but mostly looking for her reaction to me. I longed for her approval for everything I did. My grades, my short-lived piano lessons, playing my violin, my girlfriends, and eventually, my wives and kids. Her disappointment in me became more obvious over the years. I was definitely her special boy as a child. She looked at me with such tremendous pride when I played the violin, or when I brought home a good report card from school, or when I put on my best outfit for Shabbat services at the Temple. I saw the look on her face when she would brag about me to her friends at the Club. But then, when I would get into trouble, her proud expression would turn to looks of serious concern, and eventually graduate to out-and-out disbelief, and blatant disapproval. Then why do I still want to talk to Mother, to see that look of pride, and to hear her praise me as her special boy? I'm not a stupid man. In this albeit brief moment of self- reflection, I know goddamn well how Mother feels about me, about my life and my decisions. And while she used to stress about my life choices, I can tell through our conversations over the past four or five years that she has given up on me. She is resigned to the fact that I have made bad decisions and that she and Dad were good parents, as evidenced by Jimmy and Donald's successes, and the success of all of their grandchildren.

I worshipped my dad. He was tough on me, but he was always consistent and predictable. He never gave me any reason to fear him. Rather, I had him on a pedestal. He was the pillar of our community, a leader in our Temple and Country Club, a loving and dedicated husband, and a successful businessman. Times were different when I was growing up. Dad's job was to work hard and provide more, not to crawl around the floor and play with me and my brothers. He picked a perfect partner in Mother because, for the most part, she was the disciplinarian – the one whose department it was to maintain order in the house. Dad made so much more money than I ever did; I always wanted to be like him, in every way. Why couldn't I execute any of my grandiose dreams? What was I afraid of? And why am I still so mortified that my sons out-worked, and out-earned me? They can hardly stand to be around me. And they don't want their kids – my grandchildren – to be anywhere near me.

Marty spent most of his childhood running away from me, and Alan had such hate in his eyes, he even threatened to kill me if I ever hit him again. And my beautiful baby, my soft, warm-hearted Andy, shot himself in the head. Why would he do that after achieving such success? Could I have prevented that from happening? What could have happened in his life to cause him to have to throw it all away?

I'm still staring into the bathroom mirror, but now I'm

sobbing. I can't fix anything I've done in the past. I have virtually no relationship with my two remaining kids, and none at all with their kids. I have no friends, not a single one. Gail is long gone. Joan is dead, and I can't bear thinking that I might have killed her. I can only imagine what the women I've cheated with over the years think of me. And Mother. Am I being punished because the woman I've most wanted to please in my life will likely outlive me? I love her, and I hate her. I wish I knew how to please her, and how to be her special boy again. But mostly, I wish she would just die.

All of a sudden I had a moment of extreme clarity. What the hell does Rosa see in me? My God I look like shit. What does she want from me? Citizenship, money, or is there something else at play that I haven't thought of? Has she done this before – slept her way into an old man's heart to ultimately gain whatever it is he has, and she wants? Is her husband in on it? Frank was remarkably calm about Rosa's leaving him for me. Maybe it's all a ruse – a game they've played before. Have I been set up for something? I can't know for sure, but I need to watch my back from now on. Rosa may not be the angel she pretends to be. Should I tell Alan? Probably not a good idea. He'll think I'm even crazier than he already thinks I am. Am I being too paranoid? Maybe I am. I hope I am. I have to be. I love Rosa. I need her more than I've ever needed anyone before. She has to love me.

Rosa was still in the kitchen, preparing my breakfast. She didn't know I'd been crying. I needed to clean up so I wouldn't have to tell her what was wrong. If she sees that I've been crying, she'll want me to talk about it, and I don't want to. On the other hand, I always get what I want when I cry. I could just play the dementia card. So I called out to her, while the tears were still flowing. If she was truly manipulating me, two can play this game.

Rosa took me to see my doctor. I hate going to the doctor, or the dentist, or anywhere I have to wait. They give me an appointment time, and we are almost always there on time, but they are never ready to see me right when I get there. I usually sit quietly for a few minutes, but then I get up, look at Rosa and tell her I'm leaving. I shuffle out of the office, very sure she'll be following me. Sometimes I don't even tell her I'm leaving. I just get up and start walking. I look around at all the pathetic people waiting indefinitely for the doctor, knowing full well I'm now the lowest on the priority list. They don't want to see me. I'm an old miserable man who dribbles when he talks, has stains on his clothes, and who hates everyone in his path. Why would they want to give me the time of day, let alone talk to me with respect, with empathy, and with some concern about my problems? I sure wouldn't. So I just leave. Screw them all. They can see me when and if they ever keep their appointment time.

This visit was no different. We walked in, and the place was so crowded I had to sit down next to a fat old lady who was knitting, of all things. I wondered how long she'd been waiting. How many sweaters had she knitted since she arrived at the office? I would have asked her, but she didn't look friendly, or worse – she might share her life story with me, in which case I'd probably scream at her to shut the fuck up. Not to mention if I show Rosa I am able to articulate this question to this annoying woman, it might make her think I am exaggerating my memory and speech issues. So I sat down, and intentionally bumped her to establish my space. She predictably gave me a nasty look and moved over a full chair. Yes! I quickly took off my sweater and put it on the now empty chair so some other asshole wouldn't sit there, or so the super-knitter couldn't change her mind and re-take her old spot.

After waiting my five-minute maximum, I was infuriated and ready to leave. Rosa knew this. She nervously awaits my physical and emotional outbursts. I usually jump up and start my angry shuffle out of the waiting room. This time, however, she grabs my arm and holds me down before I have a chance to move. She tells me in her sweetest and most mothering tone that I should relax and be patient. She will check with the receptionist on the expected wait. She tells me (again) that this is an important visit. I need the doctor to give me the latest test results so we can understand why my memory is fading, arranging thoughts and finding words has become more difficult, and my incontinence is worse. Rosa says I've also had many more tantrums lately, and she wants to make sure that the doctor reevaluates my medications – especially the medicines I take for depression, and for sleep.

I know that I'm not the picture of health, but I'm not as helpless as Rosa thinks I am. It's true that I have some trouble with speech, depression and sleep. I have congestive heart failure, and need a cane or walker to get around most of the time. My extremities are all swollen and sore, and I have trouble breathing sometimes because my lungs often fill with fluid. I really do have trouble getting out of the bed, or standing up out of my recliner. I have high blood pressure, Type-2 diabetes, a mouth full of decay, and I forget things sometimes. But my incontinence issues are not always accidents. I remember more than I let on. And because Rosa comforts me most when I struggle with trying to say what I'm thinking, of course I remain a man of few words. I hate seeing the doctor, because I can't be 100% honest with him, for fear my slight embellishments will be discovered. The drawbacks of this are that my medications may not be exactly right for me, and I never get a true prognosis since I've bullshitted my way through another doctor visit. Besides, I don't want Rosa to ever leave my side. I don't want her to work, or to provide care to any other people, especially men. I don't want her to think she can spend more time with that bitch, Laura. I want her home, taking care of me, all the time.

Sitting there thinking about my cleverness calmed me somewhat, so the next few minutes passed quickly. My name was called, and Rosa helped me up and guided me as we entered the door of gloom. To the right was the long corridor that leads first to the scale, and the height ruler, and then the itty-biddy offices where I am usually forced to expose myself in all my un-kept glory. Luckily I should be able to avoid that during this visit, since we are here for test results. I reluctantly stepped on the scale. Two hundred fifty-eight pounds. Rosa's cooking, no doubt. I'm shrinking though. I was 5'8" at my tallest, but now I measure barely 5'6". I know what the nurse was thinking as she typed my stats into her electronic tablet. He's miserable, short, fat, old, decrepit, and taking up space.

The nurse smiled and patronized me with a, "How is your day going, Benjamin?"

I ignored her completely, following her down the corridor, navigating past all these little rooms, swinging my walker forward, taking a step, and then all over again. I could probably walk without it, but it serves two purposes – a little balance security, and of course, Rosa's sympathy. Occasionally I heard what sounded like a doctor talking or a patient moaning inside one of the closed rooms. What ever happened to doctors making house calls? I was definitely born a few generations too late.

Rosa was allowed to come in with me, as Alan had contacted the doctor's office and asked that she be able to come to my appointments and help me communicate. I'm sure he got sick and tired of the all-too-frequent calls from Rosa to come out to our place and take me to the doctor. It was better for me as well, since I was able to manipulate Rosa pretty easily. I don't know if Alan or Marty suspect I'm exaggerating my conditions, but one thing I know for sure; they would do almost anything to avoid dealing with me. The nurse had me sit on the examination table and took my temperature and blood pressure measurements. She typed the data into her tablet, and then asked me about all my current medication, and if there is anything else that the doctor should know. I just looked at Rosa, and she knew to answer for me. Once the nurse had all the necessary information, she left the room, but not before telling me that the doctor would be right in.

Rosa and I waited about five more minutes. Just as I was ready to give up and march out of there, we heard a faint knock on the door, and Dr. Richards entered the room. He reached out to shake my hand, so I slowly returned the favor, though the extreme puffiness in my hands makes it difficult to grasp anything. He said hello to Rosa, then sat down and spent about thirty seconds reading the information that the nurse had added. He had already seen all of my test results. Before he gave me the news, he wanted to administer another oral exam for dementia. He asked me about twenty questions, mostly the same or similar to ones he'd asked me before. I didn't want to come across as needing memory care, but I also didn't want Rosa nor the doctor to think I was totally fine. So some of the questions I answered correctly and some I didn't. I made sure to take lots of time to answer them all. Most were ridiculously simple questions, like… who is the president of the United States? What year is it? What city do you live in? In what year were you born? What is your birthday? What was your mother's name? I didn't even correct him when he asked about Mother in the past tense. Ha. She's still alive, lucky me.

He wrote down his observations, then proceeded with the results of the recent blood tests and brain scan they had just taken. He believed I might have suffered one or more minor strokes, since I was having trouble rationalizing my thoughts and speaking. He said the brain scan was inconclusive, and diagnosing onset Alzheimer's would be difficult without having had a previous scan to compare it to. He said he didn't think what he saw in the scan explained the worsening memory issues Rosa had reported. He attributed the incontinence to the dementia. He thought because the dementia and associated symptoms were getting progressively worse, and my recent unexplained angry outbursts, he was going to change my depression medication to 'Seroquel.' He didn't change any of my other medications or treatments for high blood pressure or diabetes. He said he wanted me back in two months to assess any memory or behavior changes, and possibly perform another brain scan if things had deteriorated.

I wasn't going to say anything, since nothing he said was going to change my situation with Rosa. One thing made me curious, however, mainly because I wasn't being altogether honest about the severity of my memory loss or my incontinence.

I asked the question in as few words as possible, continuing to show that I struggle to say everything that I'd like, "What is Seroquel?"

Dr. Richards elaborated as I had hoped he would. He explained, "Seroquel is an antipsychotic drug that treats severe depression, as well as schizophrenia and bipolar disorder. It shouldn't dull your senses, but will help stabilize moods, and possibly help you rationalize and speak better."

Hmmm. Well at least he didn't talk to me like a child. I guess I'll have to take the drug, or Rosa will suspect I'm not as screwed up as I claim. Maybe it'll make me feel better. It sounds like I'll still be able to regulate what I can or can't say. I just nodded as if to say, "Okay," and got up to get ready to finally get the hell out of that place.

We were told that the doctor would call in my prescription, so we headed out the door of our examination room, down the long corridor, back into the waiting room, and finally and mercifully out the glass doors and into the parking lot. Rosa was so proud of me for behaving, she said she would take me to lunch anywhere I wanted to go. I smiled back at her, which made her feel a great sense of accomplishment for having handled this normally-painful process so well. I felt pretty good, too. I got through it relatively unscathed and decided to throw Rosa a bone, an appreciative smile, and a kiss on the lips after we got in the car.

Another family reunion. I always dread these. I didn't want to go, but I like hearing Joan tell me over and over that it wouldn't be the same without the oldest son being there to celebrate Dad's 95th birthday. She tells me my family loves me, and would certainly be asking about me if I weren't there. I suppose she's right, but I'll have to face Mother. I'll have to listen to her subtle jabs at me, reminding me how fat I am, and how plain Joan is. She'll criticize me for having retired seven years prior, because I never made enough money while working, so how could I afford a happy and long retirement? How could I afford to come to Florida for this reunion? What do I do all day every day? And then, Mother will hand me a check to reimburse me for the trip. I'll be so angry I could punch her, but I won't be baited into reacting angrily. I'll quietly take the check and hope nobody sees or finds out about it, though I'm sure Dad will know. I'll also let Alan rent a bigger car so I don't have to pay for my own rental. I might even profit from the whole thing. Even though I can't stand the thought of having to kiss the asses of my entire extended family, at least it won't cost me anything – or more accurately, it won't cost me any money.

All three of my boys would be there for their grandpa's 95th. They have always adored him. I just don't get it. Why is Dad so much closer to my sons than he was to me? They idolize him, and he treats each of them like they are the center of the universe. He treats all of the grandkids that way, even Jimmy and Donald's kids. There are nine of them among the three of us. It's no wonder they're all so enamored with him. How does he do it? I'm glad he loves my kids so much, but I'm angry and jealous that he never treated me the same way. Shit, my own kids never looked up to me like they do their grandpa. Dad always used Mother to confront me about my life, about my choices. He went out of his way to avoid dealing with me. I can't remember the last time we had a heart-to-heart talk about my life – about my future, even sharing his investment recommendations with me. I'm sure he thought that it was much too late for any such conversations. Any hope he had for me stopped when I married Gail and moved to L.A. As politically correct as Dad has always been, I could feel his disappointment in me. I'd be a fool to attempt to engage in any deep conversations with him now.

Jimmy is the big shot of the family, or at least that is how Mother and Dad treat him. He's the most successful; and wouldn't you know it, he followed Mother and Dad to Florida, and is semi-retired and living the good life. His family seems so close, while my kids do whatever they can to avoid me. Jimmy's family always has nice things to say about each other. I can't be sure, but I'm almost positive that Marty, Alan and Andy all talk about me behind my back. I see them huddling with their cousins – and when I come close, everyone clams up. The cousins love it when Marty, Alan and Andy are together with them. Mother and Dad love it when all of their grandchildren are together. My brothers and their wives all seem happier than pigs in slop. So why am I so miserable? I look at Joan – unattractive, needing help to walk around, taking so goddamn long to walk from the car to wherever we're headed… I just want to push her off a cliff, slap my hands clean of responsibility and reenter the picture. Once again, I'd be recognized as the best-looking, smartest and most popular boy at the party. Beautiful women would be clamoring to be with me, and Mother would proudly boast of my accomplishments. Then reality strikes. Joan is still next to me, hanging on my arm, motioning me to help her find a chair so she can rest. She's not even a wallflower anymore. She's an embarrassment.

Other than Mother and Dad, the entire family stayed at the Embassy Suites in Boca Raton. As much as I hate these trips, I love the Embassy Suites. I can get up in the morning before Joan has managed her way out of bed, and before any of the family has smelled the wonderful aroma of bacon that penetrates the walls of the guest rooms, I can make three or four trips through the free breakfast buffet. If I'm going to put up with my family for three days, I'm going to eat my misery away at the free buffet. When family started to show up, I sneaked back up to our room just in time to watch Joan struggling to dry her hair, put on one article of clothing every several minutes, and finally she was ready to make her way oh-so-slowly to the elevator and down to breakfast. I had burned off the calories from the three breakfasts I'd already eaten just watching her go through her painful morning rituals. We sat quietly while various family members stopped by and offered their good morning greetings, none coming across all that sincere. My brothers and their wives sat near us and tried to engage in small-talk, but it was obvious they would much rather be sitting somewhere else. I did my best to ignore them, and Joan's conversational skills are taxing at best.

Most of the family had gone to the beach early on the day of the party. The festivities were to start promptly at 6 p.m. Mother wanted everyone dressed appropriately, and on time. We were invited to the beach too, but I couldn't go because Joan can't handle the sun or extreme heat, and I would be looked upon with even less favor if I showed up alone. So Joan and I hovered around the breakfast area until lunchtime, and went back to our room for room service, and then to watch college football until we had to start getting ready. Even if we were able to go with everyone to the beach, we would have to be back to the hotel long before everyone else, since Joan required two to three hours to get dressed and ready.

Mother rented one of the smaller ballrooms at the hotel for Dad's party. Of course she ordered prime rib for everyone, and was all over the kitchen staff to make sure the meat was perfectly cooked, and the tables were adorned with precisely the right table settings and centerpieces that she had ordered. Though she spared no expense, she made sure everyone knew how much the whole event cost. She even made reference to the money they have paid to, "…make sure all the family could attend," which, of course is a not-so-subtle reminder that she has paid for our trip. It made me wonder if my brothers would find out Mother paid me off to be there.

Dinner was delicious. I was able to quietly arrange two helpings of prime rib without Mother finding out. After taking full advantage of the open bar, I was feeling pretty relaxed. I was able to listen to Jimmy talk about his profitable semi- retirement, and his new consulting gig in Naples, and maintain a smile on my face. Donald and I talked more than we had in years. He seemed genuinely interested in how I was doing in retirement, and even in the job I had before I retired. His real estate business sounded interesting, and even more intriguing to me was the fact that I thought he was much better off than his portrayal suggested. All of a sudden I felt a comradery with him. Or maybe it was the Scotch.

Dinner was over, dessert plates were being cleared, and Jimmy stood up and clinked his water glass with his spare spoon. Great, we get to hear the great Jimmy talk. I guess I should be ready to speak too. After all, I am the oldest son. When he had everyone's attention, Jimmy announced that he had the great pleasure of introducing Dad on his 95th birthday. He didn't hand over the stage at that point, though. He talked about what a wonderful relationship he and Dad shared when he was a kid, and how that grew to an incredible business partnership and a friendship.

I was sick to my stomach. I wanted to throw up all of that great prime rib and expensive Scotch I had just consumed. I kept my straight face – thankful that Jimmy's comments were over and it was Dad's turn to get up. But before he did, Donald interrupted and asked to say a few words first. He thanked Dad for his love, his guidance, and for being such a wonderful grandfather to his two kids. Nice and short. I guess I was up. I really had no choice. I stood up and immediately saw the worried look on Mother's face. She couldn't say anything, but her face was telling me not to embarrass her, or Dad. I wanted to throw my drink on her, but I maintained my composure, also not wanting to waste perfectly good Scotch. As I was trying to think of something to say, goddammit if I didn't start crying. I blurted out that I tried so hard to please him my whole life, and that I loved him so much and wanted him to be proud of me. I said I was very happy in retirement, and that it was like being on a vacation every single day. I was mildly drunk, but aware enough to know I wasn't making much sense. I had said enough. I sat down. I didn't look at Mother. Joan put her hand on my leg. She knew just what to do to comfort me. I owe her so much.

It was Dad's turn to talk. Even though he was 95, he was as sharp and as smooth an orator as he'd ever been. He told a story about a young man who built a life for his family. He worked hard to build a successful and sustainable business. He was proud of the reputation he had earned in the Cleveland and Shaker Heights communities, and throughout its Jewish community. Then he started talking about Mother. He said she was by far the best natured person he had ever known, and he owed his happy life and much of his success to her. He talked about the three of us collectively – about being a proud father. But he focused on Jimmy when going into more depth about growing a father-son relationship into what their relationship became. I thought very seriously about walking out. Joan knew exactly what I was thinking and squeezed my hand on my lap, using all of her energy in an apparent effort to hold me down. So I let my mind wander…

I'm playing first chair violin in the orchestra at our holiday concert in the eleventh grade. All the pretty girls are staring at me, I can tell. I am following the movements, but I hear myself over all the other members. I know my music is beautiful. I am in another world as I master another classical piece, this time for the Shaker Heights High holiday show. I have a clear view of Mother, sitting in the second row from the front. She is smiling and looking around the room for other mothers or fathers she knows. She loves the bragging rights of having the best looking, most talented boy in the orchestra. Where is Dad? Then I remember Mother saying that he had an important meeting to attend.

My thoughts jump to senior year, following my performance with the Cleveland Jr. Symphony. That was such a surreal experience for me. I was a last minute addition since one of the regular violinists was sick. But I made the most of the opportunity. The orchestra members were all congratulating me backstage as we packed up our instruments, no remaining trace of the skeptical looks they'd given me before the performance. Would he fit in? Would he make a mistake and embarrass the whole? Ha. I was perfect. I enter the lobby and find Mother and Margi. The look on Margi's face tells me she wants me more than ever. And even though Mother is clearly none too pleased about Margi being here, she is also beaming with pride. She pulls me close to kiss my cheek and even calls me her special boy. It has been so long since I've heard her say that. As I smiled and remembered that wonderful time, I recalled that Dad couldn't make that performance either. He'd had to attend a business dinner with a client. As with the holiday concert the prior year, I hadn't thought much of it at the time.

I skip to another memory. I am in front of the room of people at my wedding to Gail. I have met and am marrying the girl of my dreams. She is beautiful, sweet, loving and smart, and she is crazy about me. The violinist plays as Gail walks slowly towards me. I flash instantly to the breaking of the glass, and then our first wonderful kiss as a married couple. My heart drops into my stomach as we exit the makeshift pulpit, and I see the look on Mother's face. To this day, I can't characterize it in words. One thing I know, however: that look was not joyful.

Before I tuned in to the rest of Dad's story, I briefly recalled the conversations he'd had with me over the years about investment opportunities. There were at least three I could remember. In each case, I'd turned him down – but not because I couldn't afford it, as he said each time that he would front me the money. I turned him down because I perceived his offers as another in the series of criticisms of my life choices, and a statement of his lack of confidence in my ability to do well on my own.

I had tears in my eyes when I rejoined reality. Dad wrapped up his remarks, and then Marty led the nine cousins in a rehearsed skit to honor their grandpa. All I could think of at that point was that no one would ever honor me like this. When the 'show' was over, I got up and walked over to Dad. I gave him a hug, and a kiss on his cheek. I told him I loved him. He said he loved me too. But then he turned to me and asked me a question that I couldn't, and wouldn't, answer.

He said, "I am so lucky to have such a wonderful family, such loving and wonderful grandchildren," then added, "Benjamin, what is your relationship like with your grandchildren?"
I turned away from him and walked towards Joan, feeling completely empty.

I just wanted her to hold me. I asked her to take me home.

"Rosa… Rosa, goddammit!"

I'm staring at my violin painting, trying to find the TV remote control to turn down the noise. I can't yell over it. I can't speak in anything but a soft tone or whisper without coughing up all the phlegm in my lungs. So now, I'm coughing, then yelling for Rosa, then coughing some more. Where is she? I stare in confusion while focusing on the room, the smoke coming from the kitchen, the smell of burnt chili sauce, and my side table and all that was on it now laying on the floor. As I look down towards all those things strewn all across the living room, I become aware of the blood on my lap, my shirt, my chair, and on my hands. I am still coughing uncontrollably, and can't find a tissue to cough into, so I just spew all I've coughed up all over my chin, and on to my shirt and lap. I look left and right, and turn as much as I can to see blood on the wall leading from the kitchen, to the short hallway and into our bedroom. I try to call to Rosa again, but hear no answer. I remember she had been moaning before, but no more. I hear nothing but the TV and the boiling over of the chili on the stove. Then, I hear another knock on the door. I had forgotten that the police are trying to get in. Why are the police here? Where is Rosa?

In that brief moment, I picture Mother. It occurs to me that I might have just attacked her. Did I just kill my mother? Oh my God.

I love Mother so much. I just want to make her proud of me.
I try to shout out, "Mother?" "Mother, are you okay?"

No answer. I can't move. I have to save Mother. Think how proud she would be if I am the one who saves her life. My legs are on fire. The room goes black, and I am again traveling through frames from the past, some familiar, some I don't recognize – spinning, then slowing, then coming into focus. Only this time, each visit to a specific moment lasts only a few seconds, and I am quickly pulled back into the darkness and into a new moment. I am dizzy, feeling faint but conscious, although I'm not so sure I want to be.

Mother is holding me. I have no idea when, or where we are. She is beautiful as usual, dressed and manicured to perfection. I am sitting on her lap. I am her special boy. She kisses me and whispers that into my ear, and then tells me to go play. I fall from her lap, looking back to see that smile of hers, the one where I know I am the reason for her happiness. I run off with incredible feelings of peace, love, and of extreme contentment. I feel the chills up my spine as I return to my wounded state in my living room.

I smile mindlessly as I am again transfixed by Mother's face. But it is a different day, I am not a child. Is it my wedding to Gail? She is looking at me with such disdain. Her lips don't move, yet I hear her voice telling me how disappointed she is with me. I watch as she turns and cries on Dad's shoulders. Mother never cries. I'm being pulled back from wherever this is, but I don't want to leave. I want to understand why Mother is so upset. My emotions have gone from surrounded with love to this sinking feeling of falling, alone, with no one to hold onto me. Mother is my world. My self-worth is wrapped up in Mother's opinion of me, in being her special boy.

I'm at the Club now, in the bonus room with Diane. I'm almost eleven years old, but I know that look in her eye. She likes me. She doesn't move or say a word, but I hear her voice saying she loves me. I hear that same voice telling me to kiss her, and then to do it again. I flash forward to the tenth grade. I am inside her on the floor of the orchestra room closet. Her face is turned from me, but I know she is in love with me. It is the first time for both of us. She wants me deeper, longer, and she never wants this moment to end. She is crying with joy. We are so much older now, and Diane is back in my life and telling me that she has always loved me. I have the same warm, loving and content feeling that brought me chills when thinking of Mother's love. But that feeling quickly transitions to anger. Diane is drunk, and crying, and I hate her for being the same bitch that Mother turned into. I'm no longer her special boy, so she is no longer worthy of being with me.

I'm living my dream, flying my F-86 Sabre over the skies of enemy territory. My call name is 'Bogart.' I've saved so many fellow pilots today; I'm imagining the parade waiting for me back home in Cleveland, and maybe even a bigger one in Washington D.C. The President of the United States will award me the Medal of Honor. I am a hero, riding in the back of an open convertible with my flight suit on, listening to the crowd cheer for me. Dad is driving the car, and

Mother is sitting next to him in the front passenger seat. She has never looked so proud. I briefly think about Jimmy. He isn't there. And why should he be? I'm the hero, not him. It's first thing in the morning, and I'm in a beautiful office high-rise in downtown Los Angeles. My surroundings are confusing me; so I reach into my pocket and grab one of my own business cards to see who I am, and what I'm doing there. I'm the CEO of West Coast Diner, Inc. I'm in our board room, and I'm getting the quarterly earnings reports from my staff. My accountants are weighing whether we should continue to expand in the next quarter versus waiting until next year. We already own over 100 restaurants, three different franchises in ten different states. Who cares? I am rich. In that same moment, an office administrator calls me out of the meeting to take a call. It is Mother. She and Dad are visiting us in California. She is out to lunch with Gail. She just wanted to tell me how proud she is of me, and how much she loves Gail. But in my mind, all I see is her stone face. I hear her apologize for judging Gail as she did, but her facial expression stays the same, and her lips never move.

I'm on my back on the floor, but where? It looks familiar. It's my house on College Park Drive in Seal Beach. Alan is crawling on top of me, and Marty follows behind him. They are laughing; we are all laughing. I'm jumping around our family room on all fours, pretending to be the attacking dog. They're taking turns jumping on my back, and I buck them off aiming for a soft, couch landing. Gail is in the kitchen, a big beautiful smile on her face as she watches her boys having fun together. She is holding Andy and cooking dinner. Her smile is so beautiful, so disarming, and so pure. Could I ever love someone so much? In an instant, I see Alan's red face. He is on his stomach on the carpeted floor, and I am on top of him twisting his arm behind his back. I am angry. He won't say uncle to me. Marty is crying. He is peaking from behind Gail and Andy in the kitchen, ready to run if I make any movement toward him. Gail is begging me to let go of Alan. His arm snaps, he screams, and all I see is Mother's stone face. This time, she says nothing.

Marty is in front of me now. He is speaking to a large group, fighting off tears. I look around, realizing we are at Joan's memorial service. I am being driven back to my house. Marty, Alan and Andy, and all of their wives are with me. The phone is ringing when we walk in. I answer, and it is Donald. He wants to fly here from Cleveland and spend some time with me. Probably feels guilty for not having come to today's service. He says he wants to help me. Help me? You used to look up to me when we were kids. But where have you been the last forty-plus years? You've deserted me just like the rest of my bullshit family. You were mad when I divorced Gail. You thought I was crazy for marrying Joan. Now you want to be my best friend, and give yourself some feeling of satisfaction by coming all this way to help me? But I said none of those things.

I only said, "No, thanks," and hung up. I knew he would tell Mother that he tried to help me. Goddamn suck-up. I didn't care anymore.

Boy, I sure know this awful place. I'm at Mission Manor, in my little tiny room. I can tell I've just moved in, as everything is still in boxes. Marty and Alan are here. I feel nothing but hate right now. After all I sacrificed for my kids, they are sticking me in this hell hole, with all these old, ugly, miserable bitches. They are touring me around the building trying to put on fake, happy faces as they introduce me to the staff. They're hoping I'll behave, I'm sure. They are moving faster than I am able – no doubt in a hurry to make themselves feel comfortable enough where they can get the hell out of here, and go back to their wonderful dad-free lives. But I'm stuck here. In the next moment I am fighting with Nell. And in the next, I'm sitting at Rosa's dinner table, with her entire family there. I'm living with them now. I feel as if I'm being tossed around like unwanted garbage. What did I do to deserve this?

Rosa has her finger on her lips, shushing me as she enters my room. She pulls up her dress and exposes that she is wearing no underwear. She helps me take my pants off, and climbs into my bed on top of me. We are in my bedroom at Rosa's and Frank's house. It is the first time we had sex. Frank and Laura aren't home. In a fast heartbeat, I am now fighting with Rosa. We have already moved into our own apartment. She's wrestling with me because I just hit her in the arm for being late getting home from the market. I knew she was cheating on me, or sneaking out to see her bitch of a daughter. She hits me and I am crying. In the next moment, she is lying on the bed, and my head is in her lap. She is comforting me, stroking my hair and my cheek. Now I am on Mother's lap. I am a child. I am her special boy… again.

What is this, a hotel room? I'm sitting in the room, and

watching Andy come through the door carrying a duffle bag. At first I don't say anything. I'm not sure he can see me. Then I see him pull a gun from the bag, and sit silently at the edge of the bed. He pulls out a pad of paper and a pen, writes a few things down, and sets it all down on the end table closest to him. I can't see what he has written.

I yell to him… "Andy… Andy, it's Daddy." "I love you, son."

He can't hear or see me. As I watch him load his gun and ready it for firing, I realize there is nothing I can do to stop it. He looks down to the floor, crying.

Maybe he'll think twice and change his mind. In an instant he pulls the gun up, points it into his mouth and pulls the trigger. Loud bang – jolting him backwards – blood splatters on the ceiling and the wall behind him – and then completely still.

I am back in my living room, screaming and coughing, and screaming some more. "No… No!" "My baby… Andy… No!"

I am sobbing uncontrollably, trying to fall forward onto the floor, but I can't move. My legs are in so much pain, and my arms are shaking and bloody. The TV noise is blaring, the boiling chili hitting the hot stove is getting louder and more constant, and I am bent forward, howling his name.

"Oh, Andy, my little boy. Goddammit, Andy…"

Hastened back to the present, the knocks on the door are getting louder. The police are saying my name, and asking if I'm okay. I realize what has happened in our little apartment. I close my eyes and cry silently.

Rosa put me in the shower and walked away. I hadn't seen or heard from her in at least fifteen minutes. It's not Sunday, so I didn't have to worry about her sneaking off to call Laura and arranging for a post-Church lunch rendezvous or something. I'd finished washing myself, so I started to call for her. First I called out with my lower speaking voice volume, since I didn't want to start coughing and lose my breath. But when she didn't answer, my calls got louder. After a minute of shouting out to her, I started pounding on the shower wall. Maybe she'd hear this and run to see what was wrong. But nothing. I started to panic. Did she leave me? Did I make her mad? Goddammit where are you, Bitch?

I tried to turn off the shower water, but Rosa always does this for me, and I don't know how it works. I turned the handle in one direction, and the water all of a sudden got boiling hot. I screamed in pain, falling out of the shower to escape the burning water. I didn't have the time or the strength to lift my leg over the bathtub ledge, so I fell – the plastic shower curtain coming with me, breaking the bar across the wall but also helping to break my fall. I was lying on the bathroom floor naked, and other than burns on my chest and stomach from the hot water, I didn't think I was hurt. But I was going to make Rosa pay for ignoring my cries for help. Where the hell was she where she couldn't hear my calls, or my banging on the wall? She must have finally heard the crash coming from the bathroom; she showed up about thirty seconds after I'd hit the floor.

I yelled at her, "Where have you been?" "Look what you've made me do."

Rosa was apologizing profusely. "I'm so sorry, Benny." "Are you okay? "Are you hurt?"

Am I hurt? Are you fucking serious? I'm an old man. I can barely stand on my own, and can't even run my own shower. I didn't say anything. She helped me up off the floor and was starting to wrap a towel around me when I grabbed her arm, brought it up to my mouth and bit her hard on the forearm. She screamed, and hit me hard on my left ear with her closed fist. I let go of her arm, recoiled, and fell to the floor. It hurt so much; I curled up like a baby and cried. My ear felt like it was ripped off, and my chest felt like I had just been branded.

Rosa walked out of the room, but she returned in less than a minute carrying ice in a plastic storage bag, and extra towels. She was also crying. She looked at my ear, and decided it was okay, so she used the ice for my chest and stomach areas. She dampened a large towel, poured the ice on it, wrapped it up and had me hold it against myself while she dried me off. While she was drying my crotch, she was being very rough and abrupt. Without warning, she squeezed my testicles hard with the towel, making me holler in pain. My arms flew up instinctively; my right arm struck her on her forehead and knocked her backwards against the bathroom door. She was still crying, obviously mad as hell at me. She recovered quickly, yelling at me to pick up the towel and ice and let her finish drying and dressing me. I was both angry and a little afraid at that point. I'd never seen Rosa so pissed off. But my anger outweighed my fear, by a longshot. I did not pick up the towel. Instead, I turned facing her, grabbed my penis, and peed on her as she stood at the door. I was crying and smiling at the same time. She had left me alone in the shower. It was her fault I got burned and fell on the floor. And now she is mad at me? What happened to the Rosa who loves me, and treats me like I deserve to be treated?

Rosa ran from the bathroom only to return a few minutes later with different clothes on. She said nothing, and wore an expression that reflected both anger and determination. She led me into the bedroom, put my Depends on me, then my pants and socks. She refreshed the ice-filled towel, had me hold it on my chest and stomach, and put a blanket over me. Then she guided me to my recliner in the center of the room and turned on the TV for me, still saying nothing. I asked her where she was when I was calling to her from the shower. No response.

I repeated the question, this time in a more demanding tone, "Where the hell were you when I needed you, goddammit?"

She walked away from me, ignoring my demands for answers. I watched her go into the kitchen, reach into the pantry, pull out cleaning liquid and rags, and take them into the bathroom to clean up my mess. I was so livid I could scream. But I knew screaming wouldn't work. I'd start coughing uncontrollably before I could make any impact. I didn't know what to do to make her pay for her disrespect towards me. I got up and walked slowly towards the bathroom, getting angrier with each step. When I arrived outside the open door, I set my walker aside, pulled down my pants and Depends in one motion, crouched down holding the door-jam for support, and took a shit on the hallway carpet a few feet from where Rosa was on all fours cleaning my piss off the bathroom floor. She turned around just in time to see and too late to stop me. She just stared and cried.

I instantly felt regret for having done that. I pulled up my pants, grabbed my walker and slowly made my way back to my chair. I sat down, making a mess in my Depends with what had apparently not been deposited on the hallway floor. My chest was still burning from the hot water. I would sneak a peek every couple of minutes to see Rosa cleaning – first the bathroom, then the hallway carpet. When she finished and had put away the cleaning supplies and thrown away all of the dirty rags, I looked up, sporting an apologetic, guilty and tear-filled look especially for her. When I saw her expressionless glare, I immediately grabbed my chest in pain, doubling over, coughing occasionally for effect.

I started crying, "Rosa, help me… Help me." "I'm so sorry I hurt you." Thankfully, Rosa came running over to me right away. "What's wrong,

Benny? Are you okay? Do you have chest pains? Is it the shower burns?"

I shook my head no at the last question. My chest really did hurt, but I didn't think it was a heart attack. I had Rosa's attention. And the more I squeezed my chest and buckled over in pain, the more the pain became real. Rosa called 911; the paramedics arrived in mere moments. I was poked and prodded, strapped with an oxygen mask, and loaded onto an ambulance. What an awful morning. All I wanted was for Rosa to come get me out of the shower and take care of me. Now look what she's done.

The EMT's and hospital staff rushed me to Loma Linda Hospital and into an ICU cubical. They took off my clothes and put me in one of those humiliating hospital gowns. The nurse must have seen my burns because in only a few minutes, after EKG, IV and vital sign monitors had all been hooked up, the hospital social worker showed up. I was so tired. My chest hurt. My ear still hurt. I was so mad at Rosa for doing this to me. She was doing the same thing to me that Mother, and Gail, and Joan had done to me. They turned on me. They drew me in and made me believe I was their special boy. Then they either abandoned me like Mother, or they drove me away like Gail, or they took all the life out of me and then died like Joan. The social worker asked me how I got the burns on my chest. I told her Rosa turned on the hot water. She asked why my ear was red and swollen. I told her Rosa hit me. Then she asked about our relationship in general. I said she is my caregiver, and she is mean to me. Apparently I answered everything okay, since she left me alone after that, and I was able to drift off to sleep, if only for a while.

When I woke up, I was calling for Rosa. But the doctor said Rosa was not allowed in to see me. I didn't understand why. I need

Rosa, and she needs me. We love each other. The doctor said they were going to keep me overnight to monitor my heart. When I got to my private room, the social worker was there waiting for me. She was on my hospital room phone talking to someone, and from all appearances, the person on the other end was doing most of the talking.

She kept repeating, "Okay, I understand." Then, she handed me the phone, saying it was my son, Alan. I don't remember Alan being this angry with me since he was a kid.

"Dad, when you get off the phone, you will tell the social worker the truth about you and Rosa. Tell her that it is YOU doing the manipulating, and not HER. Tell her Rosa has NOT abused you. That she is only defending herself because YOU are an abusive and nasty S.O.B. If you continue these lies, you will be put in a nursing home where they will drug and restrain you, rather than dealing with your abusive and all around bad behavior. Is that what you want? Do you understand me, Dad?"

I understood perfectly. Alan had apparently already explained all of this to the social worker. She was just waiting for me to confirm it. I didn't want to go into a nursing home. And even though my life with Rosa was not the life I dreamed of, at least I was in control most of the time. I need someone to love me, and Rosa does. So I told the social worker that I was groggy and didn't answer her questions correctly. I told her Rosa is good to me, that I want her there with me, and I want to go home with her. She told me that the police had been notified that there was a possible case of elder abuse, and they might have to investigate. In the meantime, she was going to recommend that I be discharged to a rehabilitation facility where they could watch my heart and my other wounds, and make sure it would be safe for me to go home with Rosa. I looked at her and cried. She sat on the bed and asked me what was wrong. I told her I didn't need rehab. I told her I was fine, and that I needed Rosa to take care of me.

After two days in the hospital, Alan showed up so that I could be released to a family member. The social worker had relied on Alan in deciding I could go back and live with Rosa and avoid the stint in rehab. Rosa had been allowed to visit me in my hospital room and had even brought me some of her wonderful chili last night, just to show me how much she loves me and wants me to come home to her. She apologized to me over and over again, telling me it was all her fault.

In the car on the way home, Rosa told me that she had been out front of the apartment talking to Laura on the phone and didn't hear me calling from the shower. What? You're admitting to me that you chose Laura over taking care of me? And what about my heart? You could have killed me. I managed to hide my angst, and maintain my half-smile through my tightly clenched teeth. After all, she was apologizing to me. I would get even for her picking Laura over me, eventually. Two days after being discharged, there was a knock at our front door. Rosa answered, and soon two Riverside Police

Officers and Rosa were standing in the living room where I was sitting. One of the officers said they were following up on a complaint of elder abuse. Rosa and I looked at each other, not sure who might have called the police. Maybe this was a follow up from the initial conversation I had with the social worker in the hospital. We weren't sure. The officers separated
us, each of them taking one of us to a separate room to ask us questions.

When the officer asked me how I got the burns on my chest and stomach, all I could muster was, "Rosa did it."

All his other questions required only yes or no answers, thank God. Fifteen minutes had passed since Rosa had left the room with the second officer. One of the officers handed me the telephone. It was Alan. Apparently Rosa had told the officer who was interviewing her that he was my son and had medical power of attorney for all related decisions. I grabbed the phone, and again, as before in the hospital, Alan was fuming with anger.

"Dad, what the hell did you tell the police officer? Did you tell him that Rosa is abusing you? You know damn well that you are the abuser. You are the manipulator. Didn't you hear what I told you in the hospital? If you insist on telling these lies, Marty and I will be putting you in a nursing home. Is that what you want? Well, is it? If it isn't, then tell the goddamn truth. And just so you know, next time I get one of these calls, you ARE going to a nursing home, period!"

When I gave the phone back to the officer, I told him I was sorry. I told him my memory doesn't work so well anymore, that Rosa is the only one who cares and takes care of me. I told him I turned the shower water the wrong direction, accidentally turning the water on the hottest setting. After talking on the phone to the same social worker who had talked to us in the hospital, the officers left the apartment. As they departed, they warned that the next time they were called here, one of us would be removed from the home, and the other would likely be arrested for assault and possibly face elder abuse charges.

I was glad this was over. Rosa had been so nice to me since getting home from the hospital two days prior. But even though things have really been good, as I relaxed alone in my recliner, I smiled to myself, realizing that I now have the upper hand with Rosa. After all, she's been suspected of elder abuse, and I am the poor, dependent old man with dementia.

Something was definitely wrong with me. I had been depressed for at least fifteen years before Joan died. It's been a year since she's been gone. I found myself blocks from my house walking around in my underwear. One of my neighbors was standing there, talking to me like I was a small lost child, holding my arm and leading me home. I felt humiliated, but I also needed the help, at least in that moment.

I sat in my living room after checking the mail, trying to organize all of the bills I have to pay. It's a good thing Joan arranged for my social security and pension to be direct deposited, because I'd never be able to manage making deposits, paying bills and keeping accurate balances. Marty and Alan visit every couple of months, and I use those opportunities to tell them how overwhelmed I am with my daily tasks. They don't know what to say, or how to help. So they take me to lunch, bring me home, we stare at each other for fifteen minutes and then they leave. Checked that box, again.

I was living alone in my house. I could hardly move from one room to the next, barely squeezing by on a path I had created through all of the newspapers, medication, books, bank statements, clothes, mail and other junk that's been accumulating over time. In the couple of years before her death, Joan was unable to do any housework. So we hired a cleaning lady and told her to just clean where she could reach. That meant most of the kitchen, the two bathrooms – only one of which we used – the narrow pathways in the living room, and our bedroom got cleaned. Our bedroom was also in shambles. Joan and I each had a portable TV tray on our bedside which contained collectively over a hundred bottles of prescription medicine. This was in addition to the medicine on each of our nightstands. Some of it was current, most of it expired. Joan kept track of all of it all, or so I thought. But now, it's anyone's guess what I'm taking, and whether it's expired, or whether it's even mine. The cleaning lady still comes once every two weeks. She spends a couple of hours cleaning, though I can't even tell she's done anything when she leaves.

I was driving to the market every day to pick up prepared food for my meals. I never had any desire to cook, or to prepare the simplest of meals or snacks. I drove to the bank to write a check for cash every three or four days, as I'm afraid of not having enough. I have no idea what my bank balances are, or how much money I've saved over my lifetime. I don't care either. I just wanted some hot soup from Safeway. I hadn't been to the doctor in months, because I hate being put on hold when I call, and then having to wait when I go in for an appointment. I would call only to get refills of my prescriptions, and predictably, they would nag at me to come in for a physical exam. Mostly, I sat in my house, going through the mounds of mail, mostly bills, not knowing what to deal with next. Joan did everything for me, even as sick and crippled as she was at the end. I never realized how many things there were to deal with. Groceries, cooking, bills, taxes, doctors, laundry... the list goes on. I hate her for leaving me. But I couldn't stand the thought of taking care of her for another day.

Jimmy called me to tell me he and Donald were going to throw Mother a 100th birthday party in Florida. I figured he was going to plead with me to attend, telling me it may be the last time Mother has all three of her boys together with her. Instead, he asked if I would pay one-third of the costs for the party. He thought my share would be between two and three thousand dollars. What the fuck? You want me to pay for the privilege of being insulted by Mother, and having to spend an entire weekend with people I can't stand? Will I have to buy a plane ticket? Will Mother reimburse me for the trip? How will I get from the airport to the hotel? Do I have to rent a car? I can't deal with all this, and I have no intention of paying Jimmy and Donald a nickel for anything, let alone a celebration for Mother, who makes me feel like a complete failure. Of course I shared none of that with him. I told him I couldn't come, then I hung up on him. I was sure I'd be the talk of the family, now that I've refused to take part in Mother's big birthday, but I could not have cared less.

Apparently Jimmy called Alan, and after Alan's relentless coaxing, I reluctantly agreed to go to Florida. Isn't September the hottest time of the year there? Just terrific. Alan is buying my ticket, reserving me a room at the hotel where everyone is staying, and driving me to and from the airport. Well at least I don't have to stress about making all these arrangements, and then navigating back and forth once I'm there. I guess I'll go, but I'm still not paying Jimmy or Donald for anything, although Alan wants me to pay him back for the airplane tickets and hotel room. After all I've done for him.

Maybe Mother will really be thrilled to see me? I sat back on my chair in my tiny living room, the TV blaring on the golf channel, closed my eyes and imagined what it would be like to see Mother again. I pictured her face when she first notices me. She smiles; even at 100 years old, her smile is so beautiful. She is dressed so nice, as usual. Her expression tells a story of a happy woman who is proud of her oldest son, her special boy. She holds my face with both hands and tells me how wonderful it is to see me. She says that she has missed me so much, and is so sorry about Joan. She offers me money, anything I need. She wants to take care of me. Maybe this trip will be different than the others have been. Even though I had a few weeks before we would leave, I wanted to make sure my clothes were clean, and I picked the ones that didn't make me look too fat. I wanted Mother to be pleased. I was going to show Jimmy. He might have all the money, but Mother will want to sit with me. She will have missed me the most. I needed to go get my hair cut. I decided to go buy myself a couple of new shirts.

As the day approached, my anticipation turned to anxiety. Even though it was getting harder and harder to drive by myself, I managed to make the two-hour drive from Beaumont to Alan's house in L.A. so we could go to the airport together. The trip to Florida was uneventful, but only because I managed to ignore all of the morons at the airport, on the plane, renting the car, and at the hotel. How do these people get and keep their jobs? They are so slow, and they make me wait. Whatever they are paid, it is too much. I hate waiting. I just want to hit people who make me wait. Or at the very least, I want to get them fired. But on this trip, I just let Alan deal with everything and everyone. I kept calming myself by thinking about Mother, and occasionally daydreaming about playing the violin, or dancing with Gail, or one that really takes me away – beating my dad at a footrace out front of our house in Shaker Heights. Finally, we arrived at the hotel. Embassy Suites again, and just about time for the free evening cocktails. There is a God.

I'd been sitting around one of the cheap round party tables for at least twenty minutes, awaiting the Queen's arrival. The party was being held at Mother's assisted living home. Occasionally, one of Jimmy's or Donald's adult kids came up to talk to me; but I just gave them the, "Uh huh, yeah, uh huh" response, as if I'm only partially there. They soon found an excuse to leave me alone.

Finally, Marty entered the room, pushing Mother in a wheelchair. Her room was quite a distance from the entertainment hall; and although Mother is quite capable of walking, she wanted to be wheeled there so she could save her energy. So in she rolled, and the family ran to her side like hungry flies on fresh shit. Marty helped her from her wheelchair to one of the dining chairs, and there she sat, talking to one person at a time, making sure that each person knew how much she appreciated their being here for her birthday.

I got sick to my stomach, watching my brothers, their kids, my own kids, all their wives, and all of the children clamoring for Mother's attention. I could see her face through the crowd. She looked nice, but wore a worried expression. I knew why. She couldn't find me in all of the chaos. I knew she must be frantic wondering where I was, or if her oldest son even made the trip for her birthday. I figured she'd suffered long enough. I pushed my chair out from under the table, got up and slowly started cutting my way through the crowd towards Mother. I stepped close to her, but I was still behind her, and not able to push my way any further, since the family were everywhere – kneeling on the floor, squatting, leaned over in her face, and standing right in my way. I reached my hand in between a niece and nephew of mine and grabbed the back of Mother's chair.

I knew she wanted to see me. Her head was moving left to right. I was sure she was looking for me. I knew that, if she were younger and able, she'd pop up, quickly slide between and through everyone to find me. Once she'd found me, I'd hear her yell, "Benny, Benny!" And she'd come to me, stop in front of me, put her arms around me and cry. She would tell me she's missed me, and that she's so glad I came.

I got a grip on the back of her chair and, with all my strength, started pulling it towards me, with her still sitting in it. Apparently she was not too secure in the chair, because I heard Alan yelling for me to stop. She was slipping off of it. But I didn't stop. I kept pulling her. I knew she wanted to see me. But as I was pulling her, it occurred to me she didn't even care what was happening. She was so engrossed in a conversation with her grandchildren and great grandchildren, she had no idea I was there trying to get to her. But I kept dragging her chair towards me. Finally, Marty grabbed the chair from the other side to stop its movement.

In that same instant, Alan yelled, this time louder and with authority, "Dad, stop!" Everyone in the room heard his command.

I let go of the chair. I backed away from the crowd, and from Mother. I kept looking at her, slowly realizing she wasn't looking for me after all. I was invisible to her. Eventually she saw me sitting around the head table, where she, Jimmy, Donald and their wives were supposed to sit for the celebration and the dinner. She walked over and sat down next to me.

I said only, "Hello, Mother."

She looked old. She took more time than I expected to look me over, to focus on my features. The first thing out of her mouth was, "Benny, have you gained more weight?"

I didn't answer. I froze. I wouldn't hit Mother, but I sure wanted to. I knew if I reacted inappropriately, I would be swiftly 'controlled' and escorted out. And that would be the best case. I didn't want that. So I sat there, watched Mother engage in more loving conversations with others in the family, and started eyeing the dinner buffet, which was now being set up in the room.

Jimmy got up, clinked his glass and started to talk. Then it was Donald's turn. They had both asked me when I first arrived if I wanted to say a few words, and I'd said no. So they didn't push it. I'm sure they remembered Dad's 95th and didn't want me to embarrass the family. They should all be so lucky. Marty then went to the piano and was playing some songs while a picture slideshow was being presented to Mother. I got up, walked unnoticed away from the group and towards the buffet, which contained roast beef and side dishes that were still covered as the wait staff completed their preparations. I found the stack of plates and walked over to the delicious looking meat. I grabbed what looked like the carving knife and started cutting away. I couldn't get good leverage so I put my left hand on the meat to hold it still, while my right hand carved. Finally, success. I had a thick, medium-rare piece of meat on my plate. I found a serving spoon and after removing a couple of lids and foil covers, helped myself to au-gratin potatoes and green beans. That was enough for now. I weaved my way around everyone, returning to my seat next to Mother, and I started eating. I was getting some disapproving stares, but no one said anything, at least until Mother sat down.

She looked at me with astonishment. "Benny, I raised you better than this.

Dinner isn't even ready yet. This is very rude, Benjamin."

She was not finished lecturing me, but when she took a better look at my face, she saw my rage. I was shaking. My arms tensed up and my fists were clenched. I turned and brought my face within four or five inches of her face and shot her an angry, evil smile with my mouth open and half-full. Anyone else would have been scared, mortified, horrified – pick one. Not Mother. She just shook her head in disgust, and turned her body away from me.

Just then, the chef walked up to our table and so that everyone close by could hear, told me that because I had touched the roast with my hand, I had compromised the entire meal and they would have to make everyone else wait for another hour until they could replace everything I had touched. And of course, those things I didn't touch would be ruined after sitting for an hour, so essentially he said he was going to have to rebuild dinner completely. Mother ignored me. Jimmy and Donald were livid. They were each in one of my ears telling me they weren't going to let me ruin Mother's special day.

When Jimmy said he expected me to pay for any damages, I turned to him with half a mouthful of food and barked, "Go fuck yourself!"

Food sprayed on his face. He grabbed an unused cloth napkin from our table, and walked away wiping his face.

The party was on Saturday, and after the long weekend and trip home, I finally returned on Tuesday to the house I'd shared with Joan for over twenty years. I parked my car, walked inside, navigated my way through the piles of useless crap and plopped down on my comfortable chair. I turned on the TV and cranked up the volume to drown out my thoughts. Before I got lost in an NCIS rerun, I thought to myself that this was the last time I would ever see Mother. I was also sure I would never be her special boy again. I tried to focus on the TV, but I couldn't concentrate. I just stared into the light, numb to anything and everything around me.

Rosa took me to dinner at her favorite local Mexican Restaurant, called 'Viejo Loco.' We go to this place a lot. She has been going there for years and knows everyone there. As is customary when we first walk in, the managers, hosts, waiters and cooks all say hello to us, some even coming over to give Rosa a hug. They all address us by name and lead us to what has become our table – closest to the front door with convenient access to the bathrooms. I'm not allowed to complain about the service or the food in this restaurant. I did it once, and after Rosa embarrassed me by shushing me in public, we got in a big fight and she didn't speak to me for two days. I come here because it makes Rosa happy, and she tells me this is my reward for being good. Whoop-tee-fucking-do. I get to sit here and watch all the cooks hit on Rosa, and I have to smile and enjoy the barely- mediocre food and annoying, chatty employees. Rosa appeases me by letting me drink expensive scotch, but she usually limits me to two drinks. Fine with me. It numbs me just enough. I chase it when her head is turned with sips of her Corona beer. Besides, I have learned to pick my battles.

Since getting home from the hospital, I've felt pretty good. I have to apply medicated salve to my chest and stomach areas twice a day so the burns continue to heal. They are feeling better, though I have a few blisters and some peeling skin that still bother me. I haven't had any more chest pains, though I never really did. I wish I didn't have to go through all that hospital trauma, but as it turns out, it did solve the problems of the moment. I got my burns taken care of, and even better, I created a bit of leverage for myself by telling that social worker I'd been abused. I almost got Rosa in a lot of trouble for elder abuse, but Alan came to the rescue. He told the hospital staff, and later the police, that my dementia was making me say and even think things that weren't true. If I hadn't recanted everything I'd said, she'd be in serious trouble. Sure, I had to endure the tongue- lashing from Alan, but I think it was worth it. Not only have I scared her into being nicer to me, but I've scored myself even more sympathy than I was getting before. Rosa is worried. I can tell by the change in her demeanor.

I don't know why I have to be so conniving. I feel like I've always had to be this way. From pretending I loved Diane back when I was in the tenth grade, to bullshitting Margi into daily sex in the backseat of my car, to lying to Gail about working late all those nights, to inventing golf outings so Joan wouldn't suspect I was really having another rendezvous with a lonely widow. They all started out loving me the way I deserved, but soon I felt out-prioritized by friends and family trying to take my place as the most important person in their lives. I couldn't let any of them win. Mother told me time and again what a special boy I was, and that women would adore me like she did. She said I was so good looking, and talented, and smart, they wouldn't be able to resist. It might have been true at first, but the excitement and total dedication never lasted. Goddammit, it never lasted. I hate Mother for lying to me, or at the very least, for not telling me all of the truth: That women are not to be trusted. They will pretend to love me, yet will eventually hurt me. They will move on to someone or something else that makes them happier; they will make me the fool.

Now I have Rosa. I know I'm an ugly old man. I know I'm demanding, and depressed, and need help doing just about everything. Rosa has told me hundreds of times that she loves me. She's done things to me sexually that no one ever has. She makes me feel sixteen years old again. Why would a young, attractive woman like her want to have sex and spend all of her waking hours with an old, miserable man like me if she wasn't in love? I know I'm paying her a salary to be my caregiver, and that's how our relationship started. But now, we are lovers. She makes me feel special. She tells me I am the smartest, best looking man she has ever known. She puts up with my depression, and my anger, and also things she doesn't know, like the fact that I've not been completely honest about my dementia, and my ability to say what I'm thinking. I sometimes wonder why Rosa stays with me, and even though she says it all the time, I question how she could love me.

Marty and Alan have told me that they aren't sure whether she may have selfish or sinister motives. They just can't believe that a vibrant woman could want to be with me. Caregiving is one thing, but loving me? Having sex with me? Would Rosa do all that to gain access to my money? Would she do this to gain legal residency? Even if any of that were true, do I really care? As long as she continues to take care of me, and show me that she loves me, then I can live with that. Oh, and she can never leave me.

I didn't say much during dinner, since Rosa was busy chatting with everyone. Even the manager came over and sat with us for a while. I ignored them all and kept eating and drinking. But the fact that I didn't complain about anything, including Rosa's socializing, should have made her very happy about our evening out. I guess we had gotten to the point where a non-confrontational day was the measure of success and even happiness. That wasn't exactly a proud thought. We are supposed to be in love, and that's hardly a good measure of a healthy relationship. But for me, it's a low bar that's much easier to get over than trying to be the perfect lover. Dinner was over, and after suffering through all of the hugs and tedious goodbyes from the restaurant staff, we slowly made our way out to Rosa's car.

When we got home, I got out of the car and followed Rosa into the house, struggling to keep up. She was looking and smelling especially sexy tonight. She was getting herself a glass of water in the kitchen, when I came up behind her, put my arms around her waist, and started kissing her neck. For a second, I thought she was accepting my advances and was about to turn around and start kissing me. But as she completed her turn, her hands came up from her side and she held them out in front of her, as if to establish a distance between us. Her voice was pleasant, but her words weren't. She told me she didn't want to make love to me tonight. She didn't give me a reason. She took her water and walked out of the kitchen and down the short hallway into the bathroom, shutting the door behind her.

I was both shocked and humiliated. Rosa never refuses sex with me. Even if we have been fighting, she will touch me if I want her to. She will always go through the motions, though sometimes I can tell she's not really in the mood. So what happened? Did one of the guys at the restaurant hit on her, and now she can only think of him? I started getting so angry I could hardly function. I made my way slowly to my recliner, stopping on the way to pick up one of my old photo albums from the built-in bookshelf on the living room wall. I thought maybe that would distract me from these feelings of anger and despair. I sat down, put the album on my lap and replayed her denial in my head over and over. I was pissed off, but I was also scared. I can't lose Rosa.

I opened the photo album, hoping that going through some old memories might take my mind off my current woes. Alan had gathered a bunch of pictures when he and Marty cleaned out my house, and he had put together one good- sized album for me to keep. For the first time since moving out of my house, I went through the pictures. They were even put in chronological order for me. There I was as a small child. It looked like a Passover Seder at our house on Grove Street. I recognized Mother, Dad and my brothers, but didn't recognize some of the others. A few pages later, I was sitting at the piano with Mother. I could probably identify the date within a few weeks, since I didn't play the piano very long. Then, I was at my Bar Mitzvah, with Mother on my right and Dad on my left. There were several pictures of me with my violin – some with the Shaker Heights High School orchestra, and even a couple with the Cleveland Jr.

Symphony. I recognized the Performing Arts Theater. What a beautiful place, and such a surreal experience I had playing with them on that one special night. There were so many pictures; looking at all of them really helped me get my mind off of Rosa, and what could possibly be wrong with her tonight.

Around the middle of the photo album, I came to a picture of myself with Gail, Marty, Alan and Andy. Andy looked to be about six years old. We had posed in our living room for a professional photographer. I remember vaguely having the picture done for Dad's 60th birthday. I focused on everyone's expression. The kids' smiles looked a little forced, and Gail had her trademark beautiful and sincere smile. But my attention was drawn to my own face in the picture. I really looked happy. I noticed Gail's and my hands were touching. It reminded me of what I threw away so long ago. I started thinking about the drive I had made to our house in Seal Beach on what was probably the worst day of my life – the one where I told Gail and the boys that I wanted a divorce. I remembered crying as I drove, practicing what I was going to say, and getting angrier and angrier with Gail for driving me into the arms of other women. I shut the album hard, creating a thud as the cover slammed closed. I was back to the present, both angry and worried; but the anger was taking over. I needed to teach Rosa a lesson.

I put the album on the floor, pushed myself up from my chair, held on to my walker and made my way to the bedroom. When I walked in, Rosa was already in bed, propped up on her side, reading a book. I stood there for a few moments waiting for her to look up at me, but no acknowledgment. I finally asked her what was wrong.

She put her book face down, looked up at me and only said, "Nothing is wrong."

That was it. She picked up her book and resumed her reading. I knew she was punishing me, though I didn't know what for. I needed her help getting out of my clothes and ready for bed, but I decided to start attempting to do these things alone and see how long she would let me struggle before she would offer assistance. I brushed my teeth, walked back into the bedroom, sat on my side of the bed and started struggling to take off my shoes. I heard Rosa get up, and then saw her walking over to my side of the bed. She finished taking off my shoes and then helped me get out of my pants. She quickly left my side of the bed to return to hers, and then went back to her reading. She was obviously still avoiding me for no apparent reason.

I got in bed, getting angrier and angrier at Rosa's cold shoulder. I lay there seething for most of the night, while she slept on her side, facing the opposite direction. Around 3:00 am, I had to pee. I was tapping Rosa to try to get her to help me to the bathroom, but she ignored me. I wanted to swing my arm as hard as I could and hit her in the head. Don't treat me like this. What is your problem, Bitch? But instead of hitting her, or yelling something nasty, I stood up, pulled down my underwear and started peeing on the floor, right there on the side of the bed. Rosa turned over, and saw what I was doing. She looked up at my face. I'm sure I looked angry, but I also made sure to flash her an evil smile. I'll teach her to ignore me.

I finished peeing, grabbed the extra blanket from the foot of our bed, and walked out into the living room. I sat in my chair, covered my legs, grabbed the TV remote and turned on some mindless sitcom rerun. I still had some Cutty Sark in my glass from the night before, so I chugged what was left. I could hear Rosa moving around in the bedroom, no doubt cleaning up my mess. I wanted her to come out here and apologize to me. She owed me that much.

She came out of the bedroom about twenty minutes later, holding several wet towels away from her body. She dropped them off at the washer, and then walked towards me in the living room. For a brief moment I was afraid. Had I crossed a line? Was she going to attack me? Rosa has shown that she's not afraid to deal with my outbursts, physically if she has to. But she doesn't instigate. Would she do it this time? I braced myself to be hit by some object, but it never came. Instead I felt her walk past me and take a seat on the couch perpendicular to me, but at an angle where we could look directly at one another. Finally, after hours of silent conflict, she talked to me, the whole time sobbing.

"Benny, I don't know what to do anymore. You were rude to all my friends at Viejo Loco. They were looking at me with sympathetic eyes while you ignored them, drank scotch, sneaking sips of my beer and eating like you have no manners. You embarrassed me. You say you love me, but I don't believe you. I think you just like manipulating me. What do you want from me? I need to know."

I was in tears by the time she finished. I really do love her. Maybe she wasn't flirting with the staff. Was I really that rude? I was just trying to behave, or was I?

I looked back at her and said, "I do love you, Rosa. I'm so sorry I upset you.

We're together, forever…"

She walked away with a strange look on her face, a guilty smile, if I was reading her right. I let it go, as it seemed Rosa had accepted my apology, again.

Marty called me to check in. He asked me how I was feeling, how my chest and stomach were healing, and whether I was sleeping okay. I don't usually say much when he or Alan calls, but this morning, I was feeling pretty good, and chattier than usual. Rosa had cooked me a wonderful breakfast, and I had shown her my appreciation by doing the dishes. Boy did that ever go a long way to make her happy. She knows it's hard for me to get around; and even though it took me a while, I did it myself, and even wiped down the sink and stove areas. I'm sure Rosa had never seen the kitchen looking as spotless as it did when I finished with it. And she knew, because I told her, that I had not done all of the meal dishes since I was in college. That made for a wonderful start to an otherwise ordinary day.

Rosa was walking around the house, collecting the trash from the bedroom, bathroom and living room and depositing it into the main kitchen trash can. She pulled and tied the bag, and headed out to the community dumpster to throw it away. She told me that after she threw the trash out, she was going to walk across the street to the 7-11 and pick up some half-and-half for a recipe she was cooking for us for dinner. I was temporarily alone in our apartment, and Marty and I were having a pretty good exchange, so I asked him a question that had been bothering me since he first called me to tell me the news. I asked him if he knew why Andy committed suicide.

I could tell by the way he balked that he knew something he didn't want to share. I told him I had been having terrible dreams, and in all of them I watched Andy shoot himself, and that I howled and cried out because there was nothing I could do to stop him. At first, Marty told me it didn't matter why. He tried to appease my curiosity by telling me Andy had 'demons' that none of us knew about, and it was nobody's fault but his own. But I pressed. I had a moment of complete clarity, and I think I surprised Marty on account of it.

I said, "Marty, please stop with the stalling. Did Andy leave a note? If so, what did it say? I need to know. Please, Marty. If you've ever cared about me, I need to know."

His whole demeanor changed. I know Marty. He didn't want to argue with me. He was never tough enough to deal with me head-on, and he wasn't about to start now. I wasn't in the mood to evaluate Marty's and my relationship. I wanted to know why Andy shot himself, nothing more. I think I had successfully communicated that to Marty. So he told me that yes, Andy had written a note. He then told me he didn't think I wanted to hear what Andy said.

I yelled as much as I was able, "Tell me, goddammit. Tell me the truth, now!" So he read me Andy's short note:

"I'm sorry for the hurt I will have caused my family, my patients and my friends. This is not about any of you. This is about two people. Me, and my father. To Dad: Your physical and emotional abuse, and your insane hatred of me and of everything I have loved, have left me broken. Every day I look in the mirror, I see more of you looking back at me. I am becoming the person I despise the most in this world. I just can't do that to

Marty was finished reading Andy's note. After ten or fifteen seconds of silence, Marty said, "I'm sorry, Dad."

I thanked him for calling in as polite a tone as I had in me. I hung up the phone before he could say anything else. I was in shock. I didn't know what to feel at first. I stared at the TV, and got lost momentarily in another mindless rerun. My thoughts immediately turned to Rosa. Should I tell her all of this? What will she think of me if I do? Is there anything about telling her this that will make my life with her better? I quickly decided it wouldn't, at least not right now.

I was still alone in the apartment, and left with my thoughts after having listened to what Marty just read to me. I was sure he was being truthful. No matter how much Marty might hate me, he would never tell me something like this if it weren't true. My mind was racing. I was flashing back to when Andy was a little boy, remembering how Gail shielded him from me almost every time I tried to be a father to him. The older he got, the more distant he was. He was always hiding behind Gail, even as a teenager. Andy was weak. There were no tears flowing at all. A calm came over me. I wasn't going to hold myself accountable for this. This was Gail's fault. The only thing I'm sad about is that I'll never be able to set him straight. He should know the truth. He should look up to his father.

I had a glass of water in my hand, and I wanted to throw it against the wall. My fury was building at the thought of Andy blaming me for his weaknesses, and never once mentioning his mother. My arms and hands were tense and shaking, and my jaw and teeth ready to break. I almost lost control and let the glass fly across the room, but instead I just tensed and shook even more. Just then, I heard the back door shut, so I knew Rosa was home from emptying the trash and walking to the store. I had to compose myself, but I was still so upset, my grip on my water glass was weakening on account of my shaking. As soon as I broke my grip, the glass fell, water spilled all over my lap and the glass fell to the floor. I could tell by the sounds in the kitchen that Rosa was still in a happy mood from our breakfast, and my voluntarily cleaning the kitchen. I had to conjure up my happy disposition; I didn't want to have to explain any of this to her.

I called to Rosa, reaching deep down for the loving, almost child-like voice I use when I need Rosa's help. She saw I'd spilled my water, and with all the love and sympathy I cherish about her, she quickly cleaned me up and changed my pants. She apologized for leaving me alone to go to the store, but assured me that I would be so happy because she was going to make her special boy a very special dinner.

I hadn't slept since talking to Marty. I asked Rosa for my Cutty Sark to help me sleep, but she said she was afraid of what the combination of the scotch and my Seroquel might do to me. I just wanted to sleep. I didn't want to think about Andy anymore.

I couldn't erase those words from my head, "…the person I despise the most in the world."

What a load of crap. Using me as an excuse to end his troubled life? He was living with Gail when he overdosed as a teenager. Gail and Francis were off gallivanting all over the world when Andy needed structure and guidance. I wonder how they are handling this, now. I hope they blame themselves.

After dinner, I told Rosa I needed more Cutty Sark. I had been drinking since just before lunchtime. She tried to talk me out of it, saying she is afraid that I am drinking too much, and that combining it with my medicine might make me very sick.
I repeated my demand, "I want it, now!"

Rosa knew better than to argue with me when I was upset. She also knew that I wasn't going to take no for an answer. Soon she gave in, but each glass was coming with more ice and less Cutty, so I pounced right away. As she bent over to place my glass on the table beside my recliner, seeing the significantly reduced amount of scotch and glassful of ice, I grabbed her free arm, squeezing as tightly as I could while pulling her to her knees in front of me.

She shouted in pain. "Stop. Benny, you're hurting me. Please let go."

As I let go, I grabbed the glass of mostly ice and threw it towards the TV, missing it by inches and hitting my treasured picture of the lonely violin. Luckily the picture wasn't damaged, but the glass broke against the wall and fell with what little contents there was on the carpeted floor. Rosa pulled herself up from her knees, still crying.

I said to her through my clenched teeth, "Please fill this fucking glass full with Cutty, with two small ice cubes, now!"

She said nothing, but hurriedly complied, not wanting to infuriate me further. She had no idea what was bothering me, and I had no intention of telling her that my son blamed me for taking his life. I had thought a few times in the last few days that telling her might gain me some sympathy, but I hated the thought of Rosa knowing what my son thought of me. I know she has been wondering why Andy didn't talk to me for so long, and why Marty and Alan only talk to me when they absolutely have to. I've avoided that subject for the most part, and I didn't think now was the time to tell her that my sons don't like me, and I don't particularly like them. I could never tell her that I hate the fact that they all bested me. They are all successful, with loving wives and families. If that isn't hard enough, they still have never thanked me for their lives, and all my sacrifices.

Rosa thinks I am a sweet, loving, smart and good-looking man who has been very unlucky in love. She thinks I was a wonderful, caring and doting father, and that Gail poisoned my kids against me.

She thinks Joan abused me for more than half of our forty-two years together, by playing psychological games with me on account of her illness. I have painted a picture of a woman who took me in when Gail forced me away from her. She treated me like Mother used to – showering me with compliments, and then food, and gifts, and unconditional compliance, to a fault. She lured me into a trap; I married Joan almost immediately after my divorce from Gail became final. Then she became too ill to work, and made me responsible for not only supporting us both, but for caring for her as her disabilities worsened. I've wondered for a long time if she knew about her illness even before we married. That would make sense, actually.

I should have known that Joan was using me from the very beginning. She was so nice to me. Too nice. Even when I tried to anger her, she killed me with kindness. So many times I wanted to pick a fight with her. I wanted her to find out I was screwing around behind her back, but she refused to see it. On one of our camping trips after she was first diagnosed with Lupus, I was in our trailer, wanting to get out to play volleyball with one of the cute single ladies who had joined our camping club. Goddammit she had the most perfect legs I'd ever seen. Joan was going through her usual painfully slow cooking methodology; wash the tomato, dry the tomato, wash the radish, dry the radish, wash the green onion… Holy crap. If she wasn't going to go outside with me, then move the hell out of my way so I can go play. The trailer was so small; our tiny pathway was not sufficient to accommodate the both of us. I was trying to get around her, and she wouldn't move. She tried to maneuver out of the way, but in a fit of combined anger and impatience, I pushed her towards the trailer door, and she went tumbling out the door and onto the dirt ground outside. It was her own fault. I helped her up, and I went to play volleyball while she limped back aboard the trailer to finish her arduous work. As usual, dinner was late and delivered to me in increments.

As much as I hated Joan for all of her deliberate, boring and tedious behaviors, she did everything for me, until she went into the hospital and died on me. She did all the housework and cooking, the finances, our taxes, managing both of our medications, and dealing with both of our doctors – absolutely everything. I would get so mad when my computer wouldn't work right, or when the toilet wouldn't flush properly, I would curse and throw objects around the house. I wanted things done, now. Nothing was done quickly with Joan. Come to think of it, why couldn't she anticipate what I wanted? Shit, we'd been together for so long, she should have known and just stepped up and solved the problem. What is so hard about calling the goddamn Geek Squad? Why must I walk around the grocery store, dodging all the other old bitches while they ponder what type of lettuce they want this week? Why do I have to answer questions about my social security year-end tax form? Good God, figure it out. I support you, you take care of me. Simple concept, right? Yet she failed to maintain her end of the bargain. I needed her to love me, to take care of me, to treat me special, and to make my life exciting.

I couldn't talk to Mother about it, because all I ever got in return was an "I told you so." Mother had told me since the very beginning that Joan wasn't right for me. Plain, and from the wrong 'stock'. I had heard it all. As much as I hate to admit it, Mother was right. Joan wasn't good enough for me. I could, and have done so much better. It is her fault I had to sell our house and get rid of a lifetime of memories. It is her fault I am reduced to this pathetic, dependent old man.

Rosa was back in the kitchen, and I was sipping my full glass of Cutty. It was 7:00 p.m., and a rerun of The Big Bang Theory was starting. I was hoping the combination of the scotch and TV would take my mind off of Andy and Joan, and maybe I'd be able to get some sleep. After drinking half of the glass, I lost track of the TV show. The sounds all were replaced with a blur of unidentifiable monotone noises. My eyes were wide open, yet I was in some sort of a trance. My mind was fixed on another memory.

I'm back at Loma Linda Hospital. The surgery to clean Joan's open wounds was successfully completed three days prior, but she still won't move. She's in too much pain and is too weak. Her attending physician summons me out of her room. He tells me that they will have to discharge Joan. There is nothing more they can do for her. She needs to go to a rehab facility, or receive in-home care. The doctor explains that his staff did some checking, and, unfortunately, my insurance won't cover such treatment. He is sorry. He's sorry? I'm so pissed I can hardly see straight. I want to slam every object within reach in this fucking place.

Back in my living room, seated in my recliner watching Sheldon Cooper object to another date night with Amy Farrah-Fowler,

I became aware that my eyes were extremely wide open, and my scotch had spilled all over my lap. I was suddenly panic-stricken as a sickening realization came over me and I can no longer feel anything. I struggled to focus my thoughts on that day at Loma Linda Hospital. What happened after my conversation with the doctor?

Back in Joan's room, I stare at her pathetic form in the bed. Will she ever be able to take care of me again? How much is all this rehab going to cost me? I can't live like this. I grab a pillow from the small closet and look to make sure no one is around. I push the pillow hard into her face. She struggles, but she has so little strength, it lasts only for a couple of seconds. It was easy. The moment her body goes limp, I return the pillow to the closet and walk mechanically from her room, across the hall to the open elevator. As the doors close, I hear an alarm sound from the monitors in her room. I make my way out of the hospital and into the parking lot. I find my car, open the door, sit down and close the door. I feel so tired, I need to go home and rest.

As I start the car, I notice the dashboard clock reads 2:00. How did it get so late? My face and chest are drenched with sweat. I must have been sitting here in the hot sun for at least an hour. I can't remember anything after returning to Joan's room. I am mad as hell that I will have to pay to take care of her, and convinced that is was her way of getting out of taking care of me. As I drive home, I try to make sense of things, to weigh my options for Joan's care. Entering the kitchen from the garage, I see the message light blinking on the answer machine. I listen to a message from Joan's doctor, and I immediately call him back. He tells me he is sorry to inform me that Joan has passed away.

I regained my senses and called to Rosa in the kitchen. I told her I had spilled my drink, and apologized profusely. I told her I was done drinking scotch for the night. That made her happy.

It's 10:00 a.m. I didn't sleep much last night, again. I've been sitting in my recliner since 4:00 this morning. Rosa got up with me half an hour before that to help me into the bathroom. But once I was in there she shut the door and returned to bed, leaving me there alone. I needed her to help me in the bathroom. And I didn't want to go back to bed. I wanted to get up and have something to eat; and I expected Rosa to help me to my chair, and fix me a snack. I called to her three times from the bathroom, but she ignored me. I shuffled out of the bathroom to see if she was even paying attention to me, and I saw that she had a second pillow over her head to block out my calls for help. She was ignoring me on purpose. I wanted to scream, but I knew she either wouldn't hear me, or would ignore me. So I went back into the bathroom, shut the door behind me, pulled down my underwear and left her a message in the middle of the bathroom floor that she would surely understand. You will answer me goddammit! You will help me when I need it. You will do exactly what I want, exactly when I want it.

When I was finished, I walked out of the bathroom, through the bedroom, out into the small hallway and into the kitchen. Rosa had left my morning Seroquel pill out for me on the countertop. I promptly threw it down the garbage disposal and turned on the water to get rid of it from view. No more going through life in a fucking cloud. I'm sure Rosa pleaded with the doctor to give me something that would turn me into a zombie. I'm sick of being that half-dead old man that Rosa just leads around like a wounded dog. Maybe that's what she wanted all along, a sick dog that she could mother back to health. I want to be alive. I want to have more sex, and I want Rosa to be exciting. I wouldn't know it if she was excited for me nowadays, taking that mind-altering crap twice a day. I rummaged around in the refrigerator and instead of taking that pill with a glass of water and a dry English muffin, I grabbed a tray of leftover Taquitos from the night before and ate them all, probably about ten of them. And I ate them cold. I didn't want to have to figure out how to operate the microwave, and I wasn't about to wake Rosa to come help me. I wanted her to find the pile of shit I left for her in the bathroom. I wanted her to know that when I ask for her, or need help from her, she needs to be there for me right then. I chased the Taquitos with a couple swigs of Orange Juice. I would have preferred some Cutty Sark, but I didn't want to push my luck. Rosa would surely smell it on me, and I would once again be scolded like a child.

I had moved to my chair in the middle of the living room, and was watching the early morning news broadcast. I had the volume turned up pretty loud, in part so it would wake Rosa from her sleep. She should be up and out of bed tending to me. I'll be damned if I let her think she can get into the habit of sleeping in when I'm up and in need of her help. After three hours of sitting in the living room alone and watching TV, I finally heard rustling from the bedroom. It was about 7:30. I could tell she was getting herself out of bed, and from the sounds of a hanger dangling back and forth in the bedroom closet, I knew she had removed her robe. Only seconds later, I heard her loud moan.

That was followed by a distinct yell, "Benny! Good God, what did you do?" Clearly, she had stepped into the bathroom and found my 'message'. I hoped for her sake she had turned the bathroom light on first, otherwise, she would have stepped right in it. Or maybe I hoped she would step right in it. There was about twenty seconds of silence, and then sounds of water running, and things being tossed around the bathroom. She was making sure I heard her, not just the clamoring for cleaning supplies to clean up the mess, but loud slamming and even cursing in Spanish. Hopefully she learned her lesson. When I need you, you need to come to me, anytime, all the time, and without delay.

After about fifteen minutes, she emerged from the bathroom, carrying soiled towels. She was huffing and puffing, and carrying on a conversation with herself in Spanish. I didn't understand a word she was saying, so I didn't react. I decided to wait until she was finished with her mini-tirade before I said anything. While I sat there, I thought about Joan. I remembered that she never once raised her voice to me. When I got upset about something, she left me alone until things were calm. She would bring me something special, like a fresh drink and a plate of deli lunch meats and apple slices. As annoyingly slow as she was, and as needy as she became, she would always take care of things for me without argument. She even anticipated things that she knew I would need. She agreed with me when it came to politics, and on every subject I can think of. She even agreed with me on how ungrateful my kids were. She always told me what a wonderful husband and father I was. And she would never say anything derogatory to me or about me – not to anyone, and not for any reason.

Joan did almost everything a good wife should do. Everything except excite me in the sack. That was the biggest exercise in futility of my entire life. Women in my life have always been anxious to please me in any way they could. Not with Joan. At least not after we got married. She not only couldn't or wouldn't please me on account of her Lupus, but even when she was healthy, she just wasn't exciting to me, period. I can't even count the number of times I begged her to be more 'inventive' in order to please me. When she would start trying to do something new, always after having to give her explicit direction, I would just throw her off of me and walk away. It was like giving a robot step-by-step dance instructions. No rhythm. No feeling. And definitely no desire. At least Rosa loves sex. I believe her when she tells me that she and Frank had a long and loveless marriage, if for no other reason than she can't wait to hop into bed and demonstrate her thirty years of frustration. But one thing Rosa doesn't have that Joan did is the desire to do absolutely anything I ask, whenever I ask for it. Rosa is starting to get an attitude. She is being defiant. When she acts like this, all I can see is Mother's face telling me again how I threw it all away for a life that wasn't good enough for me. She would remind me that I used to be her special boy – so good-looking, so smart and talented. Used to be? I need to punish her like she's punished me for all these years.

After more than an hour of silence, Rosa walked up to me, stood in front of me, and slapped me hard in the face. I couldn't believe what had just happened. I was in absolute shock. It took a few seconds to grasp the reality of the situation, but when I did, my blood boiled. When I went to raise my arms to fight back, she grabbed both of my wrists and put all her weight on them, holding them against the arms of my recliner. I didn't have enough strength to move her. I was so angry, I was crying. The anger and adrenaline were causing me to cough uncontrollably. Phlegm was coming from my mouth and nose – flying everywhere as I couldn't raise my arms to capture or control it. I tried to throw my head forward to head- butt her, but she quickly let go and backed away so I couldn't hurt her.

She had as nasty a look on her face as I had ever seen, and said "Never again, Benny. Never again."

Her caregiver instinct must have taken over, however, since Rosa walked quickly to the kitchen and got me a glass of water and a cough lozenge. She stood behind me, patting my back to help me clear my lungs and calm me down at the same time. But she kept her distance for fear I would retaliate. I was finally able to catch my breath and relax.

I looked back at Rosa and, through congested lungs and labored breathing I said, "You need to come to me when I need you."

Rosa said nothing. I looked at her and started to cry again. After several minutes of my carrying on, I could tell that she thought I was feeling remorse. But that couldn't have been further from the truth. I wanted to choke the life out of her. I was so angry I couldn't think straight. My muscles had all tensed beyond feeling. I could no longer hear the blaring of the TV, or Rosa – if she was saying anything at all. I had no recourse; I could hardly breathe, and had no power to get up and run after her. Rosa had made a physical stand. The bitch had bested me. I couldn't let that happen.

It took me over an hour of sitting and seething in my chair, but I finally calmed down. I convinced myself that I would get back at Rosa, and that she had not beaten me yet. Rosa had cleaned everything up and had a load of laundry going. I could tell she was starting to prepare lunch; I could hear her preparing the raw chili. She knew I liked to eat early, so I was sure she was feeling bad for having slapped me and was going to make it up to me with a special lunch. I still wouldn't forgive her. I heard her opening the cellophane wrapper and removing the chili, slicing off the stems, cutting and cleaning them, and getting them ready to boil and eventually blend them into a coarse and tasty sauce. I was still a bit full from the cold Taquitos I had eaten several hours earlier, but it was only a little after 10:00. I figured by the time the chili was done, I'd be hungry again.

The Price is Right started at 10:00, so I changed the channel and started watching. Even though the TV volume was very loud, I could hear Rosa talking on the phone, intentionally keeping her voice down so I wouldn't hear the conversation. I pretended not to notice her, but picked up the remote and started slowly reducing the volume so I could pick up on who Rosa was talking to. I was hearing bits and pieces of Rosa's end of the conversation:

"He shit on the... floor... on purpose..." "I slapped... held him down..."

"...want to leave... can't take this... don't know if I... " "...back with your father..."

I didn't hear everything, though I tried my best to eavesdrop. But I heard enough to know she was talking to that bitch of a daughter of hers, and that she was talking about me, and not in a good way. I think Rosa figured out that I had turned the TV down, possibly to listen to her conversation, so she changed it up completely. At that point, she turned what seemed like complaining into an instantly happy tone. She even started exaggerating words and sentences so I'd be sure to hear.

She said, "So Laura, how is the job going? Oh, good. And how is your father doing?"

She was rubbing my nose in it. I am sitting in this prison, barely able to move on my own, or say what I need to say. I began crying again – getting angrier and angrier, as I had been just a short time ago.

With all of the energy I had, I yelled, "Get the fuck off the phone. I need you, now!"

She heard me, of course, as this was all a performance to make sure I knew that she was in control. Still holding the phone to her ear, she walked out of the kitchen, and over to me. I had peed myself. I knew what I was doing. I had no other recourse. If I had any left inside me I would have shit in my pants too.

While looking me directly in the eyes, she told Laura, "I have to go, Benny is acting up, again."

She said goodbye and put the phone down. Her tone changed. She started talking to me like a baby. I couldn't take it anymore. Rosa was going to pay for her defiance. This was going to end right now.

I'm holding Rosa by the hair with my right hand, and hitting all parts of her face and head over and over again with my left. She is screaming for me to stop. She pulls away and falls onto the table next to my chair, knocking it over along with all it once held. She continues her fall to the floor and starts crawling away. I pull myself up, grab my walker, and with power I didn't realize I still have, lift the walker up, reach out and hit her again and again with it. I strike her legs, her torso, and her head and neck. There's blood everywhere. One side of her face looks to be completely torn from her head. Her ear is dangling. She manages to crawl away in the direction of the kitchen. I slowly settle back into my chair, put my walker back beside the chair, and close my eyes, trying to regain my senses and relax.

Rosa's crying and moaning stop after a minute or so. I yell to her to come over and help me change my pants. I want her to bring me some Cutty Sark to calm me. I don't care what time it is. Without warning, she runs up to me from behind and lunges at me with a large carving knife. I see it at the last possible second and somehow am able to shift to my left, sparing my back and head. She tumbles over my right shoulder and stabs me deep in my right thigh, continuing to roll down my legs and back onto the floor. She pulls the knife out, causing me to wince in excruciating pain. She probably wants to use it again and again, but is unable to since she is badly injured and is desperate to crawl away from me as fast as she can. She pulls on the legs of my chair, then the carpet, and then the hallway walls and drags herself into the bedroom. I am kicking her as she pulls herself away from me.

There is a lot of blood on me. The living room is in shambles; a trail of blood follows Rosa into the bedroom. The TV is still blaring, but my senses are numb. My anger quickly turns to satisfaction. Rosa will learn her lesson. It's happened before, and as before, she just needed to be reminded who is in control. Women are like that, and Rosa is no different. She understands me. She loves me. I'm sure she's in the bedroom right now getting cleaned up so she can come out, help me get changed and finish getting lunch ready. I won't even ask again for my Cutty Sark. She'll be proud of me for not drinking so early in the day. I'll even apologize. That will make her feel good.

As I settle back in my chair and start watching TV again, there is a knock on the front door. I ignore it. Rosa answers the door, not me. More knocking, louder and with purpose.

Then, a loud voice announces, "This is the Police. Is everyone okay? Open the door." I turn the TV down so I can be sure what I am hearing. The police are here. They repeat their request.
I call out, "Rosa, answer the door. The police are here. Where are you?"

She isn't responding, and the knocking continues. I am still in shock, but aware enough to start thinking about what will happen if and when the police come inside. What will they think? What will

Rosa tell them? What should I tell them? I turn the TV volume way down so I can yell something that the police can hear.

With all the air and strength I have left, I call out to them, "Please help me.

I can't move. I've been stabbed."

I hear them trying to open the door, and then a loud bang as the door is forced open. Two officers enter quickly, both slightly crouched in defensive positions with their guns drawn. At this point, I am extremely aware of what has happened, including where Rosa is, and why.

As the police finish their search and secure the apartment, I look at one of the officers and say, "She attacked me. She is my caregiver and we live here together. Please help me."

They find Rosa on the bedroom floor. She is barely conscious and calling for me. She is moaning, "Benny, I'm so sorry. I love you, Benny."

The police officers call for paramedics, and ambulances. Each of the two officers are tending to us individually, making sure we stay alert until the medics arrive. The officer who is with me is asking me all kinds of questions. What's my name? What is my caregiver's name? Do I have any family they need to contact? What exactly happened today?

I'm trying to stay focused, but I've lost lots of blood, and although I've become very aware of what has happened and how I need to handle it, it is becoming harder and harder to stay alert. I answer all of the officer's simple questions. I give him Alan's name, and point him to one of the kitchen drawers where I thought he could find the needed contact information. When he asks me again what happened earlier that morning, I decide I need to keep it simple. I didn't want to create a story that either I wouldn't remember, or that I might accidentally repeat incorrectly during some future inquiry. After all, I had gone to law school. I knew what should and shouldn't be said at the scene of a crime. So I answer him slowly, but with conviction:

"Rosa slapped me hard in the face because she was mad at me, again. A few minutes later, she attacked me with a knife, and I used all my strength to knock her off me. I defended myself and hit her with my walker. She crawled away and into the bedroom. I was afraid she was going to kill me."

I don't know what Rosa told the other officer, but I manage to overhear the two of them comparing notes. I hear them use the term, 'elder abuse,' several times. I have a half smile on my face upon hearing that term, but I quickly wipe that smile away and replace it with my damaged and frightened look, at least for the police. I hear them trying to put the timeline of events together, and it sounds like my officer was essentially buying into my short statement to build the official report. I become a little concerned when they say that they want to talk to the neighbors who had called the police. I have no idea what they might have heard, or what they had seen in the past several months that could make the police question my story.

The Paramedics arrive, and the officer who had been talking

to me directs them to Rosa, as she needs more immediate attention. A second paramedic crew arrives about one minute after the first. They come over to me and start asking me a bunch of questions about my injuries. They say they need me to lie down so they can cut my pants away and look at the knife wound. They slowly pull me from my chair and help me to the floor, away from the debris that had fallen from my table when Rosa landed on it. I am so dizzy, I feel like I'm going to pass out, but the medics want to keep me alert, so they keep talking to me, asking me more questions – most repeats of earlier ones. In addition to having lost so much blood, I have been up most of the night. I am so tired. Chaos has broken out in our little apartment. Medics bark at each other, in the living room with me and in the bedroom with Rosa. They are calling out vital signs, and starting I.V.'s, and assessing injuries. I hear the medics in the bedroom say they are going to need a respirator for Rosa. I know that's bad. But I also know she couldn't talk to the police with one of those things inserted. Probably just as well.

One of the officers stays behind to assist the Paramedics and secure the scene while the other goes to talk to the neighbor. I'm a little worried about that. I don't know what they actually heard this morning. But I am more worried about things they might have seen or heard in the last several months. Rosa is always talking to me with such a sweet, mother-like tone. Maybe they think she is a saint and I'm the devil or something? I should have been nicer to them. I only hope they have been minding their own goddamn business and, other than hearing some crashes and bangs, have nothing to say that would make the officers question my story. We don't go outside the house together very often, so they couldn't have witnessed much outside of our apartment. If we have arguments, they occur indoors, and they are rarely loud. I throw things, and Rosa throws things. I cry, and Rosa comes running to soothe me. Once in a great while, she will punish me for my bad behavior. But those are not physical punishments. Those are part of the psychological game that we play. It can be fun, when it ends in sex. But lately it is anything but fun. It is about power. She is trying to take away my power.

The one officer returns from talking to our neighbor as we are loaded on the ambulance gurneys. I try to hear what he is telling the second cop, but can't hear anything over the medics' chatter. I see Rosa being wheeled out first. There is lots of activity on either side of her gurney; but all I can see is blood, bandages, an I.V. being held by one of the medics, and another squeezing an air bag close to her face. I am being rolled out now, and towards a separate ambulance.

As we cross the front door threshold, the neighbor says to me, "Hope you're okay, Benny."

I thank her, thinking to myself that her friendly words might be a good sign. I am relaxed, fairly confident that our neighbor probably didn't say anything damaging about me.

The police are done with me, at least for the time being. I don't know what, if anything, Rosa told them, if she was able to communicate at all. Right now, I don't care. I have been poked, prodded, lifted and jerked all around. All I want to do is sleep.

Still drowsy, the first thing I notice is how dry my mouth is. I'm having trouble waking up from what feels like a drug-induced sleep. Where am I? I force my eyes open to take in my surroundings. There are machines everywhere, my bed is tilted so I can breathe better, and there is a nurse at the foot of my bed, looking at an electronic tablet, presumably my medical chart. Definitely a hospital bed. My senses return and I become more alert. I look around my bed, noticing the I.V. in my left arm, and a bag with clear liquid dripping slowly into the line. I remember being stabbed. I reach down to feel my right leg, dropping my hand on my thigh harder than I should have, causing me to howl in pain. What did that bitch do to my leg?

The nurse looks up from her tablet, realizing I am awake and hurting. She comes around to the left side of my bed, touches my hand softly and says, "Hi, Benjamin. You're in Loma Linda Hospital. You've had surgery on your leg. It's going to hurt for a while, but the operation was successful." She continues, "If you need anything, you tell me, okay?"

I look at her badge. Her name tag says 'Angela.' She looks to be in her early 50's, about the same age as Rosa. She is really attractive, and doesn't appear to be wearing a ring on her left hand ring finger. She has a sparkle in her eye when she looks at me. As drowsy and in pain as I am, a chill of excitement comes over me as I watch her tending to me.

I nod affirmatively, and realize when I tried to speak that I am short of breath, and still suffering from severe lung congestion. I start hacking like mad. Angela adjusts the bed so I'm sitting more upright, which is causing me to writhe in pain on account of my leg. She is so sweet and helpful; seeing my look of anguish, she immediately reverses the automatic bed, comes up and pats my back, holding my head to help me clear my lungs. She reaches to grab me several tissues, too. She smells so nice, and her touch is so incredibly soft. Our faces are so close to one other, I am self-conscious that I haven't brushed my teeth since at least yesterday… my breath must be atrocious. My coughing has subsided, and I'm able to ask Angela for some water. She helps me with it, gently dabbing my mouth with a soft cloth to wipe up the drips and dribbles that missed my mouth. I smile and ask her to please call me Benny. Then I ask her what happened to me.

It was obvious that Angela didn't want to elaborate on what had caused my injuries. She did tell me that I was admitted mid-day yesterday, and that I had sustained a very deep knife wound to my right thigh. She said that surgery was performed yesterday late afternoon to repair my femoral artery, and some other muscle and tissue damage. She also said that I had been evaluated for other injuries because I had bruises on my arms, hands, face and elsewhere on my torso. I was apparently fine other than my leg; but the look on Angela's face, and the tone of her voice told me that they believed I had been abused.

I measure my next question, since I don't want to seem too

overly concerned. "Where is Rosa?"

I didn't acknowledge that I remember what had happened, but with every minute that passes, I recall more and more about what led up to our confrontation, and the fight itself. I remember looking at her ear dangling from her face, and seeing all that blood. I saw her being wheeled out on the gurney by the Paramedics, and seeing the I.V. and portable respirator as she rolled by me. Angela will only tell me that Rosa is on a different floor of the hospital. She won't say exactly where, nor will she tell me anything about Rosa's condition. She said it is hospital policy not to share information with anyone who isn't immediate family. I decided it was best not to ask any more questions about Rosa, even though I was very curious how she was doing. I am hoping we can go home from the hospital together; I know my sons will want to put me in a nursing home if Rosa doesn't take me back.

It was as if Angela was assigned to help me, and only me. Maybe she told the head nurse that I needed so much attention, she was going to offload her other patients to another nurse. Maybe she wanted to be with me. I could feel the connection between us when we first looked into each other's eyes. I knew that look. Women love to feel attractive, to be noticed. And they love to be touched. When Angela walks by my bed to perform one of her duties, I raise my arm and make sure I brush it against her. A couple of times I thought she was even making her hand accessible, so our hands would touch. She looked at me and smiled. I felt excited for the first time since Rosa left her husband and we moved into our own apartment. Our first night there was so spectacular. I don't think I'd had sex like that since Diane moved from Cleveland to be with me again twenty years ago. I was picturing Angela naked and on top of me. I ask her for another blanket, not because I'm cold, but because I don't want to embarrass myself by making my excitement obvious, at least not yet. She walks by me again, and this time when our hands meet, I grab on to hers gently, to get her attention. I ask if she knows how long I'll be in the hospital. She says that on account of my surgery and having lost so much blood, I'll probably be there two or three more days, but I'll have to talk to my doctor about that. She then tells me that the hospital social worker is going to visit me because my injuries are the result of domestic violence. She left the room, giving me that beautiful smile of hers, and even a wink. She told me she would be back soon.

I don't want to talk to the goddamn social worker again. And I'm not about to be told off by my son again. He could ruin this for me. I need to move back into our apartment, and I need Rosa to take care of me. But I've already told the police that she abused me, and they saw what happened. They were at the scene. It is my word against Rosa's, assuming she'll ever be able to tell anyone anything. I am thinking that I can manipulate the social worker into believing that Rosa stabbed me and I had to defend myself; but at the same time, I would take the blame for being a difficult patient. I would tell her that I make things real hard for Rosa. I piss and shit all over the place, and she cleans it up without complaining. I would say that I was being mean to her yesterday morning, yelling at her, and not letting her to talk to her daughter. I'll say that I went too far. I took a shit on the bathroom floor on purpose, washed my pill down the sink, peed my pants so she'd have to change me, and yelled at her while she was on the phone. The social worker will have to believe that I caused this, and that it was likely on account of missing my medication.

In order for all of this to end the way I need it to, I need some private time with Rosa. She has to want me back. I have little doubt that she'll want to be with me. I'm the best thing that's ever happened to her in her otherwise boring, unhappy life. I have to find out what room she is in, and how she is doing. I need to get in there, and talk to her, and transform myself back into the special boy she first fell in love with. I'll probably have to kiss Laura's ass, too. I am getting much more clarity about how I need things to go from here on out. I don't want to be forced into a nursing home.

I nodded off to sleep after Angela left the room. Last night was probably the best night's sleep I've had in years. I needed to get a hold of whatever medicine they had given me. I didn't even crave scotch after having slept so well. When I opened my eyes, Marty and Alan were standing next to my bed. They're both asking how I'm feeling, but I can tell by the looks on their faces they are more anxious to talk about what happened yesterday morning between me and Rosa. They think I'm an old pain in the ass, and that I can't help but be a miserable prick, and more of a burden on their lives.

Marty went first. "What the hell happened, Dad?" he said with more sarcasm than concern.

Alan had a half-smile, and his eyes opened wide at Marty's

question as if to say, "Yeah, well? What the bloody hell did you do this time, old man?"

I don't want to talk to them at all right now, but I know they can help my cause, as I'm sure they would prefer that I go back home with Rosa. Living with her keeps them from having to deal with me. Going to a nursing home would require them to get a new diagnosis from my doctor. Then they would have to find the right facility based on the diagnosis, move me in, and deal with nursing home staff calling them every time there was the slightest issue. I need them on my side right now, so I keep my answer short and sweet.

"Rosa stabbed me. I defended myself," I say. They look at me with complete disbelief. Both have doubtful smiles on their faces.

Alan finally says, "Really, Dad? She stabbed you *before* you did anything to her?"

I don't say a word. I just look at them both and smile. Alan then starts talking about the potential of having to look at nursing homes. I stop him and say clearly, so as to leave no doubt, "I'm not going to live in a nursing home."

I was pretty confident they wouldn't say anything more to anyone, even if they thought I was lying about what happened. It was not in their best interest. They don't want to deal with me any more than I want to deal with them. And even though Alan is talking nursing homes, I don't think that's what he wants for me. I then changed the subject, and asked if either of them knew anything about Rosa's condition. I was being very sincere in asking that question. I really do love her, and now more than ever, I really do need her.

Marty answered. He said that he had tried to see Rosa, but they wouldn't allow him in as he wasn't family. He did run into Laura in the hospital waiting area, though. She was mad as hell, but willing to talk to him. Marty learned that Rosa was still in recovery, and hadn't been transferred to a private room yet. He said that apparently she didn't look well. She'd had major surgery to repair her face, and the doctors were trying to stabilize her before they performed another procedure to set a broken rib. They were also concerned about some internal bleeding. She was not yet conscious. The police had been hovering around the waiting area, presumably waiting to talk to her. They had already talked to Laura. That couldn't be good for me. The last thing Marty said to me was that it was doubtful Rosa would be taking care of me anymore. I was seething with anger, but I didn't want to overreact right now. I just wanted them to leave so I could relax and be focused for the next time Angela walks back into my room.

She finally returns, and scoots me over to sit on my bedside. She reads my vital signs, and marks things down on her tablet. She is so close to me; I am looking up and down at her, and at her strong but feminine hands. I can see her perfectly shaped nose and lips. She is doing her job, but is sitting on my bed doing it. She didn't have to do that. We start talking after that. She asks me about my family, and after talking about all three of my successful sons, I told her about my 102-year-old mother. I didn't talk about Gail, or Joan, or Rosa. I ask Angela if she would be so kind as to help me dial Mother's number, so I could tell her I was okay. She says that she can't dial long distance from the hospital, but that I can use her cell phone. I don't know the number, but I remember the name and location of the nursing home. Angela looks up and finds the number, dials it for me and asks for Mother's room. She then hands the phone to me, and our hands again touch in the transfer.

After I hear Mother's voice, I say hello, and tell her in as few words as possible that I injured myself accidentally and am at Loma Linda Hospital. She asks me what happened, and I repeat that it was an accident, that I had surgery on my leg but I'd be okay. She tells me she is so glad I called. She says she has been thinking about me a lot lately, and that she's wanted to tell me how much she loves me, and that I will always be her special boy. I hear her voice cracking. Mother never cries. She tells me that she has to go, probably embarrassed at having been so emotional.

But before hanging up, she says one more thing to me, "Benny, I will always love you." I hear her voice crack again. She hangs up abruptly.

I forget for a moment that Angela is watching me. I hand the phone back to her. I have tears in my eyes, but maintain control since I don't want to appear weak. Angela reaches down and squeezes my hand, then steps out of my room saying she'd be back in a few minutes.

I didn't know where Mother's sudden burst of emotion was coming from, but for a moment I was back in high school, back at the Cleveland Performing Arts Theater. Mother's arm is around me, and she is whispering in my ear that I'm her special boy… again.

I no sooner put the first bite of my tasteless hospital breakfast in my mouth, when an unfamiliar but tidy middle-aged woman dressed in a dark-blue pant suit walks into my room. I'm not sure who it is right away, but she quickly introduces herself as Janet, the hospital social worker on duty. She explains that she is there to try to understand what happened between me and Rosa. She says she has to determine what is best for me going forward. I am momentarily relieved that she isn't the same social worker who intervened in a previous issue between the two of us, one that Alan finally had to step in to resolve.

That feeling of relief is short-lived, since she almost immediately says that she is aware of another domestic incident that occurred in the not-so-distant past between me and Rosa. She has the case file in front of her and tells me that she studied it before coming to see me.

Janet is being honest and direct with me. She tells me right away that she has talked to the police, to the first responders, to my neighbors, to my sons, and to Rosa's daughter, Laura. She has also talked to the folks at Mission Manor. It had been a couple of years since Rosa or I had been there, but those people know how wonderful Rosa was. Unfortunately, they knew me too, and all about my fight in the hallway with that old bitch, Nell. My heart sinks upon hearing that this woman has spoken to Laura, and to the assholes at Mission

Manor. I'm sure I am going to be screwed. I have to think on my feet. Luckily I feel like I'm able to think pretty clearly so I won't say something I'll regret, like last time.

Janet tells me that she is confused about my relationship with Rosa. She says that from most accounts, Rosa is a good caregiver, and has been good to me, but she gets mad every now and then and lashes out at me. According to others she interviewed, I am the abuser. I have hit her, and even relieved myself on or near her to teach her a lesson. She adds that my sons think that my medication causes me to behave erratically on occasion, and Rosa has had to become physical to control me. She says that Rosa is unable to tell her side of the story on account of her serious injuries.

I tell Janet that Rosa is a wonderful caregiver, but that sometimes I act out and do stupid things, which gets her angry with me. I repeat my story that she stabbed me, but I change it up slightly. I tell her that Rosa was holding the knife and cutting the tips off red chili pods. I tell her that I was being nasty to her because I hate her daughter, Laura, and I wanted her to get off the phone with her. I continue by saying that Rosa approached me, and it was just by coincidence that she was holding the knife. I tell her that I was startled when I saw her with it, and I pushed her, causing her to spin around and fall over my chair and into my lap, accidentally stabbing me as she tried to break her fall. I got angry and my instincts took over. I got up and hit her with my walker.

I am crying when repeating this version of events for Janet. I finish by saying that after all of this happened, I was sure it was all an accident, a misunderstanding. Rosa would never harm me on purpose. I need her. I avoid saying that I 'love' her, as I knew that wouldn't go over well at all. Janet thanks me for my time. She tells me she has to meet with my doctor, and will get back with me and my sons with her conclusions and recommendations. I have to remember all that I had just told Janet. It really came out better than I had hoped. It was all an accident. I just hoped Rosa would be okay. She needs to take care of me.

I was able to take a nap after Janet left. I wake up just as lunch is being brought into my room. Lucky for me, Angela is the one delivering it to me. She has a small lunch bag with her; and as soon as she sets me up so I can eat, she sits in the chair next to the bed and says she is going to have lunch with me. I am so excited that she wants to be there with me. She has a small salad in a Tupperware container in her bag, along with a fork. As we both eat, she talks about her family, and her job. She tells me that she is recently divorced.

Upon hearing this, I can no longer concentrate on the rest of her life story. Divorced, and sharing that with me? Maybe I won't need Rosa after all. Who better to care for me than a nurse? And she's so pretty, and sexy too. What a great life I would have. She continues, talking about her two daughters, both in school, and both wanting to be nurses like their mom. She tells me she loves her work, that she likes everyone she works with, and that she feels fulfilled helping people get better. After she finishes her salad, and I finish my lunch, she clears my tray and tells me it's time for me to get out of bed and get some exercise. I really don't want to get up. My leg is aching quite a bit, and I'm enjoying Angela's wonderful lunchtime conversation. But I guess I have no choice. I smile and look in her beautiful hazel eyes, trying to get another spark like I felt yesterday when we first looked at each other.

I finally reply, "Okay, let's do this."

Angela removes the I.V. drip, leaving the tube and port in my arm for future administration of medication. Besides, I had been eating and drinking, and I guess they decided I didn't need the constant hydration anymore. She holds my right arm and I lean on her as I pull forward to stand up. Once I'm out of the bed and my feet are both barely touching the floor, I slowly put weight on my right leg, wincing a bit as I was afraid of the pain I was about to endure. Surprisingly, when I step on the ground and transfer my weight to that leg, it doesn't hurt as much as I anticipated. I had been afraid of coming across as a wimp or a crybaby, so I was glad I handled that so well. Now that I've put weight on that leg, she is guiding me slowly back and forth from the bed to the doorway. She is so close to me; it is taking a lot of self-control not to try to kiss her. I think it is probably too soon, even though I'm pretty sure she likes me. She is holding my arm, walking so close to me that our legs and hips are constantly brushing against each other. I'm really enjoying this little therapy session with Angela.

After about ten minutes of walking, she asks if I want to use the bathroom before getting back into my bed. I had peed into a plastic tube since being there, and hadn't shit once, so I jump at the chance. She asks if I need help, and as tempting as that is, I decide to go by myself. I manage to maneuver around the bathroom, and with the help of safety bars, I get up and down from the toilet, and clean up all by myself. When I finish, I open the door to her sweet smile, take her hand and let her help me into bed. She tells me I should try to get some rest. She says that her shift ends in about an hour, at about 2:30 this afternoon, but she would see me first thing in the morning. I can't wait. I close my eyes and smile, thinking about Angela as I doze off.

I had a quiet afternoon, and ate dinner by myself while watching the evening news on Channel 4, as I always did at home. After my dinner tray was removed and everything was cleaned up, I dozed off, and again it was so much easier to fall asleep with Angela on my mind. I couldn't wait to see her first thing in the morning. Maybe she would have breakfast with me, and afterwards I would show her how much further I could walk than earlier today. The evening nurse had already been in the room and given me my medicine regimen. She told me she would be back much later with another pill which would help me sleep.

I am awakened a short time later, somewhat startled to find a strange woman I haven't met standing on the left side of my bed. She has on a white coat, not a typical nurse's issue, but she looks pretty official as she checks the machine for my vital signs and looks at my I.V. line. I don't think much of her being out of uniform since I also remembered that Angela was dressed very casually earlier in the day, and looking very sexy too. I just rest, again thinking about Angela, and about waking up tomorrow morning to her beautiful smile.

I glance over again at this strange woman. She is older than the other nurses, probably in her early sixties. There is something about her that is extremely familiar to me, but I can't place it. She is picking up a very large hypodermic syringe, probably the largest I've ever seen. I can't tell what's inside of it, but it must be a foot long fully extended. I watch her insert it into my I.V. port, and push the plunger all the way in, releasing all of its contents. I don't think too much of that, but when she removes it from the port, pulls the plunger back all the way with no medication inside, and reinserts it in the I.V. port, I get concerned. As she quickly pushes the plunger in again, I start to reach for the help button on my bed. I can't find it anywhere. It's been moved. I reach to grab the arm of the woman, and she skillfully and quickly moves it out of my reach.

The woman then takes the syringe out and places it carefully in her purse, then sits down on the bed next to me. In her purse? What nurse puts used medical equipment in her purse?

She looks at me and with little emotion, asks, "Do I look familiar to you, Benny?"
I reply, "Yes, you do." I continue calmly, for the moment, "Who are you?" She sits up, closer to me now, and asks, "Do you remember Diane?"

I nod my head up and down. Panic is setting in. Who is this woman and what has she just injected into me? I have to get help, and quickly. I start to get up, and so does she. She pushes me back in the bed and tells me to listen closely. She warns me not to make a sound or she will really hurt me. I try to yell for help and she leans forward and presses her elbow against my mouth. I am trying to bite but she is pushing too hard. I'm shaking with fear, but I'm trapped. I can't move or talk. I have no choice but to hear her out:

"When you were in high school, you raped Diane. Do you remember that, Benny? Your parents paid thousands of dollars so that she and her parents would pack up and leave Shaker Heights. You didn't know that, did you, Benny? Why do you suppose they did that? Look at me closer, Benny. I look familiar, don't I? My name is Tracy. Diane is my mother."

"I was born when mom was seventeen years old. I saw her suffer for years, hating you for what you did to her, and to her family. She married another abuser and divorced him years later, but not before he raped us both. Then, she made the mistake of trusting you again, moving her entire life to be with you in California. You abused and then tossed her out like garbage, again. Have you figured this all out yet? That's right, Benny. I am YOUR daughter. And I just injected you with enough air to stop your heart cold. In a minute or so, the world will be a better place. Fuck you."

Less than thirty seconds have passed since she finished talking, and a sudden crushing pain in my chest is overwhelming me. It's like an elephant has fallen on my chest and the weight is getting heavier by the second. The pain is radiating down both arms, up my neck and has completely disabled my breathing. Tracy has let go of me and is walking out of the room. I can't move or call for help. I'm convulsing. My chest is on fire. I am trying to cough, but can't on account of the pain, and my lungs just won't work. I am struggling to take in air. Any air. The room is going dark; the pain is unfathomable. Oh God. Oh Rosa. I need you, Rosa.

Epilogue

Tracy removed her latex gloves, put them in her coat pocket, left Benny's room and calmly walked towards the elevator. Before getting on, pressing the button and watching the doors close, she looked back towards the room she'd just left. She saw the commotion starting, presumably when equipment alarms went off in Benny's room. It would only be seconds until the duty nurses found their patient dead or dying. They won't be able to save him.

She exited the elevator on the ground floor, and walked through the lobby and out the glass front doors of the hospital, undetected. She continued across the street to the hospital parking garage, took a staircase down to the lower level, and walked past ten or eleven cars to a waiting silver Ford Edge. She opened the back door on the driver's side, slid inside, sat down, put her purse beside her, shut the door, and took a deep breath.

Tracy looked to the front seat and simply said, "He's gone. We can talk later. Let's go get a drink."

She reached both of her hands forward, Marty grabbing her left hand from the driver's seat, and Alan holding her right hand from the passenger side. After a few seconds, they released their hands and Marty started the car, backed out of his space, and exited the hospital garage parking lot. They made only small-talk on the short drive to the local Brewery. Marty and Alan had decided while waiting for Tracy to return to the car that they wouldn't prod her for details. They just wanted her to be safe, and for this miserable chapter in all of their lives to be over. And they were both in mild shock that their half-sister – whom they only knew existed for a couple of months – had gone through with her plan and killed their father.

After arriving and being seated at the restaurant, Alan immediately ordered a bottle of Champagne. Seconds after the waiter opened and poured it, they made their first toast to Andy. They all cried at the thought that he had killed himself before realizing he had a sister, and before their father was erased from humanity. After all, it was his suicide that brought Tracy, Marty and Alan together.

She had been following all three of her half-brothers from afar for many years, but had yielded to her mother's wishes to spare them the potential harm that could result from sharing their story. While reading an article related to Alan's retirement last September, she saw a link to Andy's obituary published by a Sarasota, Florida newspaper. That prompted her to reach out to Alan, and then to Marty. Over the next two months, they spoke many times on the phone, becoming very fond of and concerned for one another, especially following the horror of Andy's sudden death.

After learning from Marty of the bloody battle that had left Benny hospitalized, Tracy flew immediately to Southern California. It was time she met her brothers, and confronted the monster that had all but destroyed her mother's, and in-turn, her own life. The three of them spent that first evening and all the next day catching up on each other's lives from Alan's living room in Los Angeles. They compared notes on the impacts Benny had on all of them. It was during dinner on the second evening together that Tracy told her brothers that she needed to see Benny before returning home to Cleveland. She had had a few drinks, and kept muttering about fast and undetectable ways to kill a person. Marty and Alan looked at each other, somewhat surprised at what Tracy was saying, yet not at all sure how serious she might be. After staring at one another for ten to fifteen seconds, they simultaneously shrugged their shoulders and smiled, as if to say, "So, what if she does…?"

Marty and Alan could see that the more time they spent talking to Tracy about family history, the angrier and more determined she became. They decided to drive to Loma Linda Hospital the next afternoon. Tracy chose the time she wanted to arrive there. She said that any therapy sessions would most likely have been performed earlier in the day, doctor's rounds would be complete, and the late afternoon paperwork would be in process as the nurses prepared for their shift change. There was a high likelihood that Tracy would get the alone-time with Benny that she had waited so long for.

They had no idea exactly what Tracy had in mind when she stepped out of Marty's car and entered the hospital. In fact, although they suspected she might want to kill him, they never discussed it with her. They didn't want to know, for several reasons. They were just supposed to drop off their sister, who wanted to meet her father, the monster, for the first time – and wait for her in the hospital garage.

They had prepared themselves that just about anything was possible. Maybe she just talks to him. Maybe she intends to kill him and decides she can't go through with it. Maybe she doesn't have any opportunity to be alone with him, so she abandons her plan. Or maybe she really does kill the man that she is convinced ruined their lives.

Marty lowered his Champagne glass, and making sure there was no one in the restaurant within earshot, he quietly asked Tracy if she felt like talking about what happened in Benny's hospital room. Tracy kept it short. She reminded them that she had spent her career as an emergency room nurse, and after researching the quickest and least detectable methods to do what she had to do, she decided on a 'Venous Air Embolism.' She skipped the details, obviously not wanting to relive the moment, especially in a public place. She did share that an air embolism was not traceable unless a Medical Examiner was looking for this specific cause, and even then finding and proving it was extremely unlikely. She added that an autopsy wouldn't be performed because Benny was old and unhealthy, and he had been in the hospital more than twenty-four hours.

Alan added one final question, "So how were you able to keep Benny from yelling or fighting back?"

All Tracy said was, "I'm tougher than I look." She smiled, as did they. They left it at that.

After toasting Andy, they went on to toast Gail, and Joan, and of course, Diane. And then they toasted Rosa. Although they were never absolutely certain of Rosa's intentions, Marty and Alan believed that Rosa was a kind soul who fell in love with and eventually became addicted to her abuser, though they continued to treat her as an employee to avoid having to deal with any other personal issues. They agreed to stay in touch with Rosa and her family — maybe not indefinitely, but at least while she recovered from her injuries.

Marty talked to Laura a few times over the next several days about Rosa's condition. She was getting better; progressing well enough to possibly go home in the next few days. In their last conversation, Marty told Laura that she could call him if her mother needed anything. He didn't want to go into specifics, but he did want to send a message to her that they care about Rosa, and are willing to help if necessary. Marty and Alan both hoped that she would recover, and would soon be out of their lives forever.

Exactly three weeks to the day after Benny died, Alan received a large manila envelope by registered mail. In it was a copy of a Marriage License, issued by the County Clerk of Riverside County, California. It was signed by a Judge of the Riverside County Municipal Court. Alan's jaw dropped. Benny had married Rosa about eight months prior. And Laura was one of their witnesses. Bitch.

Alan didn't recognize the name of the second witness, but one signature he definitely recognized was his father's; it was as clear as if he'd signed it twenty years ago. Holy crap. What could he have been thinking? Rosa's intentions seemed clearer, however, when Alan saw what accompanied the Marriage Certificate. There was a hand-written Post-it note stuck to the copy of the license, which read:

"Dear Alan, I am Rosa's attorney. My business card is attached. She wanted you to see this as soon as possible. We will be contacting you and Marty soon to read Benjamin's revised Last Will and Testament,

Alan pulled out his iPhone and called Marty. At first, they both practically fell over laughing. They deserved each other, for sure. But then the conversation turned to curiosity. They talked for several minutes trying to figure out what the circumstances might have been when they made the decision to do this. Assuming their father was aware he was getting married, then why? They were sure he would have told his sons, if for no other reason to rub their noses in their obvious disapproval. After some discussion, they concluded that Benny probably didn't tell them because he risked losing their support. After all, even he had to have doubts about Rosa's true intentions.

But Benny was only completely lucid when his medication was managed properly. They wondered if this wasn't Rosa's objective all along. They had discussed this ad nauseam, but had always come to the conclusion that she was just a misguided angel, suffering from a textbook case of abused spouse syndrome. They had decided that so long as they didn't have to deal with their father's constant bullshit anymore, Rosa was okay with them.

Of course, there was still the matter of his $800,000 estate.

Acknowledgement

I had a lot of invaluable help in creating, writing and editing "Benny:"

First, thank you to my son, Eric Flagel, for reading my original storyboard, and suggesting that I tell this story from Benny's perspective. "Benny" finally came to life, but not until that lightbulb went off.

Next, thank you to my wife, Kristy Flagel, and her awesome mom, Nancy Napier, for providing continuous feedback throughout the writing process.

Thank you to our friend, Pam Anderson MSN, RN, who helped me with the medical research – in particular, recommending that a Venous Air Embolism was a relatively simple but sure way for Tracy to kill Benny. I even went online and bought a 50cc hypodermic syringe so I could visualize what Tracy would be dealing with, and more importantly, what Benny would be seeing in his final moments.

Finally, thank you to my aunt Marlene Flagel, my cousins Jennifer Flagel and Alyson Goldberg, our friend Tanya Coon, and Kristy (again), for editing my manuscript in various stages. All five of these awesome people have dedicated much of their personal and professional lives to education/academia, in various capacities.

Although sad, angry and unexplainable behaviors such as the ones I've described in "Benny" certainly exist; any similarities or familiarities are coincidental. "Benny" is purely a work of fiction.